W9-ARG-047

THE UNDEAD TRUTH OF US

THE UNDEAD TRUTH OF US

Britney S. Lewis

HYPERION

Los Angeles   New York

WAYNE PUBLIC LIBRARY

OCT 1 9 2022

Copyright © 2022 by Britney S. Lewis

All rights reserved. Published by Hyperion, an imprint of Buena Vista Books, Inc.
No part of this book may be reproduced or transmitted in any form or by any means,
electronic or mechanical, including photocopying, recording, or by any information
storage and retrieval system, without written permission from the publisher. For
information address Hyperion, 77 West 66th Street, New York, New York 10023.

First Edition, August 2022
10 9 8 7 6 5 4 3 2 1
FAC-004510-22175

Printed in the United States of America

This book is set in Baskerville MT Pro/Monotype
Designed by Zareen Johnson

Library of Congress Cataloging-in-Publication Data
Names: Lewis, Britney S., author.
Title: The undead truth of us / by Britney S. Lewis.
Description: First edition. • Los Angeles ; New York : Hyperion, 2022. •
Audience: Ages 12–18. • Audience: Grades 7–12. • Summary: After her
mother's sudden death, sixteen-year-old dancer Zharie Young begins
seeing zombies, and when she meets an undead boy, he helps her
understand how love can change someone—for good or for dead.
Identifiers: LCCN 2021025271 (print) • LCCN 2021025272 (ebook) •
ISBN 9781368075831 (hardcover) • ISBN 9781368081993
(paperback) • ISBN 9781368075909 (ebk)
Subjects: CYAC: Grief—Fiction. • Zombies—Fiction. • Dating (Social customs)—
Fiction. • Dance—Fiction. • African Americans—Fiction. • LCGFT: Novels.
Classification: LCC PZ7.1.L5125 Un 2022 (print) • LCC
PZ7.1.L5125 (ebook) • DDC [Fic]—dc23
LC record available at https://lccn.loc.gov/2021025271
LC ebook record available at https://lccn.loc.gov/2021025272

Reinforced binding

Visit www.HyperionTeens.com

And what is done in love

is done well.

—Vincent van Gogh

Dear reader, I understand there may be some areas in this book that could be triggering. In the interest of transparency, it's important that you're aware of these topics before reading the story.

Content warnings: profanity, blood, gore, body horror, grief, loss of parent, abandonment of parent, death of parent, mentions of anxiety and depression.

TO YOU, READER.

Don't let the monsters of the universe keep you from living.
Take risks, fall in love, create your own path.

AND TO MY BEAR.

For proving that love can change you
in more good ways than bad.

CHAPTER ONE

FIVE DAYS. FIVE. That was how long it took for Mama to turn into a zombie.

Day one she was stoic. She refused to move from the couch, even after I turned off the TV in the evening. I still remember how frigid her face looked in the dimness of the flickering candle before I blew it out. The spaces above her cheeks were sunken in, eyes bulged away from her face. A wiggle under there, only slightly, but it did. I saw it move. I saw it twist.

And her brown skin looked frail and thin—any wrong move, and I was afraid it would tear away in small slits, revealing the tissue beneath.

"Mama..." I whispered, creeping closer to her in the darkness. One foot after the other, the floorboards creaking with each step. I wanted to know if she was okay, if she was even awake, but she didn't say anything. Looked at her again, waited. She released a deep breath, the air cracking on its way out. Sounded like something was in there, inching its way up her trachea.

I left it alone. Kissed her clammy head, pulled a blanket over her, and tucked her in, hoping she'd be fine in the morning.

And she *would* be fine. She always was.

Day two was strange. It began with her golden-brown eyes. They glazed into a cynical gray like cataracts, and the brightness that used to be in them dissipated like smoke in the wind. When she spoke, her sentences were short and sloth-like—every word a complete struggle—almost as if someone had stuffed cotton beneath her tongue.

On day three, her veins oozed a thick green sludge under her skin. They pulsed and vibrated, not quite right. And her shoulders slouched inward, like they were weighed down by a thousand invisible moons, disrupting her inner tide entirely.

As she inched closer and closer to the invisible abyss, her dark cloud of sadness stripped away the caramelized flesh from her face, leaving her disfigured.

By the fourth day, every breath came with a creaking croak. It was like watching a sped-up time lapse of a fire burning out. Everything I loved about her was gone.

We didn't dance.

We didn't sing.

She wasn't the bleeding sunrise anymore—she was the deep, deep, dark ocean.

And on November 4, before daybreak, her last breath rolled up her throat and turned her into the undead thing that I feared.

It was the worst day of my life.

I found her on the floor in the kitchen, and my throat swelled. Her body lay in the fetal position, her right hand below her heart, crumpled like an old rose.

But I didn't get it. Zombies weren't supposed to die so easily, yet Mama did.

When the EMTs came, I tried to tell them, but the words wouldn't come out. They couldn't see that she wasn't only dead—she was *undead*.

I—I, uh, my thoughts stammered; all I could do was stare blankly. How could they not see it? How was I the only one?

And she . . . she needed more time. *We* needed more time. I didn't understand. What was wrong? How did she die? Was she *really* dead?

But they rushed her out, and I couldn't move from that spot in the kitchen where I'd found her.

Couldn't force the air out of my lungs. Couldn't take any more steps forward.

I tried to hold myself, but a sharp pain in my navel forced me to my knees. I curled into a ball on the laminate floor, and the smell of the brewing coffee nestled in my nostrils, reminding me of how she was just here, alive.

She *was* alive.

Closed my eyes, warm cheek against the cold tile now. And she was gone. I knew she was because of the permanent goosies on my arms.

When Mama died, I think her soul shattered into a Postimpressionist painting filled with yellows and blues. We were the zigzagged, black lines in that painting, the birds. And I swore I flew with her soul that day, the wind still fresh between my fingers, but I couldn't reach her. Didn't matter how fast I flew, she flew farther, and the sapphire horizon created a million miles between us. It swallowed her.

They later told me that her heart exploded in her chest. *Exploded.* I didn't know how that could be humanly possible, but when they told me, I saw those colors again.

She was yellow. I was blue.

She was dead and undead, and now the earth was flooded with zombies, drowning me with the constant reminder of Mama.

Why? I didn't know why.

But why?

I didn't know why.

But I terribly, terribly, terribly wanted to.

CHAPTER TWO

MAY 15, 5:00 P.M.

To whomever still follows this thing, you may know that—due to a slight hiccup in my anatomy that I am NOT comfortable sharing with a primary care provider—I am seeing zombies.

No, not like people dressed up in Halloween costumes, roaming the back roads of Kansas City, but literal, gruesome zombies.

And they are everywhere.

You might ask, "Why, Zharie, are you seeing zombies?"
To which I'd say, "I have no idea."

But here are my theories:

- I have completely lost my marbles.
- The "Zombie" song by the Cranberries can curse you if you listen to it on repeat too many times.
- I'm not crazy—rather, everyone around me is oblivious.

The cure:

- No cure yet.

CHAPTER THREE

THERE. IN THE HEAT of the afternoon sun, on the last day of my sophomore year, I could hear the sound of the undead sloshing in my ears.

The sound was thick and wet, and each step forward brought me closer. A few feet away, on the sidewalk, in front of the school. Hot now, the yellow sun burning my brown shoulders, and in, *I breathed in*. And there they were, two of them.

The undead teens gnawed at each other in the form of a sloppy kiss. Eyes sunken and hollow; fresh skin dangling from their cheekbones, exposing their skeletal smiles as they pressed their brittle tongues around each other.

The slosh again, echoing in my ears.

I gagged, but they didn't hear it. Didn't see me or anyone else around. And they moved clumsily into each other, their boned hands intertwining, their clothes tattered and disassembled, blood falling in thick drops onto their brand-new, matching Jordans.

The red pooled around them, but no one saw. No one cared.

But how?

I shuffled past Thing One and Thing Two and climbed onto the bus, sitting exactly four rows back, where I always sat, as close to the window as I could, pushing the thought of the zombies away.

Earbuds in, I noticed a text from Mini:

For your sadness

The message had a song attached, one that was released before I was born. Pressed play, leaned back, and not even a moment after doing so, the main singer killed it, going on about love and death and the sea of loneliness.

Is it worth it, can you even hear me? the singer started. *I'm tired, and I've felt it for a while now.*

The students loaded the school bus robotically, and as I continued to listen to this punk-ass white boy band scream at me, I wondered about Vincent van Gogh and why he was the way that he was.

Before Mama died, I learned about him in my Art Theories class, and I couldn't stop thinking about him. What I found was that van Gogh was broke when he was alive. *Broke.* Only ever sold one painting. He lived off the money his brother gave him, but even then, he used it to buy coffee, cigarettes, and art supplies—a hell of a mood.

But I wondered more about who he was outside of that. Like, would he have listened to the same music I listened to? Was there even sad music to match his sad-boy persona—or did Mozart do it for him? What did he think about between the hours, months, and years it took him to paint the smallest of strokes? Could it have driven him mad, the loneliness?

Maybe.

Like him, I imagined painting myself with the same artistic expression. Small and big. Yellow and blue. Yellow and blue.

This could be my chance to break out, the singer continued. *This could be my chance to say goodbye.*

And then there it was again—another dead, undead one. She lingered outside my window on the sidewalk. Twisted jaw, blood leaking out her mouth, dripping on the phone in her hand.

A pain pulsated in my ear while I studied her, and I yanked one of my earbuds out, thinking it would help me see her better. It had been a while since I'd seen so many of them at once, all in one day.

They were here and there right after Mama died but never like this. And I tried to tell myself it was a lie. This wasn't real. . . .

The muscles in my hand jerked, insisting I wave, but I forced my fingers beneath my leg, tapping my foot rapidly all the while. I just wanted to know who she was. Why was she like this?

A small piece of paper landed in my lap, and it startled me. It was Luca. He sat to the right of me, and he smiled so wide I saw his braces before I could see anything else.

I snatched out the other earbud and paused the song. *"What?"*

"Zeezy, I've been calling you for like three minutes." Luca sat angled in the seat across from me, his spotlight burning my eyes. His foot lingered in the aisle, and I knew if he kept it there, Mrs. Whitehead would give him a warning.

I adjusted, my thighs sticking to the hot vinyl seat. "Hey, do you see that girl outside the window?" I asked, sticking my pointer finger to the glass. The window wobbled slightly when I did, in the same way that water rippled when touched, and I wondered if I pressed harder, would my finger go all the way through?

Luca stretched his neck to see out, faint bluish veins peeking through his light brown skin. "Who, Becca? Yeah, I see her. I've been noticing her all year. Why, what's up? Did she finally break up with James's sorry ass?"

The bus moved now, and I shook my head. "No." I sighed. "Never mind." Luca didn't see it—the sagging skin, the disfigured face, the weird window, the sunflower stuck in the cement.

The sunflower. Yellow. Facing the sun.

"And you know that's not my name," I snapped, realizing that he had called me Zeezy. We'd been over that, like, a million times.

"Right," he said, his ears and brows raised.

"Right..."

"So, *Zharie Young*...or whatever," he started, and I mouthed *Thank you* for getting my name right. "What are you doing for break?"

I picked at my shirt. "Haven't given it much thought."

"No dancing?"

I pressed my toes into the soles of my shoes. Felt the heat there. West Coast Swing was my thing, thanks to Mama. She was known in the dance community as Twiggy. Though, even if she hadn't introduced it to me, I would have discovered it somehow. It had been one of the most magical things I'd ever done with my body. "Honestly, I don't know," I finally said.

"Why not?"

"Um—"

Mrs. Whitehead cleared her throat, and we could see her aging blue eyes in the rearview mirror. "Mr. Santos, we talked about this. Don't make me give you a warning on the last day of school."

Luca moved his foot quickly and waved his hand as a signal. "My bad, Mrs. Whitehead. Won't do it again." He looked at me, his eyes wide behind his thick glasses, as if to say he wouldn't hesitate to do it again, and even if he got a warning, it wasn't like his family would care. He said he never got in trouble. Said being the baby in the family came with perks.

"But you were sayin'," Luca prompted.

"I was just saying...I don't think I'll really be able to dance because of, *you know.*" Code for, *You know my mom died six months ago, and she had money to provide for me, and now I'm broke, and I can't afford to spend ten dollars to dance every week. It just ain't happening, regardless of how much I love it.*

"*Oh,*" he said.

"Yup."

"Well, uh, I mean if you ever wanna go, I can cover. My pops lets me borrow his car on Thursday nights, so I got you."

"Mmh...I'm gonna pass."

"But why? It's free money, Z. Don't you think Twiggy would want you there anyway?"

I scowled at him. He didn't know her like that, didn't know what she wanted from me.

But yeah, she'd probably want me to go. Of course she would, but she wasn't here now.

"I don't know, Luca. Why don't you go to her grave and ask her?" I said, and I turned to face the window, except the window was completely gone, and I found myself floating amidst the traffic on the highway, zooming away from Luca and his questions.

I didn't need that. I didn't need anyone.

My knuckles were damned near white when I put my earbuds back in, and the horrid wind caused a stinging in the corners of my eyes.

Blinking it away, I pulled out my phone and restarted the song. The volume was up so high I thought my brain might combust.

It almost did.

CHAPTER FOUR

IT WAS MY STOP. I said goodbye to Luca and got off the bus, feeling like I had danced across the smallest of glass shards on the way down the aisle.

Luca's protruding lips and puppy eyes were all I could think about; it didn't help that our conversation ended with death and gloom and stuff.

But it was Luca. I was happy to be away from him, happy for the summer. I knew he meant well, but he was so damn suffocating. Couldn't take a hint to save his life.

It was worse because I got the unfortunate pleasure of seeing him on the bus before *and* after school. This dude always had his own soliloquy, and really, all he ever did was talk about how great he thought he was, which felt weird. Made me feel like I couldn't fully be myself around him.

I responded to Mini's text:

> Thanks for sending the song.
>
> Definite inspo for the next post

As I approached the apartment building, I noticed a family moving in. An Asian man carried two boxes out of a U-Haul, his gray shirt soaked from sweat, and a short Black woman directed two guys with a couch to the second floor, her ponytail moving with ferocity.

More boxes. More furniture. Some plastic on the ground. A new vine growing up the side of the concrete building. A whisper from somewhere, the smell of something sour nearby.

Before I really had the chance to decipher more, a boy flew past me on a skateboard, leaving a gust of wind behind. He came back up, and then back down again, and I moved to the edge of the sidewalk.

This time, on his way down, he stared directly at me, and it made my stomach tighten.

The back of his board skidded against the cement, and then there he was, barely a breath away from me.

The first thing I noticed about him was his butt chin. It reminded me of Mama's—subtle, yet noticeable. Underneath that, his Adam's apple. The way it bobbed against his chestnut skin when he swallowed, stopping himself from saying something.

Then it was his shirt. It was black with a *Pulp Fiction* photo on it. It looked oversized and over-worn at the collar; it was sloppy, but it worked for him.

Last, his hair. It was a ball of fluffy, spilling curls, and the sides were tapered. The sunlight tinted his thick black locks marigold. Highlighted his chocolate-brown eyes. They twinkled.

The atmosphere strange and enchanting now.

It was the way he looked at me. Like he knew me. Like we were close. His full lips stretching across his face, smiling at me like we were friends.

But I didn't know this dude.

Took a step back to gather the rest of him. It was awful. He was too attractive for his own good—and why . . . *why* was he standing this close to me?

"Did I scare you? I didn't mean to scare you." It was the first thing he said to me, and I didn't think he scared me, but my face must have said otherwise.

"Uh," I started, and then I shook my head in response.

He half smiled, his lips only slightly revealing the pearly white things behind them, and maybe then the girl on his shirt flicked her cigarette and the smoke traveled from his chest to my nose, causing a tickle in the back of my throat. "I just wanted to say...you're giving me major Lisa Bonet vibes."

I scrunched my nose.

"You know, nineties icon, bohemian babe?"

That name didn't ring any bells. When I didn't respond, he took off on his skateboard again. Gone. And this whole thing was weird as hell, so I started walking, closer to the steps. But then he circled around with a quick turn, his phone out.

He stopped in front of me again, and I paused. "Here." He handed me his phone. It had a Google search pulled up with images of Lisa displayed. I recognized her face.

"Oh."

"Yeah," he said, and he took his phone back and tucked it in his front pocket. Barely hidden. "So anyway, I was distracted by you, and I wanted to know if you knew how impressive you were."

Dudeee.

My eyes felt like they were going to explode. Wow. In all of my sixteen years, no guy had ever been this forward. Like, ever.

"Um, no. I guess I didn't know that." But now that he brought it to my attention...

"Welcome to reality, queen," he said, his smile big and painted across his face.

My first response was to laugh, but my spidey senses told me that would be rude. How *dare* he "queen" me, though? He didn't know me. You couldn't just "queen" someone you didn't know. It took away the value.

My second response was to leave, so I did just that. It was too damn hot to be playing games with strangers.

"Whoa, whoa, whoa." He picked up his skateboard and followed beside me. "You have a serious need for speed. You ever skate?"

"Once. With rollerskates. When I was eight."

"What about with a board?"

I stopped at the steps. "Nope."

He looked at the building and then quickly behind me at the U-Haul parked in about five parking spots. Auntie E would be pissed if she couldn't park in her regular space when she got home.

He smiled again. "That's dope. We live in the same building. You and I, we should hang out. You gotta meet my friends."

"Nah," I said, and I took the steps.

He rushed ahead of me and opened the door. "Why not?"

I shrugged my shoulders and walked past him, noticing the flickering light in the hallway. Didn't know why it was on. It was bright as hell outside. "Guess I don't have a reason to."

He mumbled, *"Huh?"* beneath his breath as I scurried past him and up the stairs to the second floor.

My hand rested on the golden knob when I got to the apartment, and I contemplated turning back around to see what he might say next, but there was no point.

Upon entering, I dropped my backpack by the entry and placed my key in a wooden bowl that had been scarred and marked by the many things that were in it.

Living with Auntie E was still weird. I would have stayed with Grandma, but since she didn't live in the city, I would've had to leave Sumner Academy. Mama wouldn't have wanted that. She liked that her only kid was admitted to a free school solely dedicated to arts and science to prep you for college—it was a pretty big deal in the KCK area, and students who were admitted (per their requirements, of course) started attending Sumner their eighth-grade year.

I mean, it was cool and all. It was my third full year, but my Sumner friends called me a hermit. It was the stillness of my room that was comforting. It was that cool, blue light from my phone and my tablet that I was addicted to. I went to a few parties but left early. Embarrassing, I knew that much. Mama would pick me up with a smirk painted on her face, and I'd bury myself in my phone, mumbling, "Don't wanna talk about it," as we sped away.

Plus, the academy was moving at a rate so fast it was hard to keep up. The last thing I wanted was to do *more*. I did try show choir once, but it was too much for me, so I stuck to shop class for theater. It was where I met Pak, Leti, and Kanyce. They were cool. We'd do McDonald's after school sometimes or walk to QuikTrip, but really, I wasn't the best at being their friend.

I was the worst, actually. And me spending most of my free time at the dance studio with Mama didn't help.

But anyway, I really hoped living with Auntie E would be a breeze, that she'd welcome me with arms wide open, that we'd connect over the fact that we'd lost someone so important. Someone irreplaceable. It was a shiny thought.

And I still remember the way she treated me when I moved in. We unloaded the boxes from the back of her SUV without speaking to each other. I followed her down the hall, to my new room, and she half smiled, but it was strange. Her brown eyes said something else. Then she grabbed her keys and left, said she had school. I was alone. My eyes dried, my throat cracking. We never talked about what happened. We never talked about what we lost, and how this was new for the both of us.

Auntie just wasn't the same since Mama died. True, we were never hip-to-hip the last few years. Her CNA job was demanding at the nursing home. She was in night school to get her bachelor's degree. But still...I thought there would be a few nights when we'd stay up watching movies till midnight like we used to when I was younger. Or maybe we'd go walking or eat dinner together. Maybe we'd spend more than five minutes in the same room.

Something. Anything, really.

It was impossible to catch her on a "good" day. Her lips were usually folded, her shoulders slouched, and any hope of having a conversation—like a real one, more than "How are you?"—was pulling. Maybe that was a point she wanted to make.

I did try. Tried to keep the sink free of dishes, take care of laundry, clean the toilet (I hated the toilet). Tried to light her favorite candles.

Tried to share my books. It was all I had, and since Grandma could only give so much money, Auntie E was always working—which meant I was always alone.

Alone and confused. Because regardless of what I tried, the outcome stayed the same.

My stomach grumbled, and to the left of me, the kitchen whispered a warm *Hello*.

I leaned against the laminate peninsula countertop that separated the kitchen from the living room and picked at a chip in the corner of it.

What was there to eat? The cabinets were bare. A small box of Cheerios, a can of corn, ramen—plenty of that—possibly a can of expired tuna. Ew. Tuna.

The fridge? A lot of condiments, which we always had. Half a jar of grape jelly, orange juice that needed to be tossed, eggs.

It wasn't appealing, but I rushed to the fridge anyway. Opened it. Expected more, but it was sorrier than I'd remembered. There was milk at least—*eh*.

An apple sat on the countertop, the redness in it dulling, the bottom of it lopsided, but it would do.

I rinsed it off and was immediately reminded that we didn't have hot water, which meant bathing tonight would be taking a quick shower or boiling pots of water for the tub. The thought of it made my skin feel disconnected from my body.

I knew Auntie E was busy, but damn. Was it that hard? This kind of thing never happened with Mama, but if Mama was here, this wouldn't be an issue.

I took a bite of the apple, the tough skin hurting my gums.

My phone vibrated in my pocket, but I ignored it because I heard a skidding of sorts outside the window.

When I checked it out, I saw him immediately, the jabbering boy with the skateboard and the quick Google search. He was on his board now, completing a kick-flip, or maybe it was an ollie. I wasn't sure.

He went back and forth on the sidewalk, and I watched him like a cat watching a laser pointer. Then he jolted in and out of the blackest of black holes. Each time he came out, the world behind him turned into a horizon where the sun was so close to the earth that the ground burst into flames.

"Will you just put the damn thing down," the woman with the ponytail said, who I assumed was his mother. She snapped her fingers.

But he didn't quit. He kept going faster and faster until he was in the air, landing on the stair railing. Back down again he went with a whoosh, the wind moving through his curls, the fire catching on the edge of his Vans.

"Bo," she grunted, neither of them seeing the fire growing from the rich horizon or the black hole growing bigger with despair.

Bo wore a wicked smile, not saying anything, but finally coming to a halt. When he did, the world returned to its usual subtle animation.

He wrapped an arm around his mother, and she pushed him away teasingly and pointed to the truck.

When Bo picked his skateboard up, our eyes met.

He waved, but I ducked immediately, the red apple falling to the carpet.

And what I remember seeing before I freaked was the familiarity in half of Bo's face. It was a partial skeletal smile and a hollowed cheekbone.

It was the weaving of the dead thing and the living thing, intertwining and messing with the nerves in my bloodstream like some sick joke.

I exhaled, and it felt like the world was breathing with me, confirming my dissonance from reality.

CHAPTER FIVE

MAY 20, 5:00 P.M.

Today I googled: *What does it mean if you're seeing zombies?*

Turns out, Google doesn't have an answer for that. Instead, the first search result I got was: "What it means if you dream about zombies."

Naturally, I clicked on that because . . . well, because that's better than nothing.

So, if I'm dreaming about (and let's add seeing here, too) zombies, it could be because of these six things:

- I am feeling overwhelmed.
- I may feel like I'm losing control of a situation.
- I may be under significant pressure.
- Something big in my life is coming to an end, and I'm unsure of what the future brings.
- I feel rejected, disconnected, and totally alone.
- I have anxiety.

Question I must ask myself:

- Are any of the above relevant to me?

Answer:

- Surprisingly, yes. Some of them. Not all, but some.
- Okay, maybe all of them.
- Also, FML.

The cure:

- Still no cure yet. Though, I have a few ideas.

CHAPTER SIX

ALMOST IMMEDIATELY after I posted to my blog, Mini face-timed me. She'd always been my most persistent friend.

"*Gurrl.* You can't possibly think you're seeing zombies. HOW'D YOU GO FROM BLOGGING ABOUT YOUR LIFE TO SEEING ZOMBIES?" she said. Mini was sitting on a couch eating popcorn, her French braids tousled as if she'd had them in for too long, and parts of an oversized hoodie peeked in and out of the frame.

It was the prolonged look in Mini's eyes that made me hold the air in my lungs. I closed my laptop, shoved it under the pillow on my unmade bed, and clenched a small piece of the yellow fabric in my hand. The flower pattern danced momentarily as I held on to them. It reminded me of Mama.

"I know it sounds crazy, but..." It was what it was, and I left it at that, shrugging my shoulders in the same disbelief.

The last time I tried to explain myself, Auntie E thought I was going through post-traumatic stress disorder. I remembered the way she stared at me. Her eyes wide, her mouth open, speechless at first.

My face was bruised blue when Auntie E said, "That's what happens when you watch too much damn TV." Auntie didn't get it. Mama had been dead *before* her death, she was this creature, and I could still hear the croaking under her snarls.

If *only* Auntie believed me.... If only she cared more.

And it was the same with Grandma. She had to pick me up from school two weeks after Mama's death because I freaked out on a girl who followed me to the bathroom. I thought she was a zombie, ready to rip me in half and shuffle through my broken parts, but she was just a student with a full bladder who I'd almost caused to pee her pants.

Grandma told me zombies weren't real, that I was hallucinating. She told me I needed to snap out of it, or I'd get kicked out of the academy.

In a way, she was right. That zombie girl didn't eat me, but even as I tried to explain it to the guidance counselor, I saw how her eyes shifted. Saw how she was categorizing me like the rest of them.

No one else could see them. It was just me on my lonely zombie-island.

So I wasn't the least bit surprised at Mini's reaction. Her jaw dropped, and some of the kernels in her mouth fell out. "Zharie, are you *serious?* I THOUGHT YOU WERE KIDDING?!?!"

I got off my bed to retrieve my white Chuck Taylors. "I wish," I said, and in between tying the laces, I sent my wishes up to the heavens, in hopes that when I woke tomorrow, the zombies would all be gone.

"Do I need to fly down there???"

"You always say that." Mini did always say that. We'd been friends for two years, but we'd never met in person. She lived in Chicago, and I stayed in Kansas City—the Kansas side. She found my blog some-how, and for the longest time, she was the only one who'd comment on my posts. We ended up connecting over our music preferences, and it went from direct messaging to swapping numbers. But now I had a little community of followers. I was sure most of them probably thought I was writing fanfic at this point.

Anyway, we'd always say that we'd meet in Chicago, or LA, or somewhere, but it just hadn't happened.

"I know, I know, but can you explain this? Because this doesn't make sense, Z. Zombies? Really? In what universe?"

"In. This. Universe," I said, trying not to let her words hit me in the chest.

She huffed, and I huffed, too.

"Does anyone else know?" Mini leaned forward, her brown face so close to the camera, I could make out the shape of her pores.

"I tried to tell my auntie and my grandma."

"And?"

"And if I bring it up again, they'll have me shipped off to some insane asylum."

"They wouldn't do that."

I twisted my lips.

"Okay, they *might* do that, but still." She took a long breath, and I could feel her salty air on my end of the phone. It didn't matter if any of them believed me. I knew it was real.

And when I thought about it, I saw Mama's very dead, *very* real body in my head.

She was still on the floor in the kitchen, her body magically covered in yellow and blue daisies. Though, this time, the daisies pillowed her in a gust of air, and she flew away with them.

She had gone again, and I still couldn't reach her.

Mini fixed her camera so I could see her better; it brought me back to reality. "Do you think it might have to do with your mom's death? You know...maybe your auntie is kinda right. It could be a weird side effect. It really hit you hard, girl."

Side effect: n. *a secondary, typically undesirable effect of a drug or medical treatment.*

Or, in my case, seeing zombies.

This wasn't a side effect, but Mini's words bruised my cheeks anyway. What I was seeing, what I was feeling...I wasn't, I *couldn't* make this stuff up.

"You don't have to believe me," I said. "I just need to figure out why this is happening."

"How are you gonna do that?"

"Well," I said, and I stood up. I could still hear the wheels hitting the cement outside my window. "I'm gonna befriend a zombie."

Mini sighed, her nostrils flaring. "Damn it, Z. No. Please explain, and please don't do anything stupid," she said, and I heard her slap her thigh.

"Chill. It's fine. It's not like zombies are real, anyway."

Mini rolled her eyes, and I promised to text her an update before quickly ending the call.

CHAPTER SEVEN

THE ZOMBIES IN MY WORLD had one consistent rule: Once a zombie, always a zombie.

Yet Bo was the anomaly, and I didn't know how or why. First, he was human. He had real human words, diction, and inflection. His skin wasn't corroded or dragging with seeping holes. Holes that exposed deteriorating organs. Holes that were yellow and green and blue. And he smelled of summer, not rotten or sour.

Then, when he looked at me through the window, it all changed. Half of his face was full-on zombie mode, while the remainder of his body was normal. Although it had been a few days since we met, the hanging skin and tissue still burned in my memory. Bo was like the rest of the unmentionables—except he was *still* different somehow; I felt it in the hollows of my bones.

A few minutes passed before I saw him. I was on the sidewalk, lingering, going the opposite direction of the sun. He leaned left and right on his skateboard, creating a deep, invisible S in the street. The wind tangled itself in his white shirt, and his arms were outstretched.

He was a bird, and the light of the day outlined him with a canary glow.

Seeing Bo again made my insides turn in anguish. Beads of sweat formed in my armpits. It was like being midair, never knowing when the drop would come.

My fingers trembled when I grabbed my phone. I opened an old app. It had been a while since I played *Pokémon Go*, but it was something to do if I wanted to get outside by myself and avoid looking stupid. Like now.

Stayed still as I waited for it to load.

The music blasted. Shit. I turned off the sound.

Did he hear that?

Just freaking breathe, I told myself. But what would I even say when he came closer? The sound of the wheels scraping the pavement grew louder, tying my intestines together.

The app was fully loaded now. Finally. I spotted a Snorlax. I tried the super spin to catch it but failed, a bit rusty. Then I tried again, succeeding. Just what I needed.

When I looked up, I noticed Bo making a beeline toward me.

Nope, no.

No, no, no.

But it was too late to turn around. Bo was already waving, his fingers wiggling, and I would look ridiculous if I dipped out. This was it. I needed to take a leap toward the orgastic future.

Or whatever it was *Gatsby* said.

My throat squeezed, and I could barely swallow the thick slime in the back of my throat. It floated there, and I raised the limp thing connected to my body to wave back.

Shit. I guessed I was doing this.

Bo stopped his board right in front of me, dramatic as hell. His actions were so quick, the breeze from it tickled the hair on my skin. What I noticed first was that Bo wasn't a zombie; he wasn't a half zombie, either. He stood tall, human as ever.

Then, his shirt. It was white, but on the center of his chest were four words printed in black: ALL MONSTERS ARE HUMAN.

I couldn't not look at Bo after that. What was this, some sick joke from the universe?

Or...maybe he was in on this. Maybe he knew zombies existed. Maybe he could morph into one whenever he wanted.

No. That couldn't be. It would be on another level of madness, and I definitely wasn't there yet, but looking at him made my blood boil from the heat; I felt it more so when I crossed my arms.

"Well, well, well...if it isn't Bonet girl. Back in action, I see." Bo smiled so wide it caused a tidal wave to the freckles on his cheeks.

I squinted my eyes and looked deeply into his gaze, trying to figure him out, hoping it would be that easy. Or maybe he'd give in. Tell me what I knew to be true.

"It's Zharie, actually."

He raised his brows. "Ah, *Zharie.*" He looked at the ground for a moment. Smirked. And he got off his skateboard. "I'm Bo," he said, and he gripped the board in his hand, keeping my gaze now.

"That's what I've heard."

Bo twisted his full lips, but only for a moment. Pensive. Yet he dropped the question he was going to ask. He leaned to the side, and I noticed then that he was an awkward stander. Which was baffling. How could one *stand* awkwardly? Maybe it was a zombie side effect.

Or maybe it was just him.

Then the words on his shirt jumbled together to read: ALL HUMANS ARE MONSTERS.

And then: MONSTERS ARE ALL.

The hell? My brain was on mass overload. I blinked, my eyes watering in the corners. The words changed back: ALL MONSTERS ARE HUMAN.

"So, uh, what brings you to the party?" Bo asked, leaning against his skateboard now.

"You mean . . . *outside*?"

"Well, that's only stating the obvious. You're supposed to ask, 'What party?'" he said, and then he waited.

"Oh, um, what party?"

Bo grinned, and his freckles held my attention again. They were intrusive, on his lips, pressing and moving in ways I'd never seen before. "The party that I'm going to tonight. Wanna come?"

I scoffed. The scoff turned into a chuckle. "Are you like this with everyone you know?"

He looked past me for a moment, and I contemplated following his gaze but didn't. "Straight up," he said. "I'm always like this. Wait till you meet my friends."

"Friends? You want *me* to meet your friends? Why?"

"Why not?"

That was stupid. That he answered the question that way. "Because you are an obvious monster," I said, pointing to his shirt.

He looked down, beaming at the fact that I noticed his shirt. "Correction. All monsters are human, Zharie."

"Are they, though?"

Bo tilted his head to the side. "It depends on what your definition of a monster is," he said, and it was clear to me, like it was with Mama, that he had no idea how many monsters were actually in the world.

Yet the slightest glimmer in his eyes made me want to believe otherwise, and I still didn't get it. Didn't get how Bo was human *and* a monster. Why could he revert, but Mama couldn't?

Bo stared at me the same way I stared at him, waiting, daring me to dive into this nameless chaos with him. My stomach tripled in knots, and I could taste the Takis I'd eaten earlier in the back of my throat.

Right now, in this very steamy moment (Because of the heat. Not because he was cute. Monsters were *not* cute.), I wished I were dancing instead. I could already imagine my feet pressing into the ground, starting at the tip and down to the sole.

Tip to sole.

Tip to sole.

And I anchored, settling my weight to the back of my foot, creating an away force between myself and my invisible partner.

The dance pattern in my head grew silent, and I fiddled with my fingers. "*If* I agree to this, do you solemnly swear that you don't have a vendetta, or a blood-driven thirst to kill me for my brain, or heart, or any other vital organ?"

Bo smirked. "You take this monster thing seriously?"

More than he would ever know, but yeah, of course I did. This was not a joke.

He shook off a laugh. "Okay, I solemnly swear that ... I may or may not do some of those things," he said, the last words squished together.

I gathered my lips to the side of my mouth.

"I'm kidding, *I'm kidding.*" He laughed, and then he held out his pinky finger. "I solemnly swear that I don't have a vendetta *or* a blood-driven thirst to kill you for any of your vital organs. I swear it."

We crossed our pinkies together, his warmer than expected, and I somewhat believed that his promise was true.

CHAPTER EIGHT

PINKY PROMISES with the dead *weren't* as crazy as following Bo
to his apartment on the third floor.

Inside, I heard the muttered sound of the television, and his apartment smelled of incense, garlic, and onions.

The space was identical to the one Auntie and I shared, but this
one was already filled with homey things. A plant hanging there. A
throw blanket draped over the couch. The couch, long and L-shaped,
one I wanted to crawl into. Books on an end table. Books with folded
corners, small promises to open them again. Family portraits on walls,
and windows covered with curtains.

Auntie E had been living in her apartment for a year or so before I was handed off to her, and she'd never bothered to buy stuff to fill it because she said we didn't need it to survive—which was technically true. We were alive, weren't we? I asked her about it once, but she gave me a look that clearly let me know I shouldn't bring it up again. It was the same look she had when I asked her about the hot water.

"Ma!" Bo called out. "Is it cool if my friend eats with us? She's comin' to Rico's after."

Bo's mother stepped out of the kitchen. She was the Black woman I remembered seeing with Bo the other day, and from the photos, the Asian guy I'd spotted in the moving truck must be Bo's dad. She was much shorter than I remembered, though.

Her smile faded. "Uh-uh. Pause. Did you take off your shoes?"

"Ope, uh, sorry," he said, and he went back to the entryway, kicked off his Vans, and placed them by his board.

She looked at me. "You too, honey," she said before going back to the kitchen. I did as she asked, untying my Chucks and then neatly placing them side by side, next to Bo's.

I guessed that was a yes to dinner.

Bo waited for me to finish, and he whispered, "No worries. My parents love everyone." Then he sat at the dining room table, and I followed him, trying my best to keep myself away from his personal bubble as I sat next to him in a wooden chair, curling my toes beneath me.

With my next breath, I sent a quick text to Mini:

> Fuh!!! It's happening! 🔊

My phone vibrated, and when I checked, it wasn't from Mini. It was from Luca. Great.

> Yoooo
>
> Zeezy
>
> You coming to the studio next week or nah?

Ignored the text and locked my phone immediately.

Moments later, Bo's mother brought plates of food to the table: steaming hot-water cornbread, mac and cheese, sautéed green beans, and pork chops.

My stomach grumbled like there was a mini earthquake inside me, and my mouth filled with saliva. I didn't think I was hungry, but all this food reminded me of Mama's cooking. From the savory smell of the salt to the slight crunchiness of the hot-water cornbread, I tried to absorb it all without touching it.

"Bo, tell me about your friend," his mother said, handing a porcelain plate to each of us. She had a smile in her eyes, and her curly hair was laid into a low bun. Perfect edges and everything. Her deep brown skin was speckled with small freckles right below her eyes. Intricate. So that was where Bo inherited them from.

Bo glanced at me, and I wondered how many friends he brought to his house unannounced. Was I even considered a friend at this point? Not that it mattered. I was just here trying to figure out why this dude looked like a zombie from time to time.

And now I was more interested in the food than trying to figure any of that out.

Bo spooned a heaping serving of the mac and cheese and placed it on his plate. Then another. In the corner of my eye, a lamp in the living room flickered. Wasn't sure why it was on—the curtains were drawn back, letting in the evening sun—but the flickering light was powerful, weird, too.

Maybe it was a sign that I should quietly excuse myself, exit this place, and never return.

My stomach growled again. But there was food. Then my phone vibrated. I hoped it wasn't Luca again.

"This is Zharie. She's cool. She lives downstairs," Bo said, answering his mother's question.

"Zharie, it's nice to meet you. I'm Angela." Bo's mother made her plate, and she sat down across from us. "What school do you go to?"

I filled my plate with all the sides, and when Angela and Bo looked at me weird for not taking any pork chops, I said, "They look really good, but I'm a vegetarian." I had been since I was twelve. Mama always said I was the worst meat-eater; if anything was veiny or had too much fat in it, it would never leave my plate.

"But to answer your question, I go to Sumner Academy."

Angela's eyes were wide, and she covered her mouth before she spoke. It was funny how she did that. It was the same look Mama had when we learned I got accepted to Sumner.

"Oh, do you? My oldest son went there, Jackson. Bo, did you tell her about Jackson?"

Bo was mid-chew, and he looked at me with dull eyes. "Oh yeah, that's *their* star child. He went to Sumner, too, and after he graduated, he joined the National Guard. He was stationed for a couple years, but now that he's done with all that stuff, he's in the engineering program at K-State."

"Ah," I said.

"Yup," Bo said, and he rolled his eyes.

"And Bo got into Sumner, too," Angela added, staring at Bo while he ate, but he didn't look at her.

"But I go to Harmon. Didn't want to go to the academy."

"Ahhh," I said again, because I didn't really know what to say, but why didn't Bo want to go to Sumner? Yeah, it was hard, but it wasn't *that* bad.

"He should have went," Angela said.

"Maaaaa," he dragged. "Just because that's what you and Dad want for me, doesn't mean it's something I have to do. I'm never gonna be Jackson. Straight up."

Her eyebrow arched. "Ooh, child. You better watch it. Don't be raising your voice in front of your little friend, now."

I gulped, trying not to lock eyes with either one of them. I would never dare talk back to Mama with friends around, ever. She'd ground me from dance in a heartbeat.

Angela continued. "You ought to be happy you have Zharie here. Which—" She paused, looking over to me. "Sorry, honey. You shouldn't have to hear all this, but it's nothing new for him." Then she looked at her son as she knifed her pork chop. "And no, Bo, I'm not gonna get over the fact that you turned down the opportunity to attend one of the top schools in the state of Kansas. It's a better opportunity than what we had."

Bo smacked his lips. His cheeks a tint of red when I glanced at him.

"Don't smack your lips at the table. And, Zharie, sweetie, can you pass me the Louisiana hot sauce, please?" Angela looked at me and winked.

I returned the wink, handing her the hot sauce, and sweet Jesus, it was so, so awkward.

I felt a little bad for Bo. His head was low, and he forked his food like it was about to walk off his plate.

"He'll get over it, honey," she said, probably noticing my discomfort.

The front door opened, and Bo's dad walked through. He barely looked a day over thirty, wide shoulders, sharp jawline, not a single gray hair in sight.

"Hey, hey, hey," Bo's dad said, taking off his shoes and finding a seat at the table.

Slid my phone out of my pocket to see who texted me. It was Mini.

> HOT SHIT Z
>
> GOD!!!!
>
> Just don't do anything stupid

Tucked my phone away. The room felt too crowded now, and what was I supposed to do if every person here turned into a zombie?

"Well, who's this?" he asked, and I could immediately see who Bo got his smile from. Really, apart from Bo's curly hair and his freckles, he looked identical to his father.

Bo introduced me to his dad, Sam, and Sam shook my hand. Then he kissed his wife, thanked her for the food, and filled his plate.

And it had been a long time since I'd had a meal with a family.

Was it always like this for Bo? Were all dads as inviting as Sam was?

I learned that Bo inherited his wit from his father. They fired jokes at each other like they were in combat, and there may or may not have been a mini knife fight over the last piece of meat.

Later, I found out that Sam was a physical therapist, while Bo's mom worked at one of the up-and-coming hair salons in the city dedicated to natural hair.

It was a little after seven p.m. when we finished up. I asked Angela if she needed any help with the dishes, and she didn't hesitate to put me on rinsing duty. Bo teased then, stating that his mother would probably invite me over again since I was the only guest who had offered to help with dishes.

When the kitchen was clean, we put our shoes on to head out, and before I got in the car with Bo and his mom, I checked with Auntie E to make sure she was okay with me leaving.

She was home when I entered the apartment, but she was in the middle of taking a bubble bath and watching *Grey's Anatomy* on her phone. The door was open, as always.

"Hey," I said, my sudden appearance causing the candle flame to flicker. "Is it cool if I hang out with Bo and his friends?"

Auntie E's eyes were locked on her phone. She moved a little, and a few waves formed in the tub. I hoped to God that I didn't accidentally see a boob. I was still traumatized from the last time. "Who's Bo?"

"He's the kid that lives upstairs."

My phone buzzed.

"Hmm," she mumbled, and I could feel Auntie's words vibrate in my shoes. I shouldn't have asked her. I knew she'd say yes anyway, but maybe a part of me hoped she'd say, "Okay, text me the address in case you need anything," or, "Let me know when you get there safely."

But instead: "M'kay. Make sure you have a ride home." And it was still weird to me how much she had changed. I'd never forget the way her face looked at the funeral. She was stone-cold, her eyes glossed from the crying. But when they closed the casket, she stopped. Not another tear shed.

I'd never seen her like that before. She had sucked them in somehow. It wasn't like she was afraid to cry, either. The last time we'd gotten together before Mama died, she bawled at the movie we watched.

This was different. Almost scarier than the zombies.

I ignored it, though, leaving the bathroom and responding to Mini's text. She sent another one:

> Did u get my last message?????

> This is IMPORTANT

>> Mini. Stop freaking out. I'm fine!

The next text came lighting fast.

> Proof or you're an imposter!

I snapped a quick photo of myself and sent it.

>> See. I'm alive!

With that, I grabbed my cross-body bag, made sure my pepper spray was tucked inside, and headed to the minivan parked out front.

Bo and I sat in the last row with several inches of leather seat between us, but it wasn't enough. The air was thick, and it felt like my throat was closing. Maybe this was too much, too soon. There was a reason why my gut twisted in knots earlier, and it felt like a warning.

Bo flashed a smile.

Um. Yeah. That was it, that was my warning, but we were out of the parking lot before I could undo my seat belt, so I sat back and took a breath.

The good thing was that Bo wasn't paying attention to me. He and his mom bickered about what to listen to, and I think she said something along the lines of "This is my car. When you get one, you can have an opinion." It shut him up real fast.

Bo rested his head back, and I imagined it sinking through the cushion and beneath the car. My brain put him back together again, and when I looked at him this time, I noticed his forehead smooth of lines. He mouthed some words from the song on the radio, and he tapped his thumb rhythmically against the seat.

The song was blue and orange. Sweet and spice. Day and night.

Some of the lyrics swirled in my head. *You turned my heart upside down. And there is . . . nothing to do for me now.*

The moments that followed in the back seat of Angela's minivan were perpetual. I could see the world moving with haste behind us; the evening colors bent in on themselves like pottery spinning on a wheel.

Bo indisputably withstood time, glowing in the same light, and I looked at him in increments, trying my best to not be so dang obvious.

He sat up; his hands folded in his lap. "I'm excited for you to meet my friends, and my cousin Rico."

"What's he like?" I said, sitting up, too.

"Hella trill. Hella BA. He's actually the guy who taught me how to skate. I think you'll like him," he said, and he nodded his head and created the hang loose sign with his pinky and his thumb.

I pursed my lips. "Cool."

"Very," he said, and there was silence.

"So what changed?" he asked, assuming I knew what he meant, but I probably looked lost as hell, so he continued with "You know, the first day we met, I asked you to hang and you said you didn't have a reason to. What changed?"

From the window, I could see that we were pulling into the driveway of a one-story home with a few kids and a barking Chihuahua in the front yard.

"Uh..." I muttered, not able to get the rest of the sentence out. I couldn't tell him the truth. "It's funny you ask," I said as the car parked, and I picked at my fingernails—the *thump, thump, thump* of me picking them amplified in my eardrums.

I took a deep breath, but there was this cracking sound that broke in the air. It sounded as if someone was struggling to breathe, like a rumble slowly rolling up an airway and released with a gasp.

And so it was the thump from my nails and the cracking that made it hard to focus.

The *thump* and the *crack*.

The *thump* and the *crack*.

"I don't know. I wanted to take a risk," I finally said, and I looked at him and smiled, hoping he'd drop the question so we could get out.

The cracking came again. Louder and laced with snarls. It was Bo. The sound was coming from Bo. His eyes in slits, blood pulsing from them. His lips blistered and stretched past his cheekbones to reveal his sagging gums and blood-drenched teeth. Bo's whole face twisted and warped into something that could only come from a nightmare.

I clutched my bag to my chest, unable to move as I watched the blood leak from his eye and down the exposed tissue in his cheek.

He was gone, and I felt incredibly stupid for letting myself sit this close to him.

A grunt rose from where his throat should be, and the gunk in his mouth bubbled into a foamlike substance. He was drooling now.

And to think, what an awful way to die.

CHAPTER NINE

MAMA WAS THE LAST ZOMBIE I'd been this close to, and soon after, she died.

Now it was Bo. The light shining through the car window highlighted how gruesome his features were, and it caused my intestines to shrivel like an old plum.

Any abrupt move and he could rip my brain from my body with the peeling things that were his hands.

Bo groaned, and that was the last straw.

"All right, kids, we're here," Angela said, and it was the only signal I needed.

"Um ... I—I think I'mma head out." I unbuckled my seat belt and got up quickly, stubbing my toe on my way out of the car. Screeched, but I kept going, noticing that Bo was following me.

Outside, the sky stained the night black and blue, and I heard the smothered sounds of the snarls. Could hear the blood gurgling and bubbling in Bo's mouth. He was catching up to me.

I zoomed past the unfamiliar faces in the front yard of Rico's house, jumped over the barking Chihuahua, and invited myself inside.

I couldn't—could hardly think straight inside. The unfamiliar smells. The flashing light from the living room TV flickered broken images against the furniture and gray walls. Kept going once I spotted a hallway to the right of me, jolting down it as fast as I could, entering the first room I saw.

Held my hand to my throat, wheezing, and that song by the Cranberries played in my thoughts like I was in a music video. It kept pestering me, asking me what was in my head.

What stuck was their use of the word *zombie*.

Zombie, zombie, zombie-ie-ie.

Inside the room, I locked the door, turned on the light. It was a white bathroom. A gray shower curtain hung to the right of me. There were matching rugs and towels.

A drip leaked from the faucet, and each drop added to the small puddle that gathered at the bottom of the basin.

My hands trembled, and I struggled to find my phone in my bag, only to realize that it was in my back pocket. But any second and he—he could be behind me. Behind this door. Slumped shoulders. Black eyes.

Texted Mini:

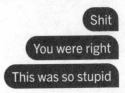

Gasped and pressed my back to the door.

He's a freaking ZOMBIE!

Mini called me. "Z, what are you talking about? Are you okay?!" The room spun, and I couldn't inhale the air anymore.

"Z," Mini pressed. "You there?"

I closed my eyes. "We were in the car. He sat next to me, and then he was a zombie," I whispered. "I got out and ran, and now I'm in some stranger's house, and I feel like I'm gonna die."

I was whisper-screaming by now. "I'm awaiting my imminent death, and I'm gonna die surrounded by people I don't even know. You were so freaking right, Mini. I feel so stu—"

"Breeeathe." Mini cut me off. "Just calm down, Z. Calm the frick down. And yeah, you *are* stupid," she said, and I was offended.

My actions were stupid, but...

"But—"

"*BUT* you are not going to die. You said it yourself. It's all in your head. Zombies aren't real! Just snap out of it. Did you say you were at a stranger's house??? How— You know what, I'm not even gonna ask. I just... I don't know what you thought was gonna happen."

My weight sank into the white door, the only thing holding me up now. "I don't know," I said, and I waited for her to tell me *I told you so*, but it never came.

A baby cried in the background of the phone line. There was another crack, possibly the signal rupturing. Then deep breathing. Long and shallow. Goose bumps trailed my arms, down my spine. A creak in the distance, somewhere down the hall.

"I—uh, I've gotta go, Z. Sorry. Babysitting." She paused. "Please text me when you get home. You've got this. Bye."

Eff. No. The call ended, and I stared at the screen in disbelief. That was my only lifeline. This was the worst possible predicament, and now I was trapped in a bathroom with no one.

A thud. The door vibrated. I lurched upright, and from the tiny gap beneath it, I could see a dark shadow cast on the hardwood floor in the hallway.

Another thud came, followed by a long, throaty groan. Something dead. Something dead and waiting.

"I—I'm kinda in here," I responded, my voice red.

He groaned again, and in the back of my mind, I heard the voice of a boy muffled in the sound that came from his chest. It was distant, like hearing a bird whistle from the tallest tree in the woods but not being able to see it.

It was Bo.

Even if he would be terrifying when I opened the door, the sound of his voice reminded me why I followed him here to begin with. I wanted nothing more than to understand why this was happening to me, and I'd never find answers to Mama's sudden death if I didn't go through with this.

I signed the shape of the cross and swung the door open with a deep breath.

The rushing air smacked me in the face, and before me was . . . well, what *was* Bo. Decaying skin now, open wounds and scars. Unblinking eyes. A feral, broken grin.

He twitched forward, and I took a step back.

Forward again, and another step back.

We played the who-could-get-closer game until I was backed into the leaky sink with my eyes snapped shut and Bo trying to communicate with me.

He placed his hand on my right shoulder, and I anticipated the moment when his claws would rip into my skin.

He can't hurt me, I thought, grounding myself and finding my center like I did when I danced. *This isn't real. This isn't real.*

Bo's voice was subdued at first, but then it flooded the space around me and filled the air. "Zharie, are you okay?" he asked, but what I heard was: *What did I do to make you so blue?*

But I wasn't blue. I was green, seafoam green. And if he moved any closer, I might vomit.

Opened my eyes, and he was leaned in. The smell sour, a gargling sound. He was half human, half zombie now, staring me down with his one normal eye and his one swollen one that leaked pus.

Just.

Freaking.

Breathe.

"You, like, sprinted away from me—*sprinted*. You look like you saw a ghost or something."

It was so much worse than that. Like, a trillion times worse.

Gripped the sink, held myself up. "I, uh . . . I wasn't feeling too good. Needed to get out of the car." Absolute lies.

His brows rose. "You sure? 'Cuz we don't have to be here. You say the words, and we're out."

"No, no." I shook my head. More lies. "We're here to be with your friends."

Half of Bo's face flickered with light, and it almost made him look more human. *Almost.*

"Shall we?" He motioned his hand toward the door, and I followed him out of the bathroom with my insides on a tightrope. I couldn't keep my eyes off the back of his head—the dead part. Pieces of his scalp pulled away, his brain mangled and exposed, cascading in lumps through his hair.

There was so much blood.

How?

We walked to the kitchen and went through a door that led to the garage. In the garage, there was another door that led to the basement. When we descended the steps, the first thing I saw was a neon sign that read PUNKS NOT DEAD hanging on the wall.

The basement was this cold, unfinished room that had poured cement for the floor and a red, dingy rug over it with a few too many questionable stains. The room was dim, no windows present, and the only light came from small lamps. There was a floral love seat with two people occupying it, seat cushions on the floor in the shape of a half-moon, an old desktop computer that rested on a desk made from plywood, and the biggest (and oldest) television I'd seen in a long time, with two beat-up gaming chairs in front of it.

The Little Mermaid played on the screen, but the sound was masked by an alternative song that came from someone's portable speaker.

Held my arms close to me and scanned the faces in the room. The first person Bo approached was this brown dude with shaggy hair, wearing a plaid button-down shirt and a graphic tee underneath. He stood on a skateboard in the middle of the room.

"My man!" Bo said, and they dapped each other with familiarity. It was strange, and maybe a little humorous, seeing a half zombie move that way. "Jesus, this is Zharie," Bo said, and after Jesus gave me the most awkward side hug in the history of awkward side hugs, I noticed how dopey his eyes were and how goofy his smile was. An easiness there. Like he'd just said the funniest joke you'd ever heard. And he was the epitome of a skater kid—with dusty Adidas, a snapback to match, and the slight stench of weed.

Then Bo hugged the two people on the couch—Mika and Andrew, I learned. Mika was a short Black girl with thick eyeliner and a black boater hat that rested perfectly on the back of her head. She rocked an oversized button-up shirt that went down to her knees, and when she hugged me, she smelled like fresh pine. There was an electric energy about her, kind of like she carried sun rays in her pockets. I hoped to gravitate toward her later and ask her where she bought her hat.

Andrew smelled similar when we hugged. He was a white boy—the only one here—and he was a foot taller than Mika. He had on a green beanie that matched his braces. When they sat back on the floral sofa, they fiddled with each other's thumbs, and I wondered if they were dating. I could see it—they were cute together.

Before I could sit, another person descended the staircase. It was an Asian kid, and I wondered if it was Bo's cousin on his dad's side. Whoever he was, he was really cute. He had an edge to him that I couldn't quite put my finger on, and a dimple that pierced his left cheek so intensely it looked like it was the aftermath of a fight. His ears were gauged, and he had one of those jaws that looked like he was constantly evaluating people. He was intimidating, and it was obvious that he was the leader of the pack.

He put his board down to hug me, and he squeezed my arms. I tensed up and looked at Bo, confused.

"Welcome to my home," he said.

Bo chuckled. "This is Rico. My cousin." They dapped, hugged, dapped, and behind him was that barking Chihuahua from earlier.

Rico told me her name was Luna. He picked her up, and she let me stroke the spot between her ears.

And last, Charlie descended the staircase. I admired her ripped black shirt and her high-waisted shorts. They hugged her better than mine did, and the only reason I knew her name was because everyone, minus Bo and myself, shouted, "Charlie!" as soon as she entered the room.

The atmosphere changed when she made it to the last step, and there were unsaid words there, a life-threatening secret.

She stood before Bo and me. Beautiful, dark brown skin, her thigh tattoos peeking up at us. Fierce winged liner, and matte violet lips.

A half smile, and when she said hi, I heard a slithering on the floor.

Bo's face flashed of death then, his lips brittle. And he morphed into the undead, keeping me from understanding anything he said when he introduced me to her.

Charlie hugged me, and she felt as if she'd been sleeping on the cement—cold and hard—but she smelled like bubble gum and cigarettes.

She tucked her short, dark hair behind her ear, and before she walked away, she gave Bo another hug—one where she squished his boned shoulders and patted the hollow in his back. She whispered something quickly to him, and then she walked away.

I rubbed my arms, still cold from the hug, and I took a deep breath as I watched everyone in the room interact with one another. Who were these people? The kids here were cool in the way society deemed otherwise, and I felt like I didn't belong, like they walked to the pace of their own soundtrack, and I couldn't even find the beat. Instead, I was an unfortunate side effect in the list of side effects that only kept coming because something good was promised.

(Spoiler alert: Nothing good was promised.)

Whatever.

Bo trudged toward the seat cushions on the floor, one of his legs delayed behind him, and I followed, sitting between him and an aquarium with a fluorescent light that made all the fish glow.

I watched the fish swim around one another, and I wondered what it was like to be in a school of fish where you were always surrounded by others, creating a barrier from potential predators in the world. But there was one lone fish at the top of the tank, his belly facing upward. The poor guy must have died somehow, and I didn't think anyone noticed but me.

Bo groaned, and the whiff that came from him smelled so rancid, I gagged. I shrugged in response to him, and I hoped he'd change back to his human form again. There were questions I had.

In all truth, even though I sat beside this monster, I didn't feel as afraid anymore. Just curious. If he wanted to kill me, he would have by now—right?

But also . . . since Bo was a zombie, did that mean he might die soon? I really wasn't sure how this whole thing worked.

A circle formed in the room, and Rico pulled a joint out of his pocket, lit it up, and passed it after taking a few long drags. I watched the joint make its way around the circle, finally getting to Bo. Bo took a puff and handed it to me.

I was exceptionally curious about weed, but I didn't smoke, so I passed it to Jesus, who sat on the other side of me.

Jesus giggled as soon as he held the joint in his hands, his feet curling. "You're missing out," he said, and he inhaled deeply. Smoke thick in the air, traveling into my lungs anyway. I figured getting contact high would be more than enough fun for one night.

"Guys, we should play a game," Mika said, kicking her biker boots off to reveal her kitten-print socks.

Rico nodded after taking another puff. "Like what?"

His eyes barely open, Jesus shouted, "Suck and blow!"

"Nope, no way, dude," Rico said, blowing rings of smoke into the air.

"Whaaat, why?" Jesus grabbed Luna—she was snuggled in a tiny ball—kissed her on the head, and held her up. "Even Luna wants to play—look at her adorable face. Isn't she just so dang cute? Can you really say no to a dog, Rico?" Luna's little brown body trembled as she dangled in the air; it made me laugh.

Rico laughed, too. "Nooooooo. We're all high. Do you think it's a good idea to play suck and blow right now? C'mon, think it through, man."

"Or maybe we could play lap chain?" Charlie suggested. She sat on the couch with Mika and Andrew, her legs crossed over them.

"Bro, what even is that?" Jesus said. "Pretty sure my idea was better."

Charlie stood, ignoring the question. "Okay, everyone stand," she said, and no one stood. "Guys. Come on. Play with me." She pouted and extended her hand to Bo, who was to the left of her in this circle of trust. He took it and stood, and although I was the only one who could see how horrifying Bo looked in the dim light and smoke, I was still baffled that *I* was the only one.

He was *right there*, blood spilling from his mouth, staining his white shirt.

The others stood, and I did, too.

"So, like, everyone needs to stay in the circle that we're in, but the idea of the game is to have everyone turn to the right and squeeze in as close as possible, making the circle smaller and smaller till we're close enough to sit on each other's laps."

"Trillll," Mika said, and she took off her hat and placed it on the couch behind her. "I'm in."

Charlie jumped with excitement, her big eyes widening and glistening. "If Mika's in, all of you have to play!"

Bo nodded and groaned something to me, and I responded with

"I'm down to play." But playing this game meant I'd have to break every zombie barrier and get as close to Bo as possible, and since Bo was to the right of me, I was bound to end up with a decaying corpse in my lap.

It also meant that I'd be sitting on Jesus's lap, and with his high level of dopiness, I didn't know if I trusted him to follow directions. It wasn't like I was the smallest girl in the room, and my biggest fear—besides Zombie Bo—was squashing Jesus to a sad, slow death.

Regardless, something told me he might be okay with that.

The group ambled forward, and we all turned to the right. We moved closer and closer to the center of the circle, until we bumped shoulders and giggles filled the room.

Bo's breathing came in fast spurts, another zombie side effect, and I was so close to him that the back of his seeping shirt pressed against my cheek, making a squishing sound in my ears.

Pressed into him again, and I could literally feel his peeling skin beneath my fingertips. The moving, the dripping of it on my shoes.

I closed my eyes, and when Charlie yelled, "Sit!" we all sat on each other's laps as planned.

Jesus's grip tightened around my waist, and it was the only thing keeping me grounded because I refused to hold on to Bo. Two seconds later, we collapsed, and the room filled with laughter.

When I looked at Bo, he was a normal teenager again, laughing, and I realized there was so, so much I didn't know about him.

"Charlie! My girl, you came through. That was actually legit," Rico said, getting off the floor. He dusted his black jeans off. "But listen, I need some fresh air. Anyone wanna take a walk?"

"Yeah," Andrew said, standing, too. Then he shouted, his fist rising in the air. "Boards!" And those who had their boards grabbed them and rushed up the steps.

Before we left, I saw that the little lone fish in the aquarium was no longer dead. He swam with his other fishy friends. Different now, scales blistering with a neon color. And I wondered if his death was only an illusion like everything else.

CHAPTER TEN

BO WAS THE ONLY ONE who'd left his skateboard at home.
I followed behind him up the steps, and when we got outside, the sun
had gone away, and all the streetlights cast a chartreuse glow on the
sidewalks.

The sky was indigo, and in it were swirls and swirls of golden yellow and baby blue. Like a painting, the lines of color were sloppy and
manicured in long, engulfing strokes, creating the illusion of wind
blowing against the clouds.

Bo and I trailed the sidewalk on Shearer Road while his friends took
on the streets like they owned them. Andrew pulled his phone out of
his pocket, and a song blasted from the speakers. A familiar tune,

but I didn't know any of the words. The sound of it created a riot in my bloodstream, and the world pivoted on its axis before returning to normal.

We were blood and fire and roses.

"So these are your friends," I said, kicking some of the broken rock on the pavement.

"Whoa, there. You say it like it's a bad thing. *Is* it a bad thing?" he asked, and boy, it was great to hear Bo's normal voice again.

I grinned and the sky liquified, the colors bleeding together. Between our steps, Bo grabbed my hand and held it. I held his back momentarily, barely enough time to feel the warmth, and then I let go.

Bo smiled still, not caring that I rejected him.

I finally responded. "No, but Jesus may or may not have held me a little tighter than he needed when we were playing the game."

"He did? Damn that kid. I can slap him up if you need me to. He probably thinks you're beautiful because, well, *you are*. And he's probably just lonely, but still."

Beautiful. Wasn't that word overrated? "Geesh, no. You don't need to physically assault anyone for me, and uh, thanks for the compliment."

"You are most welcome, Zharie. Or . . . Z, can I call you Z?"

"Sure," I said, and I watched how Bo's friends weaved around one another. They were like the birds of the streets.

"Z, have you ever been in love before?"

I shot him a look. "Wow, Bo, that's a little left field, don't you think?"

"Nope, not at all."

"Really?" I pressed. "Because there is an astronomical amount of things we don't know about each other, and *that's* the question you want to ask?"

He shrugged his shoulders, his hands deep in his pockets. "Yeah, but I'm gathering that you may want to ask me a few questions before you answer the one I asked you? True?"

"True."

"Okay. Shoot your shot."

"Uh . . . so, what grade are you in, and do all of your friends go to the same high school?"

"I'll be a junior when the school year starts again, and yeah, we all go to the same school. What about you? What grade?"

"I'll actually be a junior, too."

"Cool," he said, and he did the hang loose sign again. "So, love. Ever felt it?"

I huffed. Bo wasn't going to stop, and part of me wished my brain would turn him into a zombie again so I could ignore him. There was no desire to open up to Bo, to tell him that I'd been unable to connect to anyone on a level that deep besides Mama. Now that I was seeing zombies on a consistent basis, I didn't know if I'd ever have a normal life again.

"Romantically? No," I said.

"Never?"

"Never," I assured him. Because love was like an infected scab. It was like picking at it and hoping for a different outcome each time, but it was always the same scar that came back. "It's just an infection," I said. An invasive one. Hazardous, even.

Love was a side effect of dying.

Or, better yet, *dying* was a side effect of love. . . .

And I knew that giving too much of yourself away depleted you. It was how I felt now that Mama was gone.

"Hmm," he said, and his lips folded in on each other while the cicadas played their same old tune.

We came to a halt at the crosswalk on Steele Road as his friends continued past it. Bo went to cross and stopped in the middle of the street.

"Dude, what are you doing?"

"I'm standing in the middle of the street."

"Um, okay. Obvious. But why?"

He got on the ground, stretching out comfortably. "Why not?"

"Oh my god. Bo, a car could come! You could get hit!"

He sat up. "Come on, Z. Live a little. There are no cars coming." Bo relaxed again, his body glowing yellow from the light above him. "Join me?"

I heard a trailing behind me, and my jaw clenched when I looked. Nothing there. Looked up and down the street; still not one car in sight. A sleeping town. The stoplight turned red again, and I ran onto the pavement to lie down beside Bo.

"Woooo!" he shouted, throwing his hand in the air, reaching for *The Starry Night* that was the sky.

It startled me so much I laughed. The laughter confiscated my body, shooting up my throat in bursts like fireworks, and it was the absolute best feeling.

The *best* feeling.

I was alive, savoring every terrifying moment of this.

We looked at each other, his eyes a decaying gray. "You ever done this before?" he asked.

"Never," I said, and as weird as it was, I think Mama would be proud of me. She had always been an active (very *annoyingly* active) advocate of me stepping out of my comfort zone, and I always fought her on that.

This move was more her than it was me, and when I pressed my fingers into the warm asphalt, my body liquefied and melted into the ground. I was no longer part of the moment, part of the street. I *was* the moment. I was the long, stretched-out blackness between two crosswalks, and I think, somewhere past the filters in the sky, Mama was here, too.

A low buzzing noise clunked its way down the hill, and when Bo and I sat up, we were momentarily blinded by headlights. We fled the street, returning back to the sidewalk, and we couldn't stop the laughter from escaping our bodies. We buzzed together, like the bees. We were yellow, and black, and blue.

Bo glanced at me after catching his breath. "I don't know, Z. Maybe you've been loving the wrong people," he said. "Say it *is* an infection, right? But maybe it's only an infection because it's meant to be invasive. That kind of feeling, love, it demands to be felt."

CHAPTER ELEVEN

WHEN WE CAUGHT UP to the crew, I spotted Charlie on the edge of the sidewalk, holding her thumb out to the oncoming traffic. She blended into the night, and as Bo and I got closer, I saw a faint purple halo lingering above her head, casting a shimmering glow upon her dark hair.

A long, hushed vibrato filled the air, and the sound pulled us closer to Charlie, the entrancing melody blurring my vision momentarily. Before I caught my breath, our eyes locked and she smirked, a tingle in the pit of my stomach.

The song grew louder, piercing my eardrums, and a car zoomed past, honking.

Mika screamed and laughed, pulling Charlie away from the edge. Did everyone have a death wish? Like, wtf.

"Ludicrous," Bo mumbled, his jaw decaying as he spoke.

"But wouldn't that be fun?" Charlie shouted. I had only caught the end of her words, and I watched her wrap her arm around Mika's shoulders, squishing them.

"Hell no," Mika said.

Charlie kissed Mika's cheek. "You gotta live big, honey," she said, and she let go to look at Bo. "Isn't that right, Abraham?"

Bo shrugged, and he was a zombie again, his limbs seeping and leaving a trail behind us.

"Oh, *come on*, Abey. Those are your words," Charlie said, and she hopped on her board to catch up with Andrew, Rico, and Jesus. I heard her shout, "To the cave!"

The cave?

I turned to ask Bo but stopped, realizing how useless our conversation would be.

Mika jumped on her board then, one hand holding down her hat, and Bo grumbled, waving his deteriorating fingers. He tried to pick up the pace, but I felt like he moved in slow motion next to me.

At the end of the street and under an overpass, we followed an old sidewalk to an abandoned house.

"Do y'all always hang out in places like this?" I whispered as we approached a wire fence with a gaping hole carved from the middle.

A streetlight flickered above us when we climbed through, and I felt a small gust of wind tickling the nape of my neck.

Smacked the space there, my twists in the way, and Bo looked at me confused. I shrugged in response, and we kept moving, climbing the crumbling staircase.

At the entrance, Rico and Andrew removed the boards of wood from the doorway, placing them on the old porch. Jesus tripped on his way in, stumbling inside, and Charlie and Mika snickered, following behind him.

All I could smell when I entered was dirt and water. It reminded me of a rainy day, a couple years ago, when Mama had to bribe me to play in the rain with her. If I did, she said we'd go for General Tso's tofu—and honestly, I'd bungee jump for good tofu—but, I remembered, it took all of me to step into that first puddle of mud, the thick slosh squishing between my toes. I wiggled them, wondering if the stuff covering my feet was really fecal matter instead of dirt. And then, if it *was* poop, what if it got stuck in my nails and I couldn't get it out? What if, when I went to clean my toes, a piece of it got in my eye? How did people do this for fun?

Ugh. My stomach had bubbled and roared.

Mama had nudged me then, reading my overactive thoughts, and her nudge forced my toes deeper into the mud.

She'd thrown her head back laughing. Nothing was more fun than watching her daughter *suffer*, or try new things, what have you.

My face had twisted, but instead of going back inside I'd held my hands out and let the warm water pool in my palms. I'd closed my fists, trapping the water there, and when I blinked, I was back in the old house again, standing next to Bo, the dying kid.

The room was without light, peeling wallpaper covered the walls, and a few picture frames hung slanted, debris stuck to them. We stood on floors that were dented and bent, and next to me, a stone fireplace with the deepest, darkest hole I'd ever seen. Like the front door, the windows were boarded, and I understood why they called it the cave—there was only one way in and one way out.

Andrew started a playlist on his phone, and it cued Jesus to pull out a joint. After he lit up, he passed it to Rico, and before I knew it, the two blew smoke rings like they were battling each other, slowly filling the room with smoke.

Bo shuffled to the guys, something thick dripping from the holes in his face, and as soon as I settled into the soles of my shoes, Charlie appeared beside me.

"Hey, girl . . ."

My first instinct was to shudder, but I smiled. She had her own joint, and she tried to hand it to me. "No thanks," I said, and I shifted from my heels to my toes.

"More for me, I guess. It's Zharie, right?" She tilted her head to the side, hair bobbing, and as she stretched, her crop top rose, revealing the skin that covered her ribs.

Felt uncomfortable about my own outfit then. The lack of effort I'd put in today. The old Levi's shirt I wore had a small hole on the side.

I'd sewn it back a while ago, but it had torn again. The washers and dryers at Auntie E's apartment complex sucked; I was still missing like three socks.

Didn't say anything.

"I'm Charlie. I'm basically the mama bear of this crew. How do you know Abe?"

How many names did this kid have? "We live in the same building."

"Oh. Cool. We grew up together. Went to the same day care. He's the absolute best person in the universe. What school do you go to?"

Hard to live up to that. "Sumner."

"Really? I went there last year. We must've just missed each other. I'm at Harmon now."

There was laughter then, and Andrew dropped his board to the ground. "Bulllllshit," he shouted. Rico dropped his board, too, and he took his hat off to put it on backward.

"They're so stupid sometimes," Mika said, approaching us. "No one cares who can jump higher, but apparently they do. Bees are literally dying, and they're worried about their mass index."

Okay. She did have a point.

Mika took Charlie's joint, and Charlie rubbed her back. I wondered if they were always this close. "Don't let them throw off your vibes."

"I know. *I know*, but fuckkkk. Freaking butterballs."

Butterballs? I twisted my lips, chuckling a little, and the smell of the smoke made my throat feel dry.

Mika exhaled, and the smoke danced in circles around me until I coughed. "Wanna try?"

I shook my head.

They shared a laugh, looking at each other with strange eyes, and I felt my phone vibrate in my pocket.

> When u coming back? I ain't tryna be up forever

I sighed. The small gray bubble suffocated me. Auntie E was so twisty. If she didn't want me to leave, she should have said something. What was the point of her changing her mind now?

I put my phone away. "What do y'all do here?"

"We usually just hang. Sometimes we light up or share a drink," Mika said.

"Damn. We should have got drinks," Charlie added. "Sometimes we dance. Have you seen Bo dance? He has moves. Bo!" she yelled, and Bo turned to us for a second, the skin of his jaw gaping, tugging away in small pieces. He didn't say anything; he only stared at us like he wanted to, and then he turned back around.

Charlie scoffed. "Well, okay. Eff me, then," she said, and she rolled her eyes.

Mika handed the blunt to her. "It's cool, girl," she whispered, but I could still hear her. "Anyway." She fixed her posture. "We should do something. Play another game."

Charlie bit her lip and looked behind her again. "I don't know."

"No, we absolutely are," Mika declared, and she clapped, the sound quickly filling the darkness.

It signaled Andrew to turn down the music, and the rest of the crew looked at her.

"We have collectively concluded that a game needs to be played. It's evident that some of you—and I *won't* say who—are mongrels, but we've decided to move past that. With that being said, I suggest we play flashlight tag, and on that note...NOSE GOES!"

Everyone touched their nose but Charlie.

Her shoulders fell forward. "Come *on*, guys! Seriously?"

"Aye, those are the rules," Jesus said. "And I also want to add that I'm happy it's not me." He laughed, but no one else joined him.

Charlie folded her arms and began counting. Everyone scattered, leaving the room in seconds, and Bo came to me, his brittle lips moving. All I caught was "We...hide."

He took my hand, and his skin was so slimy I flinched.

We left the living room, entering a hallway with broken walls and creaking floorboards.

I took out my phone for the flashlight so I could see, but every corner we turned brought more darkness. I wondered if this was what it was like to be swallowed by a whale.

Bo opened a door to a bedroom. There was a bed on the right with tasseled pink sheets covering it, and from the light of the window, I could see stick figures drawn on the walls. Below each one was a name:

Alice and Bianca. The words looked like they were probably scribbled by a kid in elementary school.

Right before Bo pulled me into a closet, I spotted graffiti—one of which was a pair of boobs. Classic.

We sat on the floor, and I kept the light from my phone on.

I ran my fingers past my twists, feeling small pieces of cobwebs in my hair. My God, what else was in here?

It smelled like mildew and roadkill, and I wasn't sure if it was because the house was old or because Bo was rotting beside me.

"So," I said, looking at the floor. "This . . . is fun."

Bo grunted, and a dripping now. Small splats hitting the floor. Blood, maybe?

Just think past it, I told myself, and I faked a laugh, having no idea what his grunt meant. All this did was further prove how absolutely ridiculous this was. Clearly, I'd lost my mind, and now I was in a closet, in an abandoned house, with a zombie.

How did it get to this point?

The walls felt like they were getting smaller, squeezing us closer together. When I looked at Bo, he was looking at me, too. It was more than a look, it was like a hungry stare, a low snarl crawling up his throat.

His eyes, they were so dark, so empty.

Bo's mouth fell open, his broken air filling our space. Then he leaned in a bit, my ticker thumping, blood rushing through my veins.

I looked away. *It isn't real. It isn't real.*

He couldn't hurt me. He promised.

I counted out the steps to a dance pattern in my head, and his snarls grew louder and louder, the walls of the closet hanging over us now, pushing us together, making me feel like this was it.

I needed to break the silence. Uh. *What to say? WHAT TO SAY?*

The closet turned and croaked, and I needed air.

"So, is Charlie always like this?" I spilled out, and that was literally what I said. Of all the sentences, and all the words, *that* was what I said.

The door swung open, dust particles getting into my eyes.

Charlie flashed her light on us, her facial expression quickly changing from excitement to dissatisfaction—her irises darker than Bo's.

And as quickly as lightning struck the earth, she was gone. Never even saying a word.

CHAPTER TWELVE

MAY 31, 12:OO P.M.

"It is a truth universally acknowledged that a zombie in possession of brains must be in want of more brains." —Seth Grahame-Smith, *Pride and Prejudice and Zombies*

Yet all the zombies in my world are so unearthly different. They don't want to attack me or eat my brains (as of now, anyway).

Here's what I know about zombies:

- To date, none of them feast on living humans (or dying humans, or dead ones, to be clear).
- They groan as a form of communication.
- They smell awful.
- They can dab, and hug, and play games (also an interesting form of entertainment).

Here's what I need to find out:

- They are, in fact, decaying, but where are they getting their energy from?
- It's also hard to know if these "people" are actually dying. Are they?
- What are their motives?

CHAPTER THIRTEEN

MY PHONE BUZZED in my lap.

A notification from my blog—one new like. It had almost been a week since I hung out with Bo, but his dead eyes were sown in the roots of my brain.

After our walk that night, we exchanged numbers. There were a few times where I found myself with my phone in my hands, my thumb hovering over his contact, but I couldn't bring myself to text him.

And, yeah, I wanted to text him, but I didn't want to seem too desperate. There were rules on this, right? Texting zombies? How did one even start?

Instead, I cleared a space in my room, pushing the boxes to the farthest corners, and I stood in front of the body-length mirror against the wall, a song blasting from the wireless speaker.

The mirror was chipped on one side, broken from the move, and my reflection didn't really look like me; it looked like a funhouse version of me—long and stretched out of shape.

When I exhaled, I fixed my posture. Shoulders down and back. Arms at ease.

I triple stepped to the right, then to the left, feeling these dry bones come to life. And I glided across the hardwood floor, my feet moving with ease on an invisible slot. It was smooth, like doing the moonwalk but in the opposite direction. With the end of each pattern, I anchor stepped, digging my toes into the floorboards and then settling into the back of my feet.

Then I practiced the basic steps over and over and over again, saying the step count out loud like Mama always did in her classes.

One, two.

Three and four.

Five and six.

Mama's voice was so loud in my head. "Okay, let's do it again," she'd always say.

So we'd do it again.

Step, step.

Triple step.

Triple step.

It was like she was right there with me, leading me through each step. *Stay grounded,* I heard her say. *Not too much compression. Don't lock your arms. It's not in your arms, Zharie.*

She was always right, so I kept going, leading myself in a free spin. And in my head, I could see my twelve-year-old self tucked in the corner of the ballroom during one of her lessons. I watched her students move fluidly up and down the slot, practicing the moves they had learned that day.

Mama winked at me, her fluffy curls moving and twisting when she did.

She called me to the front of the class after, and together, we demoed the dance for them, moving apart and together like we'd been performing our whole lives. Mama was the painter when we danced; I was the blank canvas. She always made me look good. Always showed me off to her students. And I wondered if this was what it felt like for Mama when she competed.

After an hour of dance, I collapsed to the floor in exhaustion, the bottom of my feet red. When I checked my phone, I had three recent texts from Bo:

Yo. Hey. Helllooo 👍

Did u know our rooms r stacked on top of each other?

Is that weird? Also, I can hear ur music

And then a few minutes later, he sent me a song.

> play this: "Addicted" by Simple Plan
>
> it's an oldie but goodie

I clicked the link, played it.

> Hi.
>
> Hello.
>
> Hey.
>
> Listening to it now. Can you hear it?

> Play it louder

I cranked my speaker up.

> It's like we're at a party for 2
>
> But this floor is separating us
>
> Gotta change that

> And by change, you mean?

> I mean
>
> let's take away the gap between us

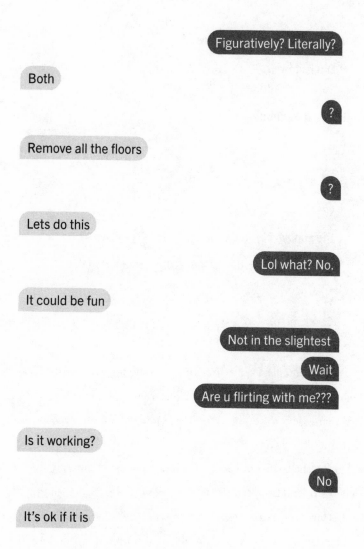

Figuratively? Literally?

Both

?

Remove all the floors

?

Lets do this

Lol what? No.

It could be fun

Not in the slightest

Wait

Are u flirting with me???

Is it working?

No

It's ok if it is

There was a tickle in the pit of my belly. It felt like I could hear him say it, but I didn't know how to respond.

So many thought bubbles

Did I scare u?

I laughed out loud.

Maybe

What's that supposed to mean?

Oh

the song is about to end

Try this one: "Sound & Color" by Alabama Shakes

Now we're really partying

Can I see u?

It was a sentence I read three times. Could he see me? I didn't know. Did I want to see him? Maybe. There were still questions I had.

When I went to respond, there was a knock on the window.

Bruh. This guy.

Ran to the bathroom and swiped on deodorant before I answered. When I opened the blinds, Bo was waving with a big, sloppy smile on his face, human as ever.

The day behind him was bright with a mix of Tiffany and baby blues. The clouds were huge and marshmallowy, and there were a few younger kids playing with a gigantic bouncy ball on the sidewalk.

"You have, like, zero patience," I said, sliding open the screen, and when I did, the heat of the day hit me in the face. I could smell the hot earth, the grass that had just been cut, and Bo.

"If you know what you want, why not go for it?" he said, and he sat down on the fire escape. He had on dark jeans and a striped black-and-white shirt. His hair seemed a little shorter, the curls not pillowing away as they usually did. Fresh cut, maybe?

I shook my head. "Being direct is cool and all, but what about boundaries?"

Bo pointed to the wall connected to the window. "There is a literal wall separating us."

I laughed. "Yet here you are."

He bowed. "Here I am. You tryna hang?"

I turned the music down on my phone. "Maybe," I said, and I looked behind me, thinking I heard something move in the living room, but it was just the wind hitting the bedroom door. Auntie E wouldn't come back for a few more hours. "I kinda smell awful right now?"

His face scrunched. "Why is that?"

"Uhhh... dancing," I said, and I felt my ribs tighten. The secret was out, though it wasn't even a secret. I didn't often tell people I danced for two reasons. A, they had no idea what West Coast Swing was. Or B, they were really, *really* shocked. It was the same reaction I got when my hair was in its natural state. People were weird.

Bo cocked his head to the side. "You were jamming out down here?"

"Kinda," I said. "Mostly practicing..."

Bo leaned forward, flashing his teeth. "Puh-lease tell me more."

"It's called West Coast Swing."

He pulled his phone out, his thumbs moving swiftly until he pulled up a video. "Whattt, you can dance like this? No way," he said after watching the video—this was exactly what I was trying to avoid. "So I'm face-to-face with an *actual* dancer. Can you show me?"

Dude needed to chill. The last thing I wanted to do was dance in front of zombie boy. "Hard pass."

"For real?"

"Yup."

"C'mon, Z. I'm harmless. I mean, you don't have to freestyle, or anything weird, and I swear I won't make fun of you. Will you show me the steps?"

"Uhhhhh…"

His face twisted to the side, and the apartment buildings were like massive sunflowers behind him, dancing in the bright sunlight. "C'mon, Z. You know you wanna…"

I pressed my lips together. Shit.

"If you show me a few moves, I can show you how to skate," he said, and he leaned forward.

"Who says I wanna know how to skate?"

"Please?" It was said so innocently, he looked years younger. It was his eyes, and his mouth, and the way a small dimple appeared at the edge of his smile. How could anyone say no to that?

I squinted. "Fine. But only because I have a few things I'd like to pick your brain about after." I wanted this to be on *my* terms, not his.

Bo jumped up and climbed through my window, bringing that tantalizing scent in with him.

Once inside, he took every opportunity to touch and look at everything. And he was fidgety, bouncing his knees and bobbing his head as he went.

"This is where your life happens, huh?" There was a grin beneath his words, and his eyes sparkled.

"Yeah, it's *so* lively," I said, staring at the blank white walls and boxes shoved into corners.

He chuckled, his fingers sliding across the bedside table, collecting dust along the way. "Is it you and your mom that live here?" he asked, taking notice of a box in the corner that had *Mama* written in Sharpie across it.

"Me and my auntie, actually. My mom passed away a few months ago." *Seven, to be exact.*

He paused, wiping his hands on his jeans. "Oh," he said. "I'm sorry to hear that."

I crossed my arms. That was the other thing: Death was like an infection, too. If it happened to someone you knew, people's faces would change—they'd squish together in an unnatural state. And then the apologies were nonstop. It made my organs curl into tight balls inside me. It made me feel like I was dying, too.

"That's what they say."

"Oh . . . got you. You've probably heard that a million times, huh?"

"A million and one now."

Bo scratched his head, his hair moving with each shake. "I get that. It's okay to not have it together. That's just the human part of us, right?"

"I suppose. The human part and the dead part. And maybe, hypothetically, the subconscious part of us, too."

He agreed. "I like your thinking process, Z. The *subconscious* part. The human mind is hella wild. Maybe the realest thing in this false world, anyway."

I fiddled with my fingers. If he only knew how strange my imagination was. How the world was alive times ten in my head. Even as my thoughts spiraled around me, the room glowed. "Agreed. So, um... steps. You wanted to know about steps." I grabbed my phone off the windowsill and turned the music back up.

"Oh, right." He stood up straight, his eyes watching my every move. When he stood, the stripes on his shirt zigzagged into one another, turning into a never-ending loop. Bo proceeded to stretch and crack his neck. "I'm ready," he said, and I fixed my posture, but the moving lines made me dizzy.

I tried to blink that feeling away, but then the lines flipped and turned. Backward and forward. In and out. There was always something up with his shirt.

I stood adjacent to him, happy to be hidden from his gaze. "West Coast Swing is danced on a slot. You see the floor? Imagine we're only dancing on these two planks of wood." I walked across the planks of wood so he could see what I was talking about. "It's also a partner dance, so you can choose to be a lead or a follow."

"Which one are you?"

"I usually follow, but I can do both."

He raised his brows. "I've never been with a girl who could *do* both, if you know what I mean."

My cheeks felt warm, and I rolled my eyes. "Really?"

"What? You know I had to. Perfect opportunity."

Okay, okay. Maybe it was a perfect opportunity. But it made me wonder if Bo had been with anyone before, and what they were like. Did he like it? Was he in love? Was it just that he wanted to? And us, being this close in my room—was it too much?

Anyway, truth was I didn't want to learn how to lead, but Mama insisted it would make me better. I guessed this was why.

Bo's voice cut through me. "I'll lead, but you'll have to show me how to follow later." He winked.

"We'll see about that," I said, and then I showed Bo how to do the sugar push, taking his hands in mine. They were soft. Not how I remembered them at all. We'd only held hands for a quick second before, so I thought maybe they'd be rough from all the skateboarding, and just in general. Bo looked like he'd have rough hands.

They were also warm, filled with light, beating like the drum in my ear.

In West Coast Swing, the sugar push consisted of a six-count pattern, and Bo caught on quickly. Then he learned how to do a left-side pass and a right-side pass right after. My envy screamed at how much of a natural he was.

And he was serious, too. Asking questions along the way, making me stop to reshow a step if he didn't understand it.

He managed to smile through it all, the freckles in his lips spreading each time I got closer to him. I tried to keep my eyes on his chest, though. Didn't want him thinking about anything other than learning this dance.

After thirty minutes of doing the same three patterns, I turned the music up even louder, and we reconnected, his hands holding mine again.

"Focus on the music," I said, tuning into the melody that played in the background.

Bo and I danced the same steps over and over again until the objects in my room melted like those in a Dalí painting. The one where the clocks were without time, and the ground was the kind of sand that we sank into until we came to a halt—where the body of water met a yellow horizon, and the foreground was strange and cast beneath the shadows of the earth.

We melted in puddles of blue.

Breathe real slowly.

Let it out and let it in.

And I wondered if, for Bo, it was terrifying . . . to be slowly dying.

Or maybe clarifying.

Let it out and let it in.

Bo gripped my hand, looking at me with swirls in his dark eyes. So much intensity. Too much; I had to look away again.

When the dance was over, the objects in my room were no longer distorted. "How long have you been dancing?" he asked, still close to me. His words vibrated in my chest.

"My whole life." I moved away from him and grabbed my phone to turn off the music. "My mom was a competitive dancer, and she introduced me to West Coast Swing before I could walk. It's how she met my sperm donor."

His eyes filled with questions as they narrowed in on me. "Dancing is *literally* in your blood."

Literally. Mama got pregnant with me during the height of her career, but it didn't slow her down. We went everywhere together. I was that one-year-old on the dance floor at midnight, but nobody cared because they thought I was cute. Besides, Mama was spectacular; everyone had respect for her. I'm pretty sure I was the face on the back of her team's shirt at one point.

"Exactly. If you extracted the DNA from my bone marrow, you'd find music there," I said, half-serious.

He laughed. "So...I'm guessing, by the name, your dad isn't around?" he asked, and he looked to my bedroom door.

A creak again.

"No," I said. The sperm donor was in California living his best life, and I didn't talk about him, ever.

It was whatever, but if Mama heard the way I thought about him, she'd probably roll over in her grave. She had always told me not to hate him, that she didn't hate him, but I hated that he left her. Hated that he assumed I was an "inconvenience."

Mama said he left us to advance in his dance career, but we still got stuck seeing him at competitions on occasion. He tried not to lock eyes with me, despite the fact that I'd see him linger in our direction at times. I used to wonder what he thought when he'd see us, if he ever missed us, but after a while I pushed away the idea that he cared.

He didn't matter to me, but even at a young age, I knew Mama felt weird about it. But she swore we'd always be okay without him. Crossed her heart. Hoped to die.

And I believed her, because it was true. We *were* okay without him. Mama won almost every competition she participated in without him, and it made me proud.

Seeing her win was the best feeling. And he looked like a total dick, too.

But the joke was on me because Mama always said I looked like him—I didn't see it. Didn't care to. Honestly, I barely remembered what he looked like.

"We don't have to talk about it," I said it in a rush. "*But* you promised me something that includes your skateboard."

Bo perked up, his chest rising. "Right," he said, and he headed to the door.

"Nope." I grabbed his arm. "Back out the way you came in." I pointed to the window. "I'll meet you outside."

"Dannnng. It's like that? Okay."

I tried not to smile, but it was something about the way he said it.

"At least you know what you want," he said, and he climbed out the window. "I'll see you in five." And the last thing he did before he left was flash the hang loose sign and stick his tongue out.

That damn boy. I rolled my eyes, shut the window, and grabbed a clean shirt from my dresser.

He was so . . . I didn't know. There was something about him when he wasn't in zombie form. Something about the way he spoke, the way he moved, the way he laughed. Something about the way he looked at me, his soul almost calling to me, his brown eyes deepening.

It wasn't something I was used to, and it was hard to believe that at any legit moment he could become a freaking zombie because of some stupid glitch in my brain.

After I rinsed my face in the bathroom, I reminded myself why I was doing this, *why* I was entertaining Bo: I needed to know his motives and what it was that made him zip in and out of this zombie persona.

When I got outside, Bo was waiting for me on the sidewalk, twirling the end of his skateboard on the cement.

"Okay, so if I get on this skateboard, what are the odds I'll fall on my butt?"

Bo pinched his lips together, and he put the board on the ground.

"That's the first step. You have to accept the fact that you might fall. Are you . . . afraid of falling?"

"Well, yeah. I'm not tryna eat the cement for dinner, so . . ."

He laughed, and it was a deep, throaty one, too. I liked the way it sounded. "Step right up." He reached his hand out for me, and the first thing I felt was his heartbeat beneath my fingertips. It was steady and thumping, completely human.

Was Bo's heart like this when he was in zombie mode? Could something dead be alive?

Bo's gaze was focused when I stepped on the board, and he kept me firmly planted on the speckled wood. "How do you feel up here?"

I wobbled at first, holding on to his hands tightly. "I feel like this could go pretty fast," I said, bending my knees.

"It could, if you wanted it to, but that's for another day." Bo waited for me to balance myself, and then he said, "You ready?"

Nope. I wasn't ready, but I sucked in a breath full of air. "Yeah," I said, barely squeezing the word out.

He walked, taking small steps while still holding on to me. "You wanna stay balanced. Find your center. Become one with the skateboard."

I focused on the wind rustling through the trees, the birds in the distance, and the beeping of something nearby. I kept my feet as still as I could, afraid the wind would take me over the edge.

"I'm gonna let go," Bo murmured. "You got this." But I didn't really want him to let go. I wanted him to stay. I needed the steady thump of his heartbeat to remind me that this new thing was okay.

He still let go. I was going on my own then. When I blinked, the cement turned into water, and I glided so effortlessly in one path that the ripples behind me turned into colorful rings of cobalt blue and honeysuckle yellow.

I was safe.

On this board, the world escaped me, and I soared, my arms spread out, the clear air rushing through my scalp, forcing my Senegalese twists to rise.

"Z," Bo said from nowhere, his voice muffled like he was speaking through a broken intercom.

My legs wobbled when I searched for his face, and gravity forced me under the deep blue tide as I held my breath.

There was a splash. The tide took me under with vigor, throwing me to the seaweed.

Footsteps slapped against the pavement, and I gasped for air. "Z, you were going so fast. Are you okay?" Bo said. The water disappeared when he came. His shadow blocked the sunlight, and I opened my eyes. We were still outside the apartment complex.

"That was . . . *fun.*" I laughed and relaxed in the grass, my legs bending at the idea of standing again.

Bo grabbed his board and sat beside me. "Really? You had fun? You 'bout killed yourself."

"It was exhilarating, though. Almost like a different world."

"Wanna try again?"

"Whoa, there, grasshopper. I'm sure I've had enough for today."

I laid my head back against the damp earth and stared at the small specks of cotton that floated in the air from the cottonwood tree nearby. "Listen, I have questions for you."

"Mmh. You're interested in me," Bo said, and I could hear a smile in his voice as he lay down beside me.

I laughed. "I'm intrigued."

"Same difference?"

"You're a mess," I said, and I wondered if he was like this with everyone he knew.

He chuckled. "I can be *your* mess," he whispered, and I noticed he lifted his head to look at me, but I ignored his gaze and continued to focus on the cotton in the sky.

"Real question," Bo said. "Who do you hang with, you know, besides me?"

I shoved him. "You mean, like, friends?"

We laughed at the same time. "That's what I said. What are your friends like?"

I folded my lips. Truth was I didn't have a lot of close friends. I *had* friends but not like Mini. Most of the friends I'd made outside of school had been through dance, but many of them were so much older than me, I stopped keeping up with them after a while. Just like I stopped responding to the group texts from my Sumner friends. It was stupid on my part, because even though I craved relationships with other beings, I never reached out to anyone.

And Mama would say it was lazy of me, but it really was easier having internet friends. The friends I made online had always been the first to reach out to me, and I got so comfortable with it that I never bothered reaching out more than I had to.

There was no pressure of having to see them face-to-face.

And better, they didn't know Mama. They didn't have to feel bad for something out of their control.

There was Luca, of course. I invited him to the studio freshman year because he wouldn't stop pestering me about it in English class . . . and then he became obsessed with West Coast Swing. For a while it felt like he was everywhere.

But did Luca *really* count as a friend if all I did was ignore his texts? I should probably respond to those soon.

"I've never met Mini in person, but she's my absolute best friend," I finally said.

"What do you mean you've *never* met?"

"Like, I met her online."

"You have an internet best friend???"

"Don't sound so shocked. It's a thing! People date on the internet all the time—what's so weird about having an internet friend?"

Bo didn't try to hold back his laugh, and I shoved him again, telling him it wasn't funny.

"I mean, I have real-life friends. People know me. I know people. But I don't have a group of close friends like you."

"Mmhm," Bo mumbled, and I wished he'd said more. Was it weird that I had more internet friends than friends I could actually see on the daily?

"I mean . . . Why'd you want to hang out with me, anyway?"

He sat up on his arms. "Me?"

"Yes, you. That's why I asked."

"Ooh. She's feisty, folks."

I chuckled.

He relaxed again. "If you must know, it's 'cuz I think you're cute. Which is blatantly obvious. But you seemed cool. Which was just an assumption, I *know*, but I wanted to see what was up. And would you look at that," he said, and he poked me. I poked him back, and he snickered, scooting closer to me. "You lived up to every expectation and then some."

This guy. This *freaking* guy. I refused to look at him again, rolling my eyes. "Okay. Another question. Is Bo your real name?" I asked, determined to change the subject. I remembered Charlie had like three names for him the other day.

"So real it hurts," he said. "But if you wanna dig into specifics, it's Abraham Cai Her. My dad wanted to name me after his dad, and my mom wanted to name me after her dad. My mom won, of course, but she didn't get by without a compromise. What about you?"

"Zharie Marie Young. Not sure why my mom named me Zharie. I think it has African origins, but I bet she just liked the way it sounded.

My middle name is Marie, like everyone else around here, but it was passed down to me. Have you always lived in KC?"

"Yup. My whole life. We used to live in a rental closer to Argentine Middle School, but Ma said it was time for a change." Bo shifted on the ground, probably trying to get comfortable. "Both of my parents grew up in KCK, too. My mom used to live over by Wyandotte Lake, and my parents met at Schlagle High School. Instant high school sweethearts. Pretty dope. My dad was also born in the city, but his parents came here from Vietnam."

"Oh," I said. "What's your family like? I remember you said something about your brother being the golden child, but don't you think you're a golden child, too?"

Bo laughed, his hand on his stomach. "I know I'm great, but they don't exactly consider me golden. Not my parents, anyway. And I'd probably never tell him this, but my brother's really cool. He's the reason I got into skating. He was raving about it one day, and then I begged my cousin to take me to the skate park with him so I could learn."

"Do you see him often?"

"Eh. He comes up every blue moon. I went down with my family to see him once. It was a little after he moved into his dorm at K-State. Have you been down there?"

"To Manhattan? Like once, I think. But I've never been to the university."

"It's huge. The buildings look like castles, and my brother's dorm was cool, but my parents were over the top, Z. They kept tryna juice me up the whole time and make me more excited than I was. Then they forced me to go on a campus tour and meet with an admissions counselor, and they kinda just ruined the whole thing after that. Haven't been back since."

"Damn. Are they always like that?" I asked. I was a little surprised, because the small moments I'd been around them, they seemed like what normal parents were supposed to seem like.

"Yup. They don't skip a beat. Enough about that, though. Is your family from around here?"

"Yeah, actually—except for the sperm donor. I can't remember if he's from here, but it's probably on Facebook."

"Woof," Bo said.

"Woof is right, but I'm over it."

Okay, *whatever*. Clearly not over it.

I looked at Bo, his arms spread out against the dark green grass, his eyes focused on the sky. "You know, Bo, you asked me this the other day, but have you ever been in love?"

I wanted to hear what he'd say, but when it took longer than thirty seconds for him to respond, I regretted asking.

"Once before." He looked at me, and with a flash, his irises turned gray.

"What was it like?"

"It was like . . . hmm. Like getting caught in the gravitational force of the universe. Like ... jumping out of a plane without a clear plan of how to get to the ground safely."

That was probably how I imagined it would be. "Sounds scary."

"It can be sometimes, but it's a good feeling." Bo focused on the sky again, and while he did, I watched his face transform into the death-ridden thing it had been in the past. Half human, half zombie.

How often did this happen? Did Bo go about living his life, doing normal, everyday stuff, and then out of nowhere, boom, he was a zombie?

"How did it end?" I asked, afraid of my own question.

He took a deep breath, and the air in his lungs rose from his throat in snaps. It smelled like rotten flowers. "In an unsettling way," he finally said, and he looked as stiff as a board. "She didn't love me the way I loved her. And I wanted her to, but you can't force that with people. You can't force love."

My agreement was in the form of a head nod, one he didn't see. Free will was a delicacy of life. But I wondered who she was and how it ended.

Bo's tone of voice changed. "Are you thinking about love, Z? I didn't take you for that kind of person."

What the hell was that supposed to mean? "That's rude." Very, very rude.

He laughed, but it wasn't funny. "It's what you said the other day," he reminded.

"Well, okay. It is what I said, but that doesn't mean I'm thinking about love," I lied.

Bo looked at me, and I didn't want to return his stare. "Do you *ever* think about love?"

I shrugged my shoulders. My biggest fear was loving someone who didn't love me back. I heard once that van Gogh said, "The more you love, the more you suffer." And, well, we all knew what happened to him.

"No," I said.

"Never?"

"Never."

Bo pinched his dead lips together, and I imagined the skin breaking on contact. "You're lying, aren't you?" he whispered, but I didn't say anything. He was partially correct. What I said was a half lie.

There was a silence that felt like forever after that. "Are you a reader, Z? Wait, of course you are. You go to an academy."

"Again, rude."

"Wait, how is that rude? It's true, isn't it?"

"But you didn't have to call me out . . . especially not in front of these birds and ants and stuff," I said, pointing to all of them. "Now they're all gonna judge me and look at me differently."

"The *ants*?" Bo said, and his face grew with color and life as he held in a laugh. Human again.

"You don't know what they're thinking!"

Bo smiled at me. "Your imagination is wild."

I smiled, too. "I know, but what was it you were trying to say about me being a reader?"

"Oh, right. That. I was just gonna say that there's all kinds of love in this world, but never the same love twice. I read that once, but now that I say it, it sounds corny as hell. Don't hold it against me."

"What book?"

"'The Sensible Thing.' A short story by F. Scott Fitzgerald."

"I haven't read that one, but he wrote *The Great Gatsby*, too," I said, and when I looked at the clouds, I could see the green light painted behind them. There was hope there.

"Yup, he's the guy," Bo said, and he sat up. "Hey, wanna go on a camping trip with me and my friends? We're tryna do it every year. It's our summer solstice trip."

"How are we gonna get there?"

"Rico. He has a van."

"I'll ask," I said, and I got off the ground and made my way back to the building.

Bo got up and followed me on his skateboard. "Where are you going?"

"To eat. I'm hungry."

"You don't wanna eat with me?"

I laughed. "Maybe next time," I said, and I waved him goodbye.

CHAPTER FOURTEEN

WHEN I WAS SEVEN, I was afraid of thunderstorms. My room was only a wall away from Mama's, but I'd climb out of bed with my favorite teddy bear and tiptoe to Mama's room. She always had a night-light plugged into one of the outlets in the hallway, and she made sure to leave her door cracked only a teeny, *tiny* bit.

I remembered pressing it open, the old thing creaking until it came to a halt. The air in her room was cooler, and it hit me in the face, smelling of rusted water and soil. Mama shifted in her yellow sheets, and the younger version of me pressed my lips together, afraid that I was too loud.

Her window was open, and rain pellets smacked against the screen, making a thrumming sound. Some of the rain splattered on the floor, and as my little toes hurried past it, the clouds crackled and rumbled.

Slowly pulling the blankets back, I threw Bear in bed first—he needed to be safe, too—and I climbed in after, snuggling as close to Mama as I could.

I moved pieces of her dark hair away, and I wrapped my little arms around her waist. It only took a few twists and turns until I settled right beneath the beat of her heart.

It was like a *bump-bump, bump-bump, bump-bump.*

And she smelled sweet like citrus, and a little like some of the peppermints we'd eaten earlier that evening. Then I moved again, and she squeezed me tight, kissing my forehead.

"Doesn't it sound beautiful?" she asked, her voice barely a whisper.

I shook my head, my cheek pressing against her rib cage. Mama loved the spring. She loved the zooming of the bugs, the green stuff sprouting from the ground, and all the water that fell from the sky. I didn't think rain was beautiful, though, and thunderstorms were downright terrifying. It was the stuff monsters were made of.

"It's okay," she had said. "Maybe one day you will." She said it as if the rain was full of secrets, and each pellet held some dying answer to the world, but it was just water.

She squeezed me again, and I remembered how much I loved her in that moment. I loved her way more than Bear, and I loved Bear a lot.

And I used to think that Mama would protect me always, that she was invincible from the world, and when I snuggled up to her, I imagined she was bigger than the sun.

I used to think that she'd be around forever, and that I'd make fun of her when she got her first gray hair. But now that she was gone, the rain didn't sound so chaotic anymore. It sounded like her favorite song—smooth and subtle, wonderfully sweet.

And if it rained hard enough, I'd run to my twin-sized bed and wrap the covers around me. I'd pretend that Mama was beside me, asking me if the sound of rain was beautiful, so I could finally say yes.

Because *she* was rain, and she was beautiful, and I loved her so damn much.

CHAPTER FIFTEEN

MY PHONE VIBRATED obnoxiously, and I didn't think this little device would betray me so soon, but it was Luca. He was facetiming me.

I grabbed my phone, staring at the flashing bright colors. "Hello?" My eyes wide, looking at myself in the camera, hoping he'd already hung up.

"Z! What's up...I didn't think you'd pick up. Uh...I'm actually outside. Wanna hang?" The camera panned to the sidewalk in front of the apartment. The familiar cement steps. The worn iron rail.

"Whaaat? What do you mean you're outside?" I rushed to the window in my bedroom, only seeing few people. A squirrel running toward a tree. Thick puffs of cotton floating against the pale blue sky again.

"I mean . . . I'm *here*. Surprise. Anyway, see you in three." He hung up, and my shoulders sagged as I shoved my phone into my back pocket. Huffing down the hallway, pulling on a pair of shoes.

If Auntie was here, I could pretend I had chores to do. Maybe start that load of laundry. Pick up a dish. Anything that didn't include me watching three straight hours of West Coast Swing on YouTube.

Outside, Luca was at the bottom of the steps, waiting. He nodded his chin toward me, his shoulders back, his chest puffed.

And I grunted at the sight of him. Loudly, deeply, intensely. Maybe it was a growl. I growled.

Somehow, Luca had always found a way to insert himself into my life. More than he needed. More than I wanted. And that was aggravating. He was always around every corner at school. Always too close to me at lunch. Always a breath *too* soon, scaring away anyone else who wanted to talk to me.

Low-key, I thought he'd be busy with work this summer. Thought he'd forget about me. Yet here he was. The sun rays bolting off his brown skin. Eyes squinted.

Another step closer to Luca, and I relaxed my shoulders, seeing that his arms were stretched open to give me a hug. He was taller than I remembered. Peach fuzz sprouted on his square chin. It had only been weeks. How had time forced this much change?

I embraced Luca, and he squished my arms before we parted.

"What's good, Zeezy? How you been? Is everything okay? Are you okay? Don't worry 'bout me. I'm good. Hell, I'm great. But you? How are you?"

"I'm okay," I said, considering, you know, my life.

He pushed his lips forward. Arms crossed tightly across his olive-green shirt. "Okay...so what's the deal? Why haven't you reached out?"

"What am I supposed to be reaching out about?"

"Dance."

"Luca. We talked about this. I can't afford to go anymore." And also, I was terribly anxious about returning to Mama's studio. That place wouldn't be the same. Those dark gray walls, that golden-brown floor. The echoing of Mama's favorite songs.

The echo. The echo.

It wouldn't be the safety net of my room that knew me all too well. My yellow, floral blanket. My head hitting that pillow. The rug that needed to be vacuumed. The cracked mirror. Leaving that would be throwing myself into an expansive, deep sea with no floaties. My skin warmed thinking about it, and I could hear the cracking of bones in my head. Could hear skin being torn from muscle, muscle being shredded. Blue veins overflowing and expanding until they busted.

Luca rolled his eyes. "Come on. Don't be like that. You know I got you. But what about me, your friend? You said you were gonna help me get better," he said, and it was true. Once upon a time, I had told Luca I'd help him with some steps. It was only to get him to stop talking so much. After Mama passed, and the sudden occurrence of zombies happened, I had truly forgotten about it.

"My bad."

"It's cool. Can we practice? I brought some shoes."

My chest tightened. "Dude. Are you serious? Are you trying to come inside? To practice *right* now?"

He pointed his thumb to a car parked in the distance. "Or we could go to the studio?"

I shook my head. "Nope," I said, and I huffed. "Fine. Get your shoes. We're going inside."

I didn't need to look back to know that Luca was smiling.

Inside, I took off my Chucks and brought the speaker to the living room. Luca noticed more than I wanted him to, his eyes skimming the room as he changed his shoes. It made me pick at my nails.

"Are y'all moving soon or something? Where's all your stuff?"

"Let's not talk about it, okay?" I picked a song. Pressed my fingers into my palm. Stood in the middle of the living room.

"What? You mad? I'm just saying, Z. If you'd come over for once . . . you'd see the difference between my place and yours." He joined me in the middle of the room. "We have a seventy-inch on the wall and this badass sound system my pops got from his friend in Texas. He said it's the newest one on the market, too, but you probably don't know anything about that, huh? You ever played a video game with a sound system before? It's some real AR shit." Luca grinned. "And we have this dope leather couch that could fit up to ten people. Ten,

Zeezy. *Ten*. Shit is wild. My mom has this cool little rock garden by the front door, and I think it's supposed to—"

"Luca, we get it. You have a nice house," I said, and it felt like the floorboards were moving beneath me, making me feel like I might trip. "And stop calling me Zeezy. It's annoying."

He held his hands up in defense. "Fine . . . but this place looks sad as hell." His words rushed out in shades of red. "It's not how your mom's place was," he said, and I studied the floor. The long lines in them. The way it felt beneath my feet.

Luca's words were painful because they were true. He'd been to my childhood home twice, maybe. Everything about that place, I loved—the reading nook, the weirdly shaped doors, the multitude of neighborhood cats, Mama's herb garden, and all her plants. The ever-present smell of wood, a sweetness that lingered. And Mama. She made the home what it was.

Auntie E's place had always belonged to her, *not* me. If she wanted to keep the walls blank, I wasn't going to hang a picture; if she didn't want furniture in the living room, I wasn't going to bring in a chair.

She didn't care about homey things, she cared about practical ones. She wasn't wrong, but neither was I. We were different.

I held my arms out in front of me, waiting for him to connect. "Two songs," I said as the one playing finally ended. "That's all you get."

Luca latched on, and he smacked his lips. "For real? That's it?"

"Yup."

He pulled me into the starter position, our ribs touching, and after two quick beats, he spun me out of it. He paused. "Did I do that right?"

My lips bunched to the side. "Technically, no."

He huffed. "Okay . . . what was wrong with it?"

"First off, you were too close to me. You gotta leave some space to fill out your partner. It's not about 'who can get the closest.' It's more of a friendly introduction. Like, are you feeling each other, are you feeling the music? Maybe it's a new dancer? Maybe the person you're dancing with doesn't want to be that close to you? Maybe you smell bad?"

"But it's a closed position, though."

"True, but just because it's a closed position doesn't mean you get to crush your partner. You've got to give your follower some space," I said, the words sounding like something Mama preached often.

Luca looked to the speckled ceiling. A moment passed. His shoulders dropped. "Not to be rude, or burst your bubble or anything, but I see people do stuff like that all the time."

"Look, if it happens naturally, it's fine . . . but you can't force people to get close to you."

"Whatever. Okay, well, can you show me the steps?"

Told myself to ignore the tone of his voice. The sooner I showed him how to do this, the sooner I could get back to watching YouTube and clearing out my Pokédex.

With a nod, we reentered the closed position, triple-stepping to his left and then anchoring away from each other. After, we did it again, and again, and it reminded me of a class I'd sat in on before.

Mama taught it, and I remembered how upset the dancers were because she made them practice the starter step for the duration of the class. It was a big class, too, and some of the students said they were tired of doing the same thing, while other students seemed to benefit from learning how different each of their partners were. West Coast Swing was about communication and body language, and when I watched them on the dance floor that night, they all did the starter step with such ease. Mama always said hard work and practice paid off. It showed.

The second song ended, and I turned off the music. Luca continued to practice the steps. "Wanna come back over here?" He said it with one side of his lips turned up.

"Nope."

But challenge accepted. He inched closer to me, triple-stepping until he was only a foot away. He reached for my hand, folding his thumbs over my fingers. Then he started again. Dancing. Swinging his head around ridiculously. And when I wouldn't dance along, he stopped, still holding my hand.

I dropped it from his grasp, and he picked it back up, squeezing it, brushing his fingers over my knuckles. Daggers flashed in the center of my eyes, confused as to why he would do that, and when I stared at him, his glasses fogged.

I retracted from him again.

"What's up?" Luca tilted his head, leaned to one side.

"Um, I'm just trying to figure out why you were holding my hand."

He shrugged. "And? What about it?"

"You know we're just friends, right?"

Luca raised a brow, and he smirked. "Well, duh."

My gaze narrowed in on him, unsure of how this conversation might end. "All righty, welp, looks like it's time for you to go."

"Damn. For real? I feel like we were just getting started. You didn't even give me the chance to show you my new moves. You might be impressed."

I pressed my lips flat, walked to the door, and opened it. Waited while the sunshine poured through. Waited while the smell of fresh-cut grass swirled in. Raised a brow and waited again.

Luca grabbed his shoes.

"When are you gonna come with me to the studio? And don't say it's because you don't have money—I got you. You know I have stacks."

"I don't know," I said. "Why do you want me to go with you anyway?" We'd never driven together; I always rode with Mama.

"Because it's weird not having you there. That, and I need more people to talk to. I'm pretty sure Rose is tired of my shit."

I laughed. Rose was one of our regulars. She was in her eighties, but she never let her old age slow her down. It was inspirational, actually, seeing her on the dance floor; she'd stay till midnight on most Thursdays. But since I'd been away, I imagined Luca had probably talked her ear off.

"I'm sure you'll find other people to talk to."

"Maybe, but you can't avoid it forever..." he said, crossing the threshold.

"See you around, Luca," I said as the door creaked closed. I locked it, wishing I could ignore every last word he said.

CHAPTER SIXTEEN

JUNE 3, 6:08 P.M.

Here's a snapshot of my day:

10:30ish a.m.	Get up. Stumble into the kitchen for oats and half a banana.
10:50 a.m.	Watch a few dance competitions on YouTube. Mama was in some of them.
11:20 a.m.	Stretch. Drink water. Gotta stay hydrated.
11:30 a.m.	Clear space in bedroom. Practice form in the mirror. Do some warmups.

2:00 p.m.	Research zombies. Why the heck do I keep seeing them?
2:05 p.m.	Google *insanity*.
2:06 p.m.	Delete Google search. The government might be tracking me.
4:00 p.m.	Distracted by memes.
4:10 p.m.	New Google search: *Are zombies real?*
4:25 p.m.	Delete search history.
5:00 p.m.	Spotted a few kids skating in the parking lot. They all looked normal. No signs of Half-Zombie Face.

CHAPTER SEVENTEEN

IT WAS TWO YEARS AGO. Mama pressed her arm against mine at the table. A signal to keep me from picking at my thumb. She hated when I did that, but I couldn't help it because he, the sperm donor, had been called to the dance floor.

It was the All-Stars social divisions at Meet Me in St. Louis, their annual West Coast Swing competition, and some unfortunate redhead had pulled his name from the glass jar.

A roaring applause for him, and the start of a fitting song: "Bad Guy" by Billie Eilish.

I kept picking. Brown thumb aching a crimson shade now. A

grappling tug at my gut, twisting. Like how he twisted her into a new position, like how she syncopated her feet to the music, to the moment.

But he was criminal.

Cynical.

Even if he was a pro at this, I still hated it. Still hated *him*.

Mama whispered over the music, her curls brushing my ear, and I jumped. "You're probably wondering how I got with someone like him, huh?"

I dropped my hands. Didn't need to follow her gaze to know who she was talking about. "No," I said, still watching him glide on the floor. Bet he didn't even know I was here. "He's gross."

"Yeah, well, he wasn't always that way. He *was* charming, you know. Used to be my best friend back in the day. We did everything together."

On the dance floor, they pivoted. In and out of motion. And so did I. Turned to look at Mama's brown eyes. Her pupils dilated now, taking up space in her irises.

Why would she say that?

"Was," I repeated. "Look at him now. You should be up there with the all-stars, not him. This should be your dance, Mama. And if he was so great, he wouldn't be ignoring us, like he always is."

Her lips thin, and I could already see it—could already see that she was gritting her teeth, that her jaw was tight. "Watch your mouth, Z," she said, her words a fire, scorching my cheeks. But I wanted to tell her that it was true. If he was this person she made him out to be, he'd still be a part of us, right?

Shifted my mouth as the music throbbed in my ears. A pulse too close to Devin's movements. More shouting and applause from the crowd. Everyone here loved him, and I'd never, ever understand that.

"C'mon, let's go to the hall," she said, her voice still low, her head nodding toward the door. I followed her through the flood of people packing the chairs, the tables, the floor. There were hundreds of us here this year. Crazy how it felt so big and so small at once. I could already feel the walls shifting, wobbling themselves closer to me, the ballroom slowly tilting itself while I suffocated.

The hallway blocked most of the ballroom sounds, and by now, I was sure Devin was exiting the stage. People passed by, and we only caught a few stares from them as we posted ourselves against the wall. I wondered if they knew Mama—if they'd ever watched her in videos or taken some of her classes.

A sliver of the sun highlighted the hues in Mama's brown skin. The yellows, and reds, and purples. So much more prominent out here.

I tried to not lock eyes with her, though. Kept my gaze on the shoe vendor table behind us. They were selling ballroom boots with suede on the bottoms of them.

"Zharie, what's up with you, huh? You know this isn't new. We talked about this. If you ever wanna compete, if you're serious about this, Z, one of the downsides is that your birth father will be part of it regardless of if you like it or not. So where's this angst coming from?"

"It's just that…" I tried not to smack my lips. "Mama. I just know—I *know* you're better than him. And it feels wrong seeing him up there with the all-stars when I know you should be there, too."

Her arms were crossed, mirroring mine, and we were almost the same height these days, but she was still taller. "I hear you, and I get it," she said, and when she lowered her head, her curls chased after. "But I'm easing my way back in. I'm not pushing myself to be as involved in this competition because I want to be beside you—this is only your second time competing—and already you're locking yourself in the hotel room, not going to some of the workshops. And you can't grow in this community if you don't give.… You can't grow *anywhere* if you don't give. I know you hate hearing it, Z, but you're more like him than you think."

"Mama, *why* would you say that?! I'm not like him! I'd never abandon you. I'd never abandon family. It's like you're defending him or something."

Her eyes narrowed, the faint lines in the corners of them deepening. The death glare. And for a moment, I was afraid I'd gone too far, said too much. I never really challenged her, didn't raise my voice often because I hated getting in trouble, but listening to the way she talked about him pissed me off.

What did she mean I was like him? Nothing about me would *ever* be like him.

Mama took a step forward. "First off, lower your voice when you're talking to me. Second, I don't need to explain anything to you. That's not how this works . . . but I can see how you think I'm defending him. I'm *not* defending him, and you have every right to be upset. He should be in your life. And if I could change that for you, Zharie, I would in a heartbeat. I promise you. I just . . . I don't want you to think he's this monster. Because he wasn't always that way, and if—"

The door to the ballroom opened, and a group of people walked out. The social divisions for the All-Stars must have ended.

She waited for some of the people to pass. They were stopping at tables, a few of them headed for the elevator.

Mama's voice was low, her words barely on the tip of her tongue. "This is hard for me, too, Z. All I'm saying is you can't categorize him to be this awful person, because we *all* mess up. Not a single person here is perfect. And I know, I *know*, it doesn't excuse what he's done, but people make bad decisions when they're desperate." She straightened her stance. "I know you think I'm the strongest person ever, but I've been in that same dark place more times than I'd like, and you've never called me a monster, because I know monsters look different to everyone."

She looked at her hands, hiding something from me. It was why she broke eye contact. She didn't want me to see her face, but even in the shadows, I saw it folding.

"This story, between Devin and me, there's more to it than you'll ever know. And . . . you might never understand it, but loving other people makes you do weird things sometimes."

She waited for me to say something, but all I wanted to do was roll my eyes. Just another excuse. Another reason for her to sidestep the fact that Devin didn't care about us. And maybe I would understand when I was older or whatever, but I didn't want to think about it anymore.

"You ready to go back in there?" she said after she realized I didn't have anything to say.

I nodded, but she didn't move. She kept staring at me, her eyes rounding by the second.

"Z, you're not doing this for me, are you? You know I'm happy if you decide that you don't want to be a dancer. You don't have to compete this weekend. It's your—"

"No. I want to compete. I swear."

"You sure?"

I got closer. I'd never been more sure. "Mama, I want this."

She smiled before wrapping me in a hug, smothering me in her curls and perfume. "Okay," she said, and then we walked back into the ballroom together. Mama didn't tense her shoulders when the cool air swept over us. She just smiled because she'd been born for places like this. She said I was, too.

And that day, I believed it.

CHAPTER EIGHTEEN

MINI WAS THE ONLY PERSON I wanted to speak to today.

Probably because I kept hearing the sound of bones popping whenever I went outside. The cracking. Felt like something followed me wherever I went, and I needed a distraction, needed someone to inspect the overflow of madness in my veins.

It didn't help that I'd just completed a book and sobbed like a baby, even though books like that wouldn't normally make me cry. I think it was the way death cursed it, how it crawled through the pages, waiting for its moment to strike. It was a tale of two teenagers who loved each other, but they had cancer, and one of them died. A strike in me because that very character made me feel the way I used to feel before the unmentionables took over.

But it sucked more because it reminded me of Mama in a way. I missed her a lot today.

Why did she have to turn into this creature and die? It didn't make sense. According to every zombie movie ever, once you DIED, you turned into a zombie. Or, once you'd been BITTEN, you turned into a zombie.

Or INFECTED.

Or there was an OUTBREAK of some sort.

No one turned into a zombie by chance. There was always a cause. So why was she the exception?

After I published today's blog post, I took a screenshot of the texts between Bo and me, and I sent it over to Mini with a message that said, *Wanna facetime?*

Another crack. Closer to me this time. Felt like it came through the walls. I gulped while I waited for Mini to respond. Then a knock on my door. I braced myself. It was Auntie. She opened it, leaned against the frame, and she looked like the past version of herself for half a second, like Twiggy's little sister. I think it was the way the light flashed in her eyes.

"Hey, you busy? Wanna go eat?" she asked. She still had her Winnie the Pooh scrubs on, and I wondered how that nursing home was treating her, but I didn't ask. It was none of my business.

We went to Taco Bell, and I ordered a potato burrito with beans and rice and a Baja Blast to go with it. She ordered a grande nacho box with potatoes, and a Mountain Dew.

This was nice. I missed this, and as I looked at Auntie while we waited, her eyes were soft, forehead smoothed. What was she thinking? Should I ask?

It was almost like that time when I was ten. Mama was in Cali, and I stayed the night with Auntie. She picked me up from school with her fresh box braids. Said we were gonna get turnt up, and the first thing she did was take me to Taco Bell. I laughed so hard because it was unexpected, and she laughed, too. I remembered we walked Oak Park Mall after that, and she bought me a pair of gold earrings from Claire's that I'd lost a few days later. Although we were never *that* close, I still thought of her as one of my favorites, but that was back when Auntie still lived with Grandma. Back before she decided to be the first in our family to go to college. Back before I turned her life upside down.

When the order was ready, I grabbed the sauce and we sat at a four-person table while we unwrapped our food. I wanted to fill the silence with words, but I was focused on how they mispronounced my name. Again, like always. Really, it wasn't their fault. English was hard, but still.

I focused on Auntie E again, searching for a resemblance to Mama. I looked for it in her deep, dark eyes; in the shape of her thick brows;

and in her rounded nose. Looked for it in her high cheekbones; her petite jawline; her smile; her smooth, dark brown skin.

Nothing.

And that pained me because I wanted to see her, be nearer to the closest piece of her besides myself.

Mama was eleven years older than Auntie, and Auntie was only nine when I was born. The two of them barely grew up together, and even then, Mama was competing on the road the moment Grandma gave her permission to.

Auntie used to tell me she wanted to be a traveling nurse, though. She said it'd be cool to randomly be in the same city as Mama, and it made me wonder if she wished Mama was around more when she was growing up.

The two of them had always been different—not just how they looked, but how they held themselves. Auntie kept her hair done, had an appointment set for every two weeks. If that wasn't the case, she had it in braids. She kept a fresh manicure, too, and her makeup was dreamy and unflawed.

Mama used to be the wildest thing that walked the earth. Big hair, dark brows, eyeliner and mascara if she had the time for it. Funky-printed clothes, baggy pants. Chipped nails. Her cheeks were tinted red because she stayed in the sun when she wasn't in the studio, and she was always smiling, always carrying that hope with her wherever she went.

And I tried to be like her. Borrowed her clothes even if she didn't know about it. Wore her bracelets and earrings to school. Practiced drawing my eyeliner the same way she used to. Watched her perpetually. Tried to mimic her smile. Tried to smell like her.

I wondered if Auntie E used to do the same thing.

Even then, re-creating any of that today still wouldn't bring her back. It didn't matter what I tried, or what anyone tried. It was so defeating.

I sipped some of the blue goodness from my plastic cup and put a bunch of sauce on my burrito before I took a bite.

"How is it?" Auntie E asked after I slowed down. She'd only taken a few bites from her nachos.

"Good." The potatoes were fresh today, and that always made a big difference. "How was work?"

"Long," she said, her usual response. She pulled out her phone, opened something, and then she slid it across the table.

"What's this?" I wiped my hands on my shorts.

"It's an email from a legal firm that dealt with your mama's estate. They were able to sell your old home, and you have money because of it."

I skimmed the email quickly. It noted somewhere close to ten thousand dollars. "This money is for *me*?"

"Well, you're not able to touch all of it until you turn eighteen. Scroll down. That's the money that you'll get for now." It was only a few hundred dollars, but that was more than nothing. If I planned it out right, maybe I could use it for dance.

"Oh," I said. "I guess that's not the worst."

"It *kinda* is. We need money, Zharie. This whole me-being-an-instant-mom thing is expensive. We have bills to pay. I know you're still grieving Twiggy's death, but it's been hard on all of us. It's not just about you. Grandma has been tryna cover your extra bills, but it ain't cutting it. I'm not tryna be hard on you, but you need to reach out to your dad. He doesn't answer my calls, or anyone's, and we all know he has money. Does he even know your mama died?"

After I gave the phone back to her, I shrugged my shoulders. My fingers throbbed at the mention of my birth father, and the potatoes at the back of my throat tasted like mush.

I *knew* my birth father knew. The day after her funeral he sent me an email, but I didn't open it, and I had no plans to. I didn't need his sympathy.

It wasn't like I asked for this. The last thing I wanted was to be a burden to anyone. I tried so hard to keep myself distant, to not cause any problems.

Besides, Auntie E couldn't make me do anything. This, *all of this*, was freaking ridiculous.

"You need to figure it out," she pressed. "And now that you're old enough, you should consider looking for a job. I know you don't have a car, but something needs to change. You know, there's a bus that comes up here now. I'm just sayin'... the time you spend on your computer, in your room, or with your head in a book, could go to earning money and helping us put food in the fridge."

The appetite I'd had was completely depleted, and I gripped my knees with my sweaty palms. My ears rang an electric blue at the sound of her staccato tone.

She couldn't do this. *She couldn't.*

Job? Car? The fuck?

I didn't want to work to pay bills. If I got a job, I wanted it to be because I liked it or because I wanted to pay for dance competitions. Not because I had to. Not because I didn't have a choice. Not because we didn't have money.

The room flashed a dark gray, smoke stains covering the once-colorful walls. The light that poured through the back windows painted Auntie E a muted yellow. No, a dull copper, almost the same color of a dusty, unpeeled potato, and the room smelled of rich soil.

"Are you gonna say anything?" she said, leaning back, her arms crossed.

My cheeks burned, and I felt the crimson in my mouth.

I wanted to say all the words. I had paragraphs and paragraphs in my head, but when I opened my mouth to speak, nothing came out. My tongue was spaghetti noodles, and we were just two people in one of van Gogh's early paintings. We were loose brushstrokes, a dull palette, and peasants sharing potatoes.

And everything, *everything*, sucked.

CHAPTER NINETEEN

WHEN WE GOT BACK to the house, I stayed outside.

The thought of going into the apartment with Auntie E made my brain explode into the tiniest of emerald fragments. Instead, I walked the outskirts of the complex with the *Pokémon Go* app open on my phone. There was a virtual gym a few yards away, and I was determined to battle every Pokémon in it and take it over.

The farther I walked, the less I heard the world at play. No swishing from the cars zooming by. No tapping from the woodpeckers. No distant chatter from the people in their homes. Just my steady footsteps, a dying sunflower across the way, and the unkempt sidewalk, eroding crevices filled with weeds.

As I trailed along, a part of me wished the earth was a dance floor. All I wanted to do was put on my old dance shoes and slide across my problems like they were dried sweat stains between the planks of hardwood.

But there would be no dancing. No dance floor. No dreams. Nothing.

Apparently, I needed to look for a job.

Once I made it to the Pokémon gym, it took me less than fifteen minutes to battle it and take over. Before I walked away, I left behind one of my best Pokémon, a shiny Vaporeon.

It was eight in the evening now. The lightning bugs were out, and so were the mosquitoes. The trees hung over the path like spiderwebs, and the light bled in and out of the gaps like a flickering candle.

The cars passed me with their bright lights, but no one noticed me. I thought I saw a zombie in one of them, arguing with another in the passenger seat, but I remembered that zombies couldn't really speak. I imagined it would have been deep groans of anger instead.

Just then, I heard a choir of short, rasping breaths behind me. When I looked over my shoulder, there was nothing there, just trash twirling in the wind.

But the sound dragged against the dry cement. Long and heavy. The rasping coming again, long and hushed.

My muscles tensed, and I clenched my fists, digging my thumbs into my knuckles.

If I looked again, what would be there?

I kept my head down, walking faster, my heart pinching in my chest, my teeth pressing into my lip. But I remembered then, it wasn't windy. It hadn't been the entire walk until now, so what was behind me?

The hair on the back of my neck rose, the sound in my ear, the feeling against my shoulder, a whisper in my throat.

Finally, I looked, and when I did, Mama was beside me.

It was her feet dragging, one behind the other, broken, almost as if they were in fourth position. She was so close to me, strands of her black, curly hair brushed my shoulder, and it sent chills down my spine and to my toes, paralyzing me momentarily.

My voice tore when I tried to say her name, but I was taken by her distorted face, her sinister stare.

Her bones cracked with each movement.

Pop. Pop. Pop.

And the sound came louder and louder. Her breathing heavy, jagged, torn.

She looked like Mama, but her aura felt different. Her tattered skin stretched until the tissue spilled out. Her stare hungry, her mouth open.

Still, I wanted to touch her so bad. It had been months, almost a year, and I wanted to be beside her, her arms around me. I needed to know that I would be okay.

But the look that came from her eyes was dark, unlike any of the zombies I'd seen before, and if my imagination were to kill me, today would be the day.

She groaned, the skin on her cheekbones parting, and it triggered me, making me move. I clenched my teeth and picked up my pace, but she mimicked me, her bones still breaking beside me.

Eff. Eff. Eff. I broke out into a jog, warm tears spilling from my eyes, cascading down my face. I didn't look back when I ran; I had to keep going, and I went at full speed until coming to a halt at the front door of the apartment.

When I got to my room, I hid beneath the blankets and clamped my eyes closed. The tears continued to come, and I gripped my phone in my hands, still seeing images of her in my head, hearing the sound of snarls in the walls.

I hated my brain so much.

Just please, please go away.

CHAPTER TWENTY

BEFORE MAMA DIED, I had only competed a few times. The most recent time was at a local competition in Kansas City, the Midwest Westie Fest.

This was how it went for me.

I sat. Leads were on one end of the ballroom; follows were on the other end. I waited. Things were said by a moderator. My organs pounded. I tried to breathe, tried to swallow some of the slime in my throat. Tried to force my over-rising chest to look normal. I waited. Still.

Then they called me. "Lucky for you," they said. "Follows get to choose." I stuck my sweaty brown fingers into a plastic cup, pulling out a folded piece of white paper.

They said his name. The crowd cheered, and I looked for Mama in the crowd. She was there, neck stretched, waving. We walked to the middle of the dance floor. We smiled. He was familiar. Silence grew. We stood in close proximity. In closed position. I wondered if the crowd knew how old I was. Did they think I was here because I was Twiggy's daughter?

Then . . . there was always this moment. The moment in the first three seconds of the song, recognizing that song, and visualizing how my body might move during that song.

After two measures, we moved, the acoustic guitar rising in my eardrums. In the past, I remembered Mama saying that those first fifteen seconds in closed position were sometimes the most important. Maybe I messed those seconds up, but maybe the judges didn't catch it. It was my feet I was worried about. They weren't doing what I wanted them to do. They were doing too much, actually—off time, sloppy, half-done.

It was my wild thoughts that trapped me. I wanted to know what the crowd thought of me, but it was that exact thing that kept me from stylizing my moves. It kept me from being the person I wanted to be. And I was better than this; I knew I was better than this. I had taken first place in my division last time. But those fifteen seconds swiftly pushed past a minute, and before I had the chance to breathe properly, the song was over.

Less than two minutes. That was all I had, but I had forgotten how to move in my own skin, forgotten how my ligaments worked.

The crowd cheered again. We bowed. He partially smiled at me, but his eyes were dull, his nostrils flared. The moderator said something again, and we were no longer the focus.

We later found out that we were chosen as alternates. That was who they picked if any of the finalists couldn't perform.

We didn't place. We didn't even place. And *I* was Twiggy's daughter. Z, the girl who didn't place.

Later, Mama told me that I was so worried about what the lead's feet were doing, I never looked him in the eyes; I never connected with him or gave the impression that I enjoyed our dance.

My overthinking broke me.

That was the last time I competed, and I failed her.

But I failed myself, too.

CHAPTER TWENTY-ONE

THE NEXT EVENING, when the sun melted far behind the horizon, I found myself buried deep into the center of my bed, sinking.

Song lyrics stained my thoughts.

It's a blue world without you.

Then my phone buzzed. It was Bo.

Any more questions for me? 🫣

I rubbed my eyes. Right. I had forgotten about that. What else did I want to know about Bo?

Fire escape?

After I sent it, I didn't wait for a response. I pulled on a crewneck sweater, twisted my hair into a bun, and climbed onto the fire escape. Took the steel steps to the third floor and tapped on Bo's window. He opened the blinds. He had on an oversized gray shirt and cotton shorts. I could see the TV in his room had a game displayed on it. It was paused. *A first-person shooter game?*

"Well, well, well. Look how the tables have turned," he said after he opened his window, and he smelled of sweetness, on the edge of a grapefruit mixed with something I couldn't place. "I didn't expect to see you out here. Did you miss me?"

I shook my head, the humidity sticking to my face. "I don't give away secrets, Bo."

"Ahh, I see." He chewed his bottom lip, pausing momentarily and then looking behind him. And to me, he looked different than the last time I'd seen him. It wasn't a physical thing, nor was it a zombie thing, yet *something* had changed.

"Wanna go to the rooftop?" Bo asked.

"Uh, sure. Never been up there."

"Dope," he said, and he slipped on his slides, grabbed his phone, and I followed him to the roof.

The roof of our apartment was flat and square. There was a slight breeze up there, and to the right of us was a tree line so thick we couldn't see past it. To the left, our dingy parking lot. We sat on the flat surface, and I held my knees close to my chest, looking at the colorful sky.

"This can't come close to some of the views you get downtown. Have you ever seen the city lit up at night?"

"Never."

"Never," Bo responded, but it wasn't a question, and he picked at some of the gravel on the roof. "You say that a lot, like you're so sure."

"When you know definitely, you should speak definitely."

He didn't blink, and I could tell he wanted to say more, but he looked back to the sky. "Well, the city, it's beautiful," he said.

Oh, God. Please don't say it...

"Like you," he finished, and I rolled my eyes. "What—why'd you do that?"

"Hella cliché."

"You're saying a skyline is cliché?"

"I'm saying your use of the word *beautiful* is cliché. It's tired. Overused. Been there, done that. And skylines are, too."

"Wow."

"I'm just saying."

"You know what, I don't even care." He smiled, his teeth peeking through. "Cliché or not, I bet you'd look beautiful against the skyline at night."

I pulled the sleeves of my sweater down to cover my hands. "You know what I see when I look at the sky at night?"

"What?"

"Sometimes I see that painting . . . *The Starry Night.*"

Bo squinted. "By dude who cut off his ear?"

Covered my mouth when I chuckled. "Yeah, van Gogh."

"Do you see it now?"

"Mmhm, except the moon is smiling back at us, and we're all these small, colorful strokes," I said, and when I did, the sky grew closer, hovering over us like it wanted to reach out and wrap us in the stars. Strange as it was, I was slightly comforted and amazed at its oddity. I wasn't sure why—probably the same reason I saw zombies—but van Gogh's paintings had been haunting me since Mama passed. I remembered they were one of the last things I studied before her death, and now . . . now they were always everywhere.

"Really?" he asked.

"Really," I said, and I knew I sounded crazy. "Is that weird?"

"No," he said definitely, and it made me grin. "What else do you see?"

I shrugged. "Too much. I see humans, but no humanity." I figured that was close enough to zombies, but it was still only half-true.

"It's all hypotheticals," I added in a rush, feeling like I'd said too much already. It was the madness stirring up chaos in my brain, a side effect of being human.

Bo swallowed, his Adam's apple bobbing in the yellow moonlight. "I feel you," he said. "It's like we're all just surviving, but the world is so bent. It makes us cold."

The night breeze hugged me when he said it, my body agreeing with him inaudibly, and we sat in silence for a moment, watching a couple get out of their car and enter the building.

"You know what?" Bo jumped to his feet. "I'm gonna prove it to you. Prove that skylines are beautiful." He held his hand out to help me stand. "Up for a challenge?"

I crinkled my nose. "Where you tryna go?"

Bo wiped his hands on his shorts. "I know a place. Wanna come?" My next word was going to be no, but when I took a deep breath, he interrupted. "C'mon. *Come.*"

I laughed in disbelief. Tonight wasn't part of the find-out-why-my-mom-turned-into-a-zombie plan. Tonight was derived from selfish loneliness and fear.

But...if I didn't go, what would I miss out on? I could potentially learn something that could alter this whole zombie thing.

I straightened my posture. "Okay," I agreed, and as soon as I said it, the look in Bo's dark eyes changed.

I folded my lips. Unsure of his look. What *was* that?

Bo told me to meet him on the sidewalk in front of our building in exactly fifteen minutes, and then he disappeared into the night.

In my room, I packed my cross-body bag with the essentials: a phone charger, pepper spray, water, and gum. Then, quiet enough to not wake Auntie, I took the fire escape to the first floor and waited on the sidewalk with my hands tucked in the waist of my shorts.

Ten minutes had passed, and I had this overwhelming feeling that someone was behind me, but when I looked, nothing was there. I shifted my weight to the left side of my body and tapped my free foot.

Step, step.

Triple step.

Step, step.

Triple step.

The silence reminded me of Mama again, and my gut twisted. Where was he?

It was a little after midnight when I checked my phone, and after a few more shallow breaths, Bo appeared.

Thank *God.*

"Hey," he said, and I noticed he'd changed into jeans. He also had on a backpack, and his smile was bigger than mine when he held on to the straps. "Ready?"

I nodded, and then I followed Bo down the sidewalk and out of the community. A streetlight flickered when we turned onto a new path, and the shadows of the night looked mangled and wry. Bo explained that we needed to take the back roads since it was so late. Otherwise, we could risk getting caught by the cops since it was past curfew for kids under eighteen in KC. Which was stupid. They were always changing the restrictions on us.

My gulps were loud, but Bo didn't hear them, and it was hard to explain how I felt in these rushed moments because this experience was so new. My arms were locked, though, and I couldn't stop clenching my jaw.

Then my thoughts went haywire. Like, what if Bo knew he was a zombie and this was a ploy to kill me?

No. That was stupid.

But *what if?*

No. The zombies were only in my head. And again, he pinky-promised he wouldn't.

In spite of that, what if there were other zombies? Scary ones with soulless eyes, like how Mama was?

I swallowed, unsure of my imagination. Then we came face-to-face with a tall chain-link fence. The light here was muted yellow, and I contemplated grabbing my phone out of my pocket, but I was too afraid I'd need to use my hands as weapons.

Bo looked back at me, parts of him devoured by the night. "Ever climbed a fence before?"

I gripped my bag again. "No," I said, the words barely escaping my mouth.

Bo turned on his phone flashlight, and he sized up the fence. Then he looked behind us, his neck stretching as if he saw something in the darkness.

"What is it?" I said, looking too. The darkness curved in on itself, and I looked away before my imagination created shapes that weren't there.

"I thought I heard something," he mumbled, and then he fixed his posture. "Do you wanna go first, or do you wanna watch how I do it?"

"You can go first."

Bo nodded and put his phone away. I watched him climb up the fence like he'd been doing this kind of thing his whole life. Swung his legs onto the other side, and then he jumped, landing on both feet with ease.

Damn. How was I supposed to follow that up? I stuck my Converse into one of the holes, and then did the same with my hands, pulling myself slowly up the fence, one foot after the other.

Bo watched me diligently. "You've got this," he said, and I looked away from him, focusing on the climb.

When I made it to the top, I got stuck. It was a far jump down, and if I fell, I could seriously hurt myself. This was a terrible decision.

"It's okay, Z. You still got this," Bo said again, his arms out, as if he were waiting to catch me.

I swung my right leg over, then my left, and I held on to the top of the fence, the wire digging into my palms.

Just when I conjured up a thorough plan to get down, I heard a tree branch break in the darkness. "Did you hear that?"

Bo pulled out his flashlight again, squinting. "Yeah . . ."

Ohgodohgodohgod.

I placed one foot into a hole, then the other, my legs trembling on the way down.

And then there was a snap and loud rustling, almost as if someone was running through the trees on the edge of the path.

The sound stopped me in my tracks, panic piercing me.

"Shit," Bo said, his voice shaky. "Z, I heard it again. C'mon, you gotta jump."

But I couldn't jump. It wasn't that easy. There was too much distance between me and the ground, and what if I tore a ligament, broke a bone? I needed my legs to dance, to run, to escape.

"C'mon, Z. *C'mon*," he pressed. "If you fall, I'll catch you."

I ignored him, carefully placing a foot in each hole on the way down.

The sound came faster.

"Jump, Z. *Jump!*"

My thoughts spun, and I finally let go, landing on my butt beside Bo. He helped me up, and we sprinted down the empty street, my lungs crashing against my chest like a wave.

Bo was so much faster than me, his long legs taking him farther, but he grabbed my hand, and I caught up with him.

In between the gust of air and bugs that smacked us in the face, I saw Bo's body morph into the undead. It was only for a moment, but it was the scariest it had ever been, and after ten seconds, I let go of Bo's sticky grip.

We both stopped, taking time to breathe.

"I think..." Bo huffed, looking behind him. "I think the coast is clear."

When I looked, I didn't see anything, and I laughed hard, my chest rumbling from the thrill. I was just happy we'd outrun what was behind us, but I was still nervous about what would happen next.

Bo laughed, too, and he started walking again. "That was legit *too* close."

I agreed, following him, and after a few more minutes of walking, we turned onto a new path that had sand covering parts of it.

Ahead, I could see that we had made it to a playground on top of a hill, overlooking parts of Argentine, a small neighborhood in Kansas City. Beyond the hill was a swirly yellow-and-blue horizon and a sleeping neighborhood.

"We made it," Bo said, moving quickly ahead of me to the monkey bars. He raced to the top, raised his fist in the air before smiling at me, and jumped off. Then he motioned me to the slide, and we climbed it, reaching the center between two openings. It was a perfect spot, and the view was so much more like *The Starry Night* than it had ever been in the past.

Bo opened his bag and pulled out a fleece Pokémon blanket.

I gasped. "Wait, do you play, too?"

He nodded his head. "Ohhh yeah, baby."

"Please don't ever call me that again."

Bo laughed and spread the blanket out so we could sit on it. "Fine. I'll stick to Z."

"Thanks," I said, and I made him open his app so we could share friend codes. "I can't believe you play. No one does anymore."

"Right. It was something my brother and I used to do. Kept it on my phone after that. But all my friends play, too."

"What team are you on?"

"The best one around. *Clearly.*"

I waited.

"I'm on Team Instinct."

"What? No way. It's like we're becoming friends. I'm on the same team."

"*Or,*" he started, and he held his finger up. "Maybe we were always meant to be friends, and this is just the result of everything coming together."

I sat, crossing my legs, trying my best to hold back a smile. "Sure."

Bo sat down beside me. "We're gonna watch the sunrise," he said, and he set his backpack down. "Ever done that?"

"Nope," I said, taking it all in. "Have you?"

"For sure. Many times. But you're here, so that makes this different." He looked at the night, his eyes reflecting the stars. I wanted to ask him who he'd done this with, or if he ever came alone, but I pushed the thought aside.

Bo opened his book bag and pulled out a small pail. Inside the pail were two travel mugs. "Here." He handed me one. "This one is for you."

I slid open the lid and sniffed it. *"Coffee?"*

Bo wiggled his brows. "Yup. Straight from the motherland."

My face soured when I took a sip.

Bo sat up straight. "What? You hate it?"

"It's missing, like, *sugar*?"

"Z, get on trend. Everyone drinks their coffee black now."

"That sounds like an awful life choice."

Bo pursed his lips and rummaged through his bag. "Wait for it," he said after a moment, and he pulled out a plastic bag. "Cookies!" He handed me one, and I knew this wasn't the time for it, but I really, *really* hoped his hands were clean.

"It's oatmeal chocolate chip. Put one in your cup. It'll sweeten it up," he suggested.

I took a bite first. It was a damn good cookie. "Did you make these?"

"Noooo. No. *Nooo*. This was Angela's doing."

"You mean your mother?"

Bo grabbed a cookie and finished it in a single bite. "Yup, that's the one. My brother's in town, so it's time to put on a show."

"What's the deal with you and your brother? You said y'all were cool, right?" I finished the cookie and went for another one to put in the coffee.

"No deal, really. He's just Mr. Bougie and the star of the family, and I'm not."

"Does that bother you?"

Bo grabbed his mug. "It *should* bother me, but it bothers my family more that it doesn't," he said before he took a sip. "And the thing is, I'm okay that my brother and I are different. We don't need to be replicas of each other, you know?"

"Yeah," I said, having no real concept of sibling life. I had a cat once. He lived for twelve years, but anything past fighting over toys (which, to be fair, they were the cat's toys anyway) was foreign to me.

"But, honestly, how are you so happy all the time? How is it that nothing phases you?"

He wiped some crumbs off his shirt. "It's not that *nothing* phases me. It's that... I can't let them bring me down. I don't exactly need their approval to be happy. We share the same blood. *And?* What's that got to do with anything? Doesn't mean I have to agree with all the choices they want for me."

Pushed my lips forward. "Like not going to Sumner?"

"Right."

"Your family seemed pretty adamant about it," I mumbled.

"They're adamant about everything. Don't get me wrong, Z. Sumner is a great school. It's cool that you go there and all; it's just not for me."

I nodded. It was understandable. I'd had friends who didn't want to go to Sumner for the same reason. It was a college-prep school. You had to keep a certain GPA to stay in, or they'd kick you out. And if it weren't for Mama, I didn't know if I'd still be there today. Dealing with grief, seeing zombies, *and* holding a decent grade point average was hard AF.

Bo continued. "I don't know if you've ever dealt with this, Z, but my family is so narrow-focused. All they talk about is getting my head on my shoulders. This, that, and the other. But what's so wrong with my choices? What's wrong with my dreams? It's like... they forget that so often the world shows one version of success, and there's more to life than that. I mean, shit, look at all of this in front of us. Are they gonna tell everyone they didn't 'make it' because they still live here?" he said, his voice projecting over the swing set.

He paused then, his shoulders dropping. "This is home. And even if I end up somewhere else one day, this will *still* be home. It won't matter if they bring in a stupid Whole Foods. If the blocks change, and the people don't look like us anymore. This will always be where we started."

He sighed. "Anyway. My parents don't get it. Success isn't black and white."

"Are you going to tell them that?"

He shrugged. "I've tried. They don't listen. But it doesn't matter. I've got this life to live, Z. I'm just tryna live it, you know?"

"Yeah," I said. I felt that. "What are your dreams, anyway?"

Bo half smiled. "Ah, the million-dollar question."

I chuckled, waiting.

Bo chewed part of his lip, and there was a moment that made me believe he wouldn't tell me. It was how he looked at me, how his eyes shouted words that were unfamiliar to me. Another second passed, and I was about to drop it. Bury it beneath this park. Pretend I'd never said anything.

"I wanna see the world and skate on every surface while documenting the whole thing. And I don't wanna have to worry about where I'm sleeping that night, what I'm eating, or counting extra change. I just wanna be free of all that," he said, the words falling in his lap, sticking to his blue jeans like stains. He didn't look at me after, even though I swore he would have.

I bumped his shoulder with mine, feeling the compression, wishing I could be dancing on a night like tonight.

"What?" he said, noticing my silence.

"Were you not gonna tell me?"

He looked at the sky. "I don't know. Did you think it was stupid?"

"Your dream? No . . . I think it's kind of brilliant, actually."

"Really?"

"Absolutely. It's a million-dollar dream, Bo."

Bo grinned, and then we sipped our bean juice in silence for a while, the gap between us slowly closing.

"What do you wanna do after you graduate? What are your dreams, Z?"

Gah. I used to think I'd go straight to college, somewhere close. Maybe study the arts. But so much had changed.

I hummed. "I don't even know if I have a grasp on it anymore. But all I think about is dance, Bo. I dream about it almost every night. And I don't wanna go to some dance school. I wanna be there, in the middle of it all. I wanna compete and go places. Like my mama did. . . ."

Bo set his mug down, and I noticed how close his right hand was to my left one. Any closer, and our fingertips would touch, his warming mine, mine shooting blue electricity through his.

His voice sliced through the air and to the moon. "It's cool if you don't wanna talk about it, but what happened to your mom?"

My heart slid down to my stomach, creating air bubbles. I shouldn't have opened the door to be so personal. I gripped the mug, thinking of how I would tell him because, really, what could I say that wouldn't make me sound irrational?

The chills forced me to sit up straight, and far below, deep in the sleeping neighborhood, I could see some of the undead slumping tirelessly through the dimly lit streets. Their legs dragged behind them, their heads low, almost against their shoulders.

"They told me her heart exploded," I said, recalling the day. That part was true. "But a few days before it all happened . . . she was just *so* different. It was weird."

Bo looked to the neighborhood, too, but I could tell that he didn't see what I saw. If he had, his eyes would have dilated. His body would have ignited with fear. "Different *how*?"

"She, like . . ." I shrugged my shoulders. "She wasn't her usual self. She didn't dance or teach any classes that week, which was weird because that's what she fought to do her whole life. She didn't move from the couch in the living room. There was this day where I literally watched her watch TV. It was like she was looking but not *really* seeing," I said, and I set the mug down to fiddle with my fingers, watching them melt and deform due to my skewed reality, the humidity, and the darkness of the night.

And my hands looked like Mama's hands.

We shared the same hands, the same grip, the same smile, the same walk. But now I shared those similarities with no one.

And Bo, he would never really know that. No one would.

Bo looked at me while I stared at my fingers; I could feel his eyes burning a hole in my cheek. "It was like her soul was gone. It was like she was part of the undead," I said.

"D-did the doctors say she was sick?"

I shook my head. "No . . . no one could see what I saw." My voice felt small.

"Damn, Z. I'm sorry it went down like that. Do you think she was depressed?"

Depressed? She was the happiest person I knew, and we shared everything with each other. *Everything.* If something was up, she would have told me.

"No." It was all I said, and I dropped my hands.

When I did, Bo grabbed my fingers, squeezing them, and the colors mixed together, creating a vibrant umber.

We were idiosyncratic colors tonight.

After I took my hand back, Bo smiled in a way that was so much more than understanding. It was one of those rare smiles, like he was feeling what I felt, too. And I knew this moment would stick to my insides forever.

The sky called me again.

"What even is life?" I asked Bo. We looked at the sky together, his eyes set on Orion's belt, mine on splashes of cyan and neon-green colors spilling into each other.

"It's galaxies," Bo said. "It's moments like this."

"What *are* moments like this?"

There was a croak in the back of Bo's throat, coming from the deadness within. "It's feeling safe. It's belonging. . . ."

"Hmm," I said, and the cicadas paused in unison.

"Z," he said, his voice creating a word bubble in the sky.

"Yeah?" I responded, my own bubble appearing beneath his.

"You know, it's okay to feel lost in this world," he said, the bubble bright. But I felt so much more than lost.

"Just know that I'd never judge you for anything. Okay?" His bubble glowed, and when I responded, it faded away.

"Okay."

"And if you need anything, I'm always here. Okay?"

"Okay."

"And I really meant what I said about family back there. You can make your own family, make your own life. You can be whoever you want to be. Okay?"

"Okay," I said, my word bubble merging into his.

"Okay," he said again, and I wished the words would stay up there forever, but they vanished again.

Bo and I talked more, and not once did he turn into a zombie. It was like my craziness had crawled back into the farthest corner of my brain and tucked itself away for the rest of the evening.

My eyes burned when the sun came up, and I looked at Bo. He had created a countdown on his phone. The corners of his eyes were red when the timer went off—but his smile. It was still there after all these hours. Even after we almost fell asleep. Even after we counted the stars. Even after we talked about our fears. Still freaking there.

We sat up and looked to the east, but I wanted to turn my head, to look at him, to see if anything had changed.

He poked my side, a reminder that it was the sky that was changing. It shattered violently with warm colors, and I held my hand to where the stars once were, to where the sun was now waving at us. And I wished I could grab it, catch the light of the world in my hands, feel the heat from the yellow thing in the blue sky.

"It's lit," Bo said. Then he laughed. "Get it? It's lit because it's the sun, Z."

I pressed my lips together, laughing so hard on the inside, but not conveying it to him in the slightest. "Something like that."

"Now you can never say that you've *never* seen the sunrise."

"Truth," I said, and we both stood. After we packed Bo's bag, we headed back to the apartment complex, taking the normal route now that the sun was up.

At the fire escape, outside of my window, Bo stood awkwardly again, his legs doing that bowed thing that they did. I could tell he wanted to hug me, but instead he said, "Next time, I get to learn more dance moves, right?"

"Right," I said, holding my arms close to my chest. "You'll have to be sure to practice the moves I already taught you, though. I'll know if you haven't."

"Oh, I have. YouTube works wonders."

I grinned. "I'll see you around, Bo," I said, and I waved goodbye and climbed through my window.

Bo stood on the fire escape for a second longer to make sure I made it in okay. He waved and winked before making a grand exit.

I threw my things on the floor and climbed into bed. Before I went to sleep, I googled *insanity* again.

I needed to know if my vivid imagination would kill me someday.

CHAPTER TWENTY-TWO

IN MY SLEEP, I STOOD in the center of a dance floor. A single light shined on me, and I was surrounded by darkness.

The sound of a needle scratched a vinyl, and it was like lightning before the thunder, the sound of wood crackling from fire. When the music came, it was gentle at first, then immediately immersive.

Darkness, then light.

Bo appeared in front of me, holding my hands. His grin was soft and eager, and in a flash, we stood in the starter position. His hand on my lower back, my forehead resting against his chest. The dance wasn't always this close; it wasn't with everyone that I heard the echoing thud of the heartbeat. It was just with Bo. It was just now.

And somehow, it felt like he knew the words caught in my throat. That he knew me deeply, that he knew this dance inwardly. It was the serenity I felt in his arms that made me relax.

Breathed in, my ribs expanding into his abdomen.

Breathed out, my body settling, my posture forming.

He stroked my chin with his thumb, and *what* was that feeling?

Bo. I hadn't admitted it to him. Not to myself. Not to anyone. But I liked the way it felt, I liked the way *this* felt, and maybe I could like Bo for more than the specimen I treated him as. That idea was scary because even in my sleep, he could change. He could morph into the undead. He could rip me apart.

The lights dimmed, and a hidden audience applauded in anticipation of the dance. I realized then that we were at a competition, that our contestant numbers were pinned to our backs.

Bo, still human, led me through a six-count pattern like he'd been practicing for decades, and he was so lyrical when he moved, sweeping through each step like we were tethered together. A boat and an anchor.

The rush pushed me to stylize like I never had before—my arms breezing in the air above me, my feet tripling, doubling, singling like I had practiced with Mama.

This dance felt different than the last time I competed.

The wild thing in my head was hushed.

Still, Bo was human.

As he spun me, tiny green vines wrapped through my hair, undoing my twists and freeing my curls. They traveled down my arms and to my toes. They encased themselves around Bo, crawling up his torso, weaving around the sides of his face. And at the ends, they flowered. The smell of summer releasing with them.

The petals bounced around us like glitter in a snow globe, and we danced in them, kicking them back in the air.

With the final steps, Bo wrapped me in his arms, and then he spun me away from him so we could bow. Bo applauded me, and I tried to thank him, but I couldn't catch my breath.

The crowd cheered loudly, but it sounded like a single voice.

When the lights brightened, they revealed the audience.

The crowd was Mama. She stood, clapping fiercely. Her face mirrored mine with surprise and eagerness.

Mama looked proud of me, her chin raised high. But when I tried to reach out to her, she disappeared, taking the ballroom with her.

They were all gone, and then it was me. I was wrapped in vines all by myself.

Darkness again.

And all I could smell were the flowers beginning to rot right before I woke.

CHAPTER TWENTY-THREE

JUNE 10, 9:45 P.M.

Are zombies beautiful? Inherently, no . . . but maybe their human side is still searching for what their dead side craves: connection— the kind that can only be reached through the heart and brain.

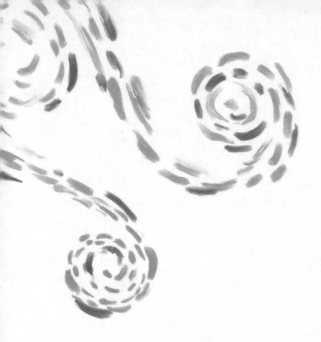

CHAPTER TWENTY-FOUR

U read, right? Wait. Yeah. We went over this. Of course u do

Again, rude

Just needed to confirm

Also it's not an insult to read

Just so u know

Do I seem offended?

Hella

Like BIG MAD offended 👎

Lol okay. I get your point. What's up?

have u read Looking for Alaska?

It's by that John Green guy. U kno the one that
wrote that sad book about those kids with cancer?

Yeah, I know who you're talking about.

I recently read that one

It completely broke me, so yea.

Devastating.

But also, no, I haven't read the Looking for Alaska one.

You NEED to read it

I finished it just now and I thought of u

You thought of me?

Why

Besides the obvious

It was this part about the labyrinth and it reminded me of how there's still so much life left to live

But it reminded me of u because I feel like you're holding back on life

And that you're stuck

And because you're stuck, u stop yourself from leaving ur bubble of safety

U stop yourself from seeking the "great perhaps"

The "great perhaps"????

Yes. What I said. The "great perhaps"

It's some dude's last words in this book

The MC is obsessed with that kind of stuff

Anyway, u gotta read it

I'll let you borrow my copy

Okay. If you insist . . . which it sounds like you do.

I do

Okay

I also expect a full report once you're finished

Lol

So, r u gonna come hang with us for the solstice? 👏👏👏👏

Maybe

U should come

Seriously

Don't bail

Come

Damn, boy. Let me AT LEAST think about not going.

Nope

CHAPTER TWENTY-FIVE

I REMEMBERED THAT DAY because it was so odd.

It was a Saturday morning when Mama was alive, and I had to finish my chores before I could talk to Mini or get on my laptop.

She sat in the kitchen at the small wooden table that she'd found bargain shopping with one of her dance friends. She held on to a mug I'd made in my fourth-grade pottery class and stared down at her phone. The steam from the coffee rose and swirled around her face.

At the time, I was finishing up the last item on my list: watering the plants. We had so many of them, and our kitchen was starting to look more like a nursery than a place you'd actually cook and eat in.

But Mama said our kitchen was the perfect spot for them because of the big skylight.

"Okay, all done," I said, dumping the rest of the water in the sink and drying my hands on the towel that hung from the oven.

When I turned to look at Mama, she still had her nose in her phone, and she smiled, her ears rising a bit.

"Hey, Mama, I'm all done," I said again, but she didn't hear me. I tried her again, the corner of my lips turning upward. "Earth to Mama. *Hellooooo.*"

She snapped her head up, her eyes blinking a few times. "What was that, Z?"

I twisted my lips to the side and tapped my fingers on my leg. "Just letting you know that I'm all *done*," I said, emphasizing the done part.

She looked down again, lost in her phone world. What was so interesting with her phone, anyway? I felt like she was pulling a move I'd do.

I cleared my throat and leaned forward. "Also, are you social dancing tonight?"

Her eyes skimmed whatever was on that device, ignoring me.

"*Hey!*"

She looked back up, gaze as wide as it could be.

I smiled, amused that I'd scared her. "Are you social dancing tonight?"

"Yeah, baby. I need to support the community. Wanna come with?"

I nodded, still smiling.

She furrowed her brows. "Why are you in such a smiley mood?"

"*Me?* I was just thinking the same thing about you. Got something interesting in your DMs?" I fluttered my eyelids, trying my best to look flirty.

Mama squinted her eyes, and her cheeks turned a tint of pink. "Girl, go on." She waved her fingers at me to leave the kitchen, and I knew that whenever she said that, it was because she wanted me to mind my own business.

Her smile was bigger when she looked back at her phone, and I rolled my eyes as I danced away to my room, smiling, too.

CHAPTER TWENTY-SIX

JUNE 18, 2:15 P.M.

What's new with the zombie complex?

A few things.

The word *zombie* was derived from the Kongo word for *soul*, known as *nzambi*.

After slaves were taken to Haiti, and the practice of the Vodou religion grew, the concept of zonbi was birthed.

More on this finding:

- For those who practice Vodou, all people die in two ways: naturally *(like natural causes, old age, sickness)* or unnaturally *(murder... basically)*.
- At death, souls are vulnerable and can be taken by a powerful sorcerer *(bokor)*.
- These sorcerers can trap souls in a bottle and control their undead bodies.

Most interesting part of finding:

- Haitians don't fear zombies, they fear *becoming* a zombie against their will.

CHAPTER TWENTY-SEVEN

MAYBE IT WAS STUPID, but today I couldn't stop thinking about the email the sperm donor had sent.

It was still at the very bottom of my inbox, unopened and highlighted.

I sat on the floor, my back against the bed. Chewed at some of the dead skin on my lip and tapped my foot obnoxiously as I stared at my phone with the email app opened. The colors burned together, my eyes strained, and after five minutes of looking at the blank subject line, I imagined my phone crumbling into pieces and rolling onto the floor beside me.

With a blink, it snapped back together again, and I hovered over the message with my thumb before pressing it. It was just an email. What harm could it bring, anyway?

From: dsinclairdancingcoach@kcmail.com

Date: November 16, 1:30 AM

To: zmyoung06@kcmail.com

Subject: <no subject>

Hello, Zharie.

I'm sorry I didn't call.

I don't have an updated number for you, but I remembered your mom shared your email address with me a long time ago.

I'm sorry I couldn't make the funeral. It would have been a lot for me, and maybe a lot for you, too, if I was there.

I am sorry for your loss.

Twiggy was a wonderful woman.

All the best and take care,

Devin Sinclair

A split in my chest, a crack in my throat, and I yelled until I caught fire, until my cheeks warmed. I threw my phone across the floor, and it slid on the hardwood, picking up dust along the way, until it came to a thunk, hitting the unopened box in the corner.

It was stupid. The whole thing was stupid. And I couldn't believe that was what he said—that was *how* he felt. I, his flesh and bone, and he said, *Take care.* Of what? Myself?

That was already par for the course, and I knew he was awful; I remembered this feeling too well, but I'd *hoped* . . .

I'd hoped, and I shouldn't have. I'd hoped, and it took me back in time to when I *had* hope.

My room flashed a dark blue and black, and I slammed my fist into the floor, rolling my knuckles into the wood. This place was the roaring ocean now, the tide pulling and engulfing the shore, the water spitting on my face. The salt stinging my eyes, blurring my vision.

The tugging on my tendons. I felt it in my back, a ripping up my spine, moving my insides and making them sour. Another second, and it would break me, push me under.

I screamed again, my voice tearing. The sound scared the colors away, and the ocean vanished. Stood, my soles sticking to the wood. Grabbed my phone. Wiped my face.

I don't need him.

Took a deep breath and played my West Coast Swing playlist. I kicked away the rug, dust particles swirling in the light. Shoulders back, chin up, arms at ease. And I danced.

It didn't matter what he said or would ever say. I still hated him.

I'd always hate him, and I wouldn't let his actions dictate me.

CHAPTER TWENTY-EIGHT

DESPITE THE CONVERSATION I'd had with Auntie E a couple weeks ago, she agreed to let me go on this trip with Bo and his friends.

There was one brief moment when she almost seemed like herself again. I wasn't sure what had happened to her that day, what caused the minute change in our chemistry, but she smiled at me, her eyes brighter than the sun.

Something about her was different, like, her brown cheeks had color in them, and her shoulders were relaxed. She'd told me a little about her job that day. A little about school. Not the usual, but it felt good to hear. The colors shifted. The plant she'd brought home the week before stretched. We shared a smile, and she didn't ask about me looking for a job. Didn't ignore me. Didn't do those things she normally did.

I wished it could have stayed that way.

The day after was like all the others. Our universes had flipped again. A croak from somewhere. The sound of something heavy dragging against concrete—the ripping of it, the pulling. The undead mocking me.

The summer solstice trip was in twenty-four hours, so I packed and facetimed Mini on my phone. Tried to also forget the dream I'd had about Bo. Didn't want to make it weirder than it needed to be.

"Damn, Z. How much stuff are you going to bring?" Mini watched me put three pairs of black shorts in a duffel bag.

"Enough to be prepared for the unexpected."

"Girl. That's like three pairs of the same exact thing."

I shrugged and kept moving.

"Where are you going, again?"

"Some small town in Kansas," I said, and I stopped moving to look at her. "It's like an hour drive."

Mini pouted. "Boooo. I wish I could go. I could be your sidekick, and it sounds like fun, even if you *are* seeing weird shit."

"You know what, you should come. Meet us there."

"Oh yeah, I'll have my dad order me a flight right away." She twisted her lips. "I wish, Z! But I can't. Hella broke."

"At least you can't say I didn't invite you."

"True. But are you *sure* about these people? You barely know them." Mini shook a bottle of blue nail polish before she opened it.

"You could also argue that I barely know you," I said, winking at her.

"Zharie, we've been friends for years. You know what I mean."

"I get it, but Bo's friends seem cool. They didn't make me feel weird or anything. I think I'll be fine. I've dealt with worse."

"Yeah . . . but what would your mom say? Going on a road trip with six strangers sounds a bit crazy."

"She'd want me to go. Absolutely. So just . . . stop worrying so much about it. Your stress is stressing me out," I said as I paired some socks together and tossed them in the bag.

Mini gritted her teeth, fighting back other words. She said she'd been working on holding her tongue, but it *was* Mini. I doubted it. "I know. I know. I just don't want anything to happen to you . . . but if they're *your* friends, it's whatever," she said, and she relaxed her jaw, continued focusing on her nail-painting technique. Mini was silent for a second, long enough for me to hear a reality TV show in the background. Then she took a break from painting to take a sip of Dr Pepper. "Wait." She paused dramatically, her eyes big. "Wait, wait, *waiiittt*. Do you have the hots for Bo???"

"Uh, what?" I smiled.

"OH MY GOD. You do!"

I tried to force my smile away, but I failed miserably. "I mean . . . he's cute, I guess. Has the whole skater thing going for him."

Mini paused our video call. "What's his last name?"

"Are you looking him up?"

"Would I be a good friend if I wasn't?"

I sighed. "It's Her."

"Who?"

"No, that's his last name."

She grinned, her lips bulging, holding it in.

Oh. "Not funny, Mini."

She laughed anyway. "Just let me live my life. But fine. You're right. Bad joke." Mini mumbled, "Bo Her, Kansas City, Kansas," under her breath as she searched for him. "Found him!" she said.

"Please don't add him as a friend."

"It's okay, I won't. I mean, I want to, but I won't. His page isn't private, so I can see everything I need to." Mini was silent for three seconds, and then: "Damn, Z! This. Boy. He's gorgeous. Ew, look at his face. How could you not tell me he looked like this? No wonder you're obsessed with him. I can't believe you've been holding back on these important details."

"I'm *not* obsessed with him."

"Right, and the sky isn't blue. But okay, *okay.* I see you, hunty." Mini unpaused her video so she could give me a look, and then she went back to snooping.

I grabbed my phone from the windowsill and searched for his social media pages so I could scroll through his photos, too. He was cute, but when I was with him, I wasn't focused on that.

"All right, I need to see these friends you're about to run away with."

"I'm not running away." I exited the app to return to our video call.

"Riiiight," she corrected. "I need to see the people who are about to kidnap you. I bet they're tagged in his photos."

I laughed. "You're a mess, Mini."

"The sloppiest," she said, and I could hear her smile. "Hmm. Looks like Bo and his friends are just a bunch of emo kids. You'll fit in perfectly."

"First off, rude of you to judge them. Secondly, I'm not emo."

"Girl, don't lie to yourself. You know more sad shit than I know sad shit, and let me tell you, *your* shit is sad."

My throat collapsed, and I felt my insides turn green. *Whatever.*

Mini unpaused her video for good this time and went back to painting her nails. "You like him..."

"We're friends."

"Friends with benefits?"

"No."

"But doesn't he live upstairs? You should just go up there and kiss him." Mini made kissy faces at the camera.

"No."

"Z... he is so beautiful, though. That man is basically the Blasian Jesus. If you don't let him bless you, he could bless someone else."

I laughed. *"Mini."*

"I'm just saying... if it were me, our tongues would be tied. What if he tries to kiss you on the road trip?"

"Uhh." I hadn't considered it. The last time I kissed a boy, I was thirteen, and it was sloppy, and there was slimy stuff, and our noses felt weird pressed together. Meh. Didn't really like him. We had danced together a few times at one of Mama's competitions. He was competing in the junior league, but I'd sat that one out. Wasn't interested. He was cute, though, and it was an opportunity I wanted to take since I hadn't kissed anyone yet.

"Or, what if he tries to kiss you, and then he turns into a zombie?"

"That would be terrific."

"You'd like that?"

"No, it would be terrifying."

"Oh. Gotcha," she said, and she downed the rest of her pop. "Since we're on the topic of zombies, what was up with that one post? Do you think zombies are *beautiful?* Clearly, Bo is beautiful, but is he even a zombie? And how can a zombie be beautiful? They're dead, Z. Super dead."

I sat on the bed, about to say what I only just realized recently. "It's a hyperbole, Mini. They aren't beautiful in the way that you think they are. They aren't supposed to be... but maybe it's beautiful that they want to connect with people, and the only way they know how to do that is to eat people's brains and hearts."

Mini made a sour face, and I laughed.

"Why the face?" I asked.

"It's just too much. Uh-uh."

"It's not *that* much."

Her lips shriveled.

"But, like, this is my reality, Mini, and it's the only way I can make sense of what's happening to me. It has to be some kind of metaphor for something—it's like my brain is tuned into the wrong frequency."

She sighed. "I know, and I am here for you. I'm just afraid for you, too."

I nodded in agreement.

"Getting to know Bo, has it helped you understand any of this?"

"I'm not sure. It's confusing. The last two times I've seen him, he's been in and out of zombie mode."

"Do you think it's getting better?"

"Maybe," I said, but definitely maybe not. And I truthfully had no idea when my life would return to normal. There were no signs to look toward; my world was still covered in hues of blue and yellow. But even though this new life was suffocating, would normalcy be any better?

Mini and I talked for a little while longer, but then I told her I had to go because I felt myself getting anxious about the trip. The more I talked about it, the more I continued to see little jellyfish floating around my empty room.

They had small, jittering lights in the center of them. With each bounce, their lights flickered a new color. Tried to blink the images away—the yellow, the purple, the blue, the green—but they danced so wonderfully, their tentacles frolicking in the air like we were surrounded by water. Like we could breathe every good dream together.

We exhaled.

And I joined them, turning on my Bluetooth speaker, kicking away the rug. I practiced my dance moves until my limbs felt as soft as the jellyfish looked. Till my body felt warm and drops of sweat ran down my neck and slid through the twists in my hair. I tried to keep up with the jellyfish, but they were always faster than me.

The jellies and I danced in harmony, and when my stomach was no longer tight, and my fists were no longer balled, the jellyfish disappeared.

When it was all said and done, I grabbed my towel and showered.

After, I couldn't stop thinking about Bo. I knew it was unusual, but with all my attention geared toward the undead, I hadn't had an adequate chance to stalk him or any of his friends on social media.

Chips first. We had Fritos. They weren't my fave, but they'd do. I climbed into bed and opened Google. Typed in his name. Five clicks, and I found him.

On Instagram, he posted a lot of videos. Local skate parks. Nature. The city. Art shows. Smoke clouds. Laughing. Sad boy music. A skyline. The rain. And he had a lot of photos. His coffee mugs. His board. The boys. Late night basketball. His freckles. There was also one where someone captured him holding a camera on his skateboard in the middle of the city at night. The lights were blurred.

An easy favorite was one of him sitting on that funky floral couch in Rico's basement. His smile was so big, it was hard to make out his eyes.

There were a lot of photos of Bo goofing around with the closest people in his life.

He really loved them, and they reciprocated that love.

And, honestly, I had FOMO like no one's business. It was simply that Bo's world, and the connections he'd formed with his friends, was something I'd never really had before. But I wanted that. Craved it. Longed for that feeling to play on repeat over and over again.

There was one photo I inspected longer than any of the others. It was taken eleven months ago. Bo was in the background behind all of his friends, and his eyes were locked on Charlie, and *Charlie's* eyes were locked on his.

They looked at each other like the world would stop spinning if either of them stopped breathing. Like all of life depended on this singular moment.

It made my chest hurt.

So naturally, I stalked Charlie's Instagram next. She had a lot of photos of her practicing yoga, skating with her friends, a collage of new tattoo ideas, a random baby goat, her kissing some boy, another yoga pic, her and Mika doing best friend stuff, dyeing her hair.

But I could only really creep on her for a total of five minutes because Charlie was conventionally attractive, and she made everything look so damn better than me—the color black, baby hairs, eyeliner, hoodies, torn jeans, breathing...

There was one last picture I looked at. It was a selfie of Charlie and Bo with a caption that read, *This is the greatest boy in the world.*

Fuh. That was it. No more.

In my attempt to log off completely, I accidentally double-tapped Charlie's photo, adding another like to her already hundreds of likes.

Hot damn. I let my phone fall off the bed, and I slid beneath my sheets, hiding my shame from the world. Stupid freaking Instagram. Stupid freaking thumb.

Good night, world.

Stupid.

Stupid.

Stupid.

While I slept, it stormed, and the pellets hit the window so hard, I thought Bo was knocking on it. Between dreams, I kept looking over my shoulder, thinking something was behind me, but it was only the wind getting through the window, causing the blinds to move ever so slightly.

Mama haunted my dreams. She followed me down long, winding paths that folded in on themselves. Her toes came to perfect points as she stood high on the tips of them, and her arms stretched far, wanting to grab on to me like twisted tree branches.

I walked faster away from Mama, hoping she'd disappear or undo the deadness she had become, but she was always a foot behind me. She tried hard to communicate with me, her voice coming in small spurts through her groans, but I covered my ears.

"I miss you, but not like this," I said, the words falling out of my mouth and onto the ground in a pile of word vomit.

But even with saying it, I didn't think she heard me. Her face kept blurring, and she was relentless, keeping her pace behind me.

The road finally came to an end, and before me was a burning forest of zombies. There were no other options, so I held my breath and ran into the forest. Terror ripped through my skin when I sprinted through the fire, ash falling in my hair, zombies pulling at my limbs.

On the other side, there was a burning yellow light that poured from the sun, highlighting a hill made of sunflowers. I didn't hesitate. I jolted toward the hill and landed on a petal, finally finding rest. The sunflowers bloomed as I laid on a seed, rising to the sky, dancing beneath the sun.

There was no sign of Mama.

No sign of the zombies.

I was safe.

CHAPTER TWENTY-NINE

MY BLACK ADIDAS were tied when I plopped on the bed to text Bo.

> In the words of John Green, "I go to seek a great perhaps."

Side note: these weren't really John Green's words; they were actually the last words of fifteenth-century French writer François Rabelais. I learned that after finishing the book last night. I sent another text.

> In the words of myself, "This damn trip better be worth it."

Bo responded quickly.

> It's so worth it

> Just wait. You'll see

> Did u like the book?

> > Dude. It made me angry.

> > But I get it. I just hate that it made me cry

> U CRIED???

Frick. He knows.

> > Just pretend you didn't read that last text.

> > Are you ready?

> Yup. Heading down in 5

> And no, im not gonna forget

My lips folded, and I grabbed my bags. Auntie E was in the living room sorting through mail when I got my keys. She didn't lift her head when I walked past her, but I overheard her talking to Grandma on the phone. When I got closer, her voice got quieter. It seemed serious, but regardless, it only made leaving easier. Didn't need her to pretend to be interested or care, and I didn't want to let myself down. I'd just have to get used to this. It would be okay.

It was a little after one in the afternoon when I checked the time. The day was hot, ridiculously hot, and sweat escaped my pores just standing. I set my bag down and stood on the front porch of the apartment building, watching a trail of fire ants crawling over the Kansas snakeroots that grew beside the entryway.

After three minutes, Bo came. He swiftly stood beside me, his sweet scent filling the space, and we smiled at each other. Most of his smile was in his eyes. He looked at me like he was excited to share the biggest secret in the world, but his lips didn't part for a second.

But his lips. It had been a while since I'd noticed them. They were different hues of pink, a few freckles sticking to the edge of them. Soft. And the sun made them shine. Were they bouncy? And *if* they were bouncy, what did they feel like ... ?

We were silent, and I wondered if he could hear my heart pounding in my chest. It expanded like a balloon as it filled with warm blood, and I waited, waited, waited for an explosion.

Just one more look ...

A single shared breath ...

I released a sigh and looked away from him. A car leaving in the distance. A zombie ambled past with high-tops and a snapback. Low moans. A hole in his chest. Blood pouring from it and leaving a mahogany trail behind him.

Then another. Male, copper skin. He followed the first, crawling behind because he couldn't walk. His elbows were scarred, and I could see the cartilage beneath. Each scoot forward caused more skin to rip away. The pain was there in his green eyes. His pupils dilated, and yellow gunk clustered in the corners.

He noticed me.

His eyes grew wider. He turned with a charge, maneuvering in the slick grass now. Arm stretched out. Growling and moaning loudly, saliva spilling from his tongue.

My face warmed. Chest rising. Vengeance, but *why*?

Bo squeezed my hand, and my thoughts scattered away from me. Normalcy again. The zombies gone.

An old Dodge Caravan pulled into a free parking spot in front of us.

"That's them," he said, and I could see his friends waving at us. More specifically, I could see Charlie—her smile big through the glass, her arms waving like one of those blow-up things outside a car dealership. Was she okay that I was coming on this trip, too?

I cleared my throat and Bo grabbed our bags, put them in the back of the van, and we climbed into the car.

I sat in the last row, next to Mika and Andrew. Right away, Mika handed me a pack of sour gummy worms, and she told me I smelled good, which made me happy.

"Thanks for the worms," I said, opening them, and I noticed Mika didn't have her cool hipster hat on today. Instead, she rocked her natural curls and a pair of black overall shorts with a plain white tee.

Bo sat up a row, beside Jesus. Rico drove, and Charlie sat shotgun.

"How are you?" Andrew said, his voice so deep it startled me at first. How old was this dude? He sounded more like a twenty-year-old than someone who was only sixteen.

Mika interrupted. "That's a loaded question. Who asks 'How are you?' anymore?" she said, her voice almost mocking.

"Everyone," Andrew said. "It is literally the vein of humanity."

I ripped a gummy worm in half. "Uh, I'm good. Thanks for asking."

"See?" Mika hovered her hand protectively over me. "You made her lie." Mika turned to look at me, and she whispered, "It's okay, Zharie. Wait . . . it's Zharie, right?" She leaned forward to Bo. "It's Zharie, *right?*"

Bo nodded, and I swallowed the worm and responded. "Yeah, it's Zharie. You can also call me Z if you want."

She relaxed again and nodded her head. "Z, don't feel like you have to answer any of Andrew's questions. He's still learning about the complexities of the human brain."

Andrew scoffed. "*What?* No. Don't listen to her, Z."

"*Andrew.*" Mika lowered her voice. "You have to admit . . . it was an awful question."

"The hell I do. I ain't admitting to nothing. If anything, you should be the one to apologize to me for *calling me out in front of our new friend.* What the fuck," he said, his pale hands lifting in the air, but all I heard him say was that *I* was a new friend.

That was cool.

"It's okay," I said to both of them. "And, in respect to honesty, I'm not good. I slept like crap. Terrible dreams." I took another bite of a worm. "Really, though, I don't know the last time I was actually good when someone asked that question," I said, and I felt my ribs crack open.

Mika's eyebrows were set high in surprise mode, and then we all leaned forward as the van came to a sudden halt.

"Sorry!" Rico shouted. I could see his hands slamming on the wheel. "There was a squirrel. Gotta keep nature intact."

"Thank you for being honest," Andrew said once the van started again.

"Yeah, that was unexpectedly appreciated," Mika said.

I shrugged and smiled. "Um, thanks for caring," I said, and when I did, Bo snapped his head back to smile at me. Then he stuck his tongue out and flashed that stupid sign again.

I rolled my eyes and turned my attention to Mika. "So how did you two meet?" I asked, taking a bite of another worm.

"Rico," Mika said, and I wondered if he was a matchmaker. It seemed like everyone spoke so highly of him.

"But we also go to school together," Andrew added.

"Yup, but don't forget to tell her how wicked obsessed you were with me," Mika said, and she smiled, leaning her head back on the old polyester.

Andrew showed all his teeth when he smiled, and he shook his head. "You always say that, but it's not true."

"Don't listen to him, Z. It is true. He's always had the hots for me. He thinks I'm the most beautiful woman in the world."

Andrew rolled his eyes, but he couldn't erase his smile, and he leaned over to kiss her. It was cute how playful they were with each other, but I wondered if it ever got annoying.

I also wondered if Bo and Charlie were ever like this. From where I sat, I could see Charlie nodding her head to the song that played while she flipped through stuff on her phone. She chuckled, maybe at something Rico said, and then I noticed Bo.

Bo wasn't focused on Charlie in the slightest. He had the *Pokémon Go* app open, and it looked like he was trading a Weedle to Jesus. A sorry trade for sure, but Jesus seemed okay with it. Must have been a task or something.

And even though Bo and Charlie weren't facing each other, I could totally see how the two of them could have meshed well together at some point in time. Not by personality, but on looks alone. They complemented each other like bees complemented flowers, and the whole thing reminded me of Vincent van Gogh's love life—all unrequited, all left unfulfilled.

Yet van Gogh wrote so highly of love even when it stripped away his will to live, and I kind of wanted that; I wished I knew what it was like to have someone turn my heart inside out. In the story I read last night, John Green's main character wanted so badly to know about this Alaska girl. The mystery of her ignited him, and getting to know her only fueled that energy for him.

Even Mama spoke highly of love. She had always told me that she *loved* love, and when it happened to me, I'd know instantly. She said I'd feel it in my toes; she said it'd be like dancing all over again.

I wanted something infinite. Maybe that was love, maybe it wasn't, but whatever it was, I wanted to hold it in my palms, push it into my pores.

It wasn't usually like me, but I wanted to know so badly.

When we were on the highway, Charlie cranked the radio up, and the start of an unfamiliar song played, but everyone turned with a strange excitement, looking at one another with animated smiles. They knew the words instantly, chanting it more than singing it.

The longer the song progressed, the more I realized I'd heard it before, multiple times, but I could only remember the chorus.

"Sweeeeet Caroline! Bah, bah, BAH! Good times never seemed so good!" I sang, sitting up straight, my fists tightening.

Everyone yelled, "SO GOOD, SO GOOD, SO GOOD!"

"I've been inclined! Bah, bah, BAH! To believe it never would... but now I... Look at the night, and it don't seem so lonely," I sang until I couldn't remember any more words, until my wrists relaxed.

Everyone around me continued to sing—Mika's hand in the air, Bo's chin to the sky, Andrew's deep vibrato in my ear. I could see Rico tapping the steering wheel, and Charlie and Jesus serenaded each other.

They all moved in slow motion around me, their lips curled, their eyes sparkling. I'd never felt so much yellow in my life; I'd never been so captivated in space like this.

And it was good.

So, so good.

A little after the song ended, my phone vibrated in my pocket. It was a text from Bo:

> I'm happy u are here

I reread it, my body sinking so deep into the seat, I could feel the unevenness of the road. When I looked up, Bo was looking at me, and his stare created a fuzziness inside me. He tilted his head to the side, his freckles falling, and I felt myself melt into the floor. Was this what living felt like?

When the air refilled my lungs, I thought long and hard about what Mini had said: What if Bo kissed me and turned into a zombie? I *knew* the zombies weren't real . . . though, really, I didn't know. . . .

That last zombie looked eerily disturbing and after me for some reason.

But would the kiss feel weird and squishy and rotten?

And could kissing a zombie turn me into the unknown—could it strip away the rest of the sanity I had?

Only time would tell.

There was commotion. Apparently, Andrew wanted to play *Call of Duty*, but Jesus wasn't down—he suggested playing some impostor game instead, and Andrew stomped his foot and huffed.

Mika whispered to me, "Don't mind him. He's a big baby sometimes."

Jesus scratched his nose, his eyes glossing over. "So, are you in or out? Our waiting room is already filling up."

"Fine. What's the code?"

Mika snickered and Bo ruffled Andrew's shaggy blond hair. "Glad you're playing, man."

Andrew rolled his eyes. "Shut up. Let's do this. You two better hope I'm not the impostor, 'cuz your asses are dead."

"Hey!" Charlie chimed in. "I'm playing, too. And don't even think about killing me off. I'll get the squad to turn on you in no time." She batted her long eyelashes.

"Ha. Yeah, we'll see about that." Andrew scoffed.

Mika bumped my shoulder and rolled her eyes playfully. "You'll get used to it."

I smiled, and I noticed she was reading a long document on her phone. "You're not playing?"

She pursed her lips. "I don't have time for these squids," she joked. "Plus, I'd dominate if I played anyway. Figured I should let them win while they can."

Hm. I chewed my bottom lip, leaned in. Instant word vomit. "Hey, so, do you know if Charlie is cool with me being here today?" Shit. Shouldn't have done that. Shouldn't have asked. Too late now.

Mika furrowed her brows. Damn. "Charlie? Yeah, of course." Her voice was lowered. "She's like the glue in all of our relationships. Maybe she's more handsy than she needs to be at times, but honestly, she just wants everyone to be happy." Mika's eyes brightened. "Why? Are you worried about something?"

I leaned back, breathed deeply. "No, no. Just curious, is all. Thanks." I forced a smile, looked at my phone, and pretended to be disengaged, even though I could still feel Mika's eyes on me. I didn't know what to think, but maybe that was the problem. Maybe I was overthinking.

Thirty minutes later, we pulled onto a gravel road, and I could hear Charlie directing Rico on where to turn next. The van went off road, past a small stream, and through a few trees until we reached a clearing.

In the distance, I could see a small wooden stage. Everything else around the line of trees was green and flat.

"It's the alter field," Charlie said, and Rico turned off the van.

"Yo, we're here!" Rico said, and he spun the key ring on his finger before jumping out.

Bo woke Jesus from his nap, and Andrew stretched, freeing his long limbs after so much time crushed in the back of the van.

When I got outside, Charlie set her bag down to give me a hug, squeezing my arms. "Hey, beautiful. It's great you're here." She released me, patting my shoulder, and my muscles tightened from her touch.

Beautiful? Great I'm here? Did she really think that, though? The last time I saw her, she made it seem like I'd released a tornado in her world.

Like Mika said, maybe this was Charlie being Charlie.

I sized her up. Charlie and I were born a month apart (thank you, social media), but the piercing look in her brown eyes made her seem years older. Her short, dark hair was pulled into a half-up, half-down sort of thing, and she had a few green highlights that I hadn't noticed before.

Charlie was lightning, adventure, and that book I never finished but really wanted to.

And I'd hate to admit it, but seeing her in person after stalking her on the web made me feel less than myself.

"Yeah . . . I'm excited to be here," I said, rocking to my heels. When I said it, I swore I heard something behind me. It wasn't the sound of people grabbing their stuff from the van, but something different. It was like a rattling, or maybe more like a rustling, but when I looked, nothing was there.

"You good?" she asked, and she pulled out a vaping device. It was silver and shiny—all I could look at afterward.

"Yeah—yeah. I'm good." I smiled, and Charlie touched my arm and winked. It was so clear how powerful Charlie's presence was. How could Bo *not* be magnetized by that?

Before I knew it, I was being led in the opposite direction, Bo lightly tugging at my fingers. When I looked behind me, Charlie was swallowed in a cloud of smoke.

We got to the other side of the van, where the sun was, and it was hard to see Bo in the harsh golden light. He leaned against the car, and I mimicked him at first, but the heated metal stung my arm.

"Hey," he said, and he flashed the hang loose sign.

I wanted to roll my eyes, but I didn't. Instead, I smiled. "Hey," I said, and I also flashed the hang loose sign.

Bo stood up straight, tilting his head. "*Whaaat*, you? I didn't think I'd ever see the day when you'd let your hair down."

"This is what life is supposed to be like, right? I'm hanging loose. I'm exploring what it means to live in the world."

Bo didn't say anything at first, but his lips were twisted, and I stared at them. "Hell yeah," he said, and he took a step forward, his shadow blocking the light of the sun. "Hell *fucking* yeah," he whispered, and all I could see was the fire in his eyes.

And I couldn't help but think about how determined I'd been to avoid the fire until this very moment. Really, burning wasn't that bad.

CHAPTER THIRTY

THREE SECONDS. That was all it took for the dandelion to be engulfed in flames.

I watched Rico pick up another one. His thumb pulled the trigger on the lighter.

One.

Two.

It was gone again with a big poof. Rico looked at me, a wide smile painted in his eyes.

"That was legit, huh?" He flicked the stem and it fell, blending into the grass. "Need help with your tent?"

When I stood up, my butt felt sticky from the condensation, the earth leaving a residue on my thighs. I wiped my hands on my shorts. "I didn't actually bring one," I said, looking off to see the others set up the camp site. I'd assumed I'd be staying with the girls, but when I saw Mika with Andrew, and Charlie slinging a hammock over a tree, I figured I was screwed. Wasn't about to snuggle up to Bo, but maybe he'd simply forgotten to tell me? Not that I had camping items, anyway.

"You're saying my cousin didn't find the need to tell you you'd be camping and shit?" He scratched his thick black hair, cocking his jaw, then relaxing. "You know what, don't worry about it. You can use mine. I was gonna hammock."

"No, you don't have to do that." I followed him to the van.

"Doing it anyway." Rico picked up a long black case and walked to a patch of grass near Andrew, Mika, and Jesus. "Is this spot okay?"

The sound again, like a whisper, rising from somewhere. It had to be a branch breaking in the thick of the trees, being swallowed by whatever was back there. What was that saying? If a tree fell in the forest, and no one was around to hear it, did it make a sound?

"Hey, Z, you good?"

Nodded fast. "This works."

Rico unzipped the bag and handed me a few metal pieces. The tent went up swiftly, in less than ten minutes, and all the while, I found myself getting distracted by Charlie practicing yoga moves on the grass.

Why was she doing yoga in the first place? It was hot as hell, bugs everywhere.

Rico must have noticed me looking because he tapped the top of the tent to get my attention. "She's tryna get more zen or whatever, but anyway, you ready for this hike?" He almost looked like Bo when he said it. I think it was the subtle way his eyes kissed in the corners, or maybe it was the shimmer riding his irises like a wave.

But. I raised a brow. Hike? "*What* hike?"

He laughed and walked away, and I watched him stop to say something to Bo, pointing his thumb in my direction. Bo turned his attention toward me, his shoulders rising, and I felt an unstableness growing in me. "I hear you're excited about this hike," Bo said as he approached me.

"Not exactly. It's like a million degrees out, and y'all wanna hike?" I kept my grunt to myself, but this was total white people shit. No offense, Andrew.

"*Y'all?* We're in this together, Z. Wait, what was that you were saying about hanging loose?"

I released a very slow breath, annoyed with him already.

"And the *Great Perhaps*," he said, pulling out his phone and flashing it in my face. "Those were your words."

"Right. About that . . ." I laughed. He was good. "Okay, whatever. Let's do this."

Bo grabbed my hand, and I followed him, exhaling through my nostrils and telling myself that the high temperature was only a figment of my imagination.

Pit stains didn't lie, though.

We left the clearing, entering a wooded area where the trees provided a cover from the harsh sunlight. The branches wrapped around themselves, holding on to one another like arms. The forest smelled like algae and soil muddled together, and we followed a small stream, walking along a rocky path beside it.

As I listened to the buzzing and humming that lived in the trees, I couldn't stop thinking about what I'd learned about zombies.

It was that blog post from not too long ago, and the website that mentioned the Haitian folklore of zombies. Some believe zombies were deceased people who were revived from the dead under the control of a bokor. They were essentially enslaved by them for personal gain, having no will of their own.

It was that part that stuck: *personal slaves.*

So if the zombies I saw were metaphorical, what or *who* was Mama enslaved to that turned her into a zombie before she died?

Like Mama, Bo seemed to be enslaved, too, but I felt worse for him because he was always so in and out of it.

Why, though? What was it about them that made my brain cast them in this light?

And was there a cure? Not for them, but for me? Like, if I figured this out, would that mean I'd stop seeing zombies all together?

It was puzzling, but all this brain chatter led me elsewhere. It took me back to the start, back to the ideology of a bokor. What if it wasn't a person that was enslaving them? What if it was a *thing*?

Just as I found myself on a roll, Charlie yelled to us in the back, scaring away my good ideas. "C'mon, guys, we're almost there," she said. Even though she wasn't looking at me in particular, I knew her comment was for me.

Fuh.

I was the only one in the back of the line, and hot damn, I was moving as quickly as I could. This whole fast-walking and breathing thing was more difficult than nailing down an eight-count pattern, and why, *why* did people do this for fun?

Fifteen more minutes passed. Sweat dripped from my brows and down the sides of my face. The path narrowed like it would never end. Green ferns, mushrooms, and decomposing leaves. A deep breath of wind forcing itself through my twists, stealing the air from my lungs.

I paused, catching my breath, resting my hands on my knees and staring at the broken rock and dirt beneath my feet. A tree branch snapped behind me, another whisper, and it felt like someone was breathing down my neck, low snarls rising in my ears.

My throat swelled, and when I looked, no one was behind me.

Squinted past all the green, looking, looking, looking. Blinked, the sweat catching in my lashes. No culprit. It was a squirrel. It had to be. Those things scattered quickly. Or birds, or chipmunks. Something besides the haunting, empty forest.

Another creak. It was Bo. He paused, noticing I'd fallen behind, and he looked around, his brows meeting in the middle. Maybe looking for it, too. His face asked a million and one questions, but he chose: "You good?"

He said it, and I couldn't look him in the eye. Didn't want him to see me like this. I wasn't good. I was my own struggle party, and pity was the last thing I wanted from him. From anyone.

"Golden," I said, forcing my eyes on the drawn path, and I carried on.

After a few more minutes, the trail came to a halt, turning into a deep slope down, and at the bottom was a waterfall.

Great.

Getting down there would require carefully navigating the rocky wet path ahead of me, and honestly, at this point that water looked more terrifying than it did quenching.

Jesus and Andrew were the first to make it down. They lifted their arms in excitement, shouting toward oblivion, but all I could hear was the water rushing toward the edge like there was no tomorrow.

With what lay ahead, there might not be a tomorrow for me. I took one step, feeling the mist on my face, and I truly thought that maybe I couldn't do this. My Adidas didn't feel secure on the wet rock, and no amount of balance I'd learned from dance could save me if I tumbled all the way down.

Squeezed everything in. Took another step, another breath. It seemed as if everyone else took the path so effortlessly. They glided down like they'd done this a million times. Skipping almost.

Charlie danced at the bottom, her chest to the sky, and Mika kissed Andrew beneath the waterfall, and I was frozen on the third rock down, feeling like a total imbecile.

Bo turned around. His cheeks sunburned red, his eyes full of promise. He had slowed down significantly. If he wanted, he could be down there with his friends by now, enjoying his best life, but I knew he was babysitting me. Just knew it.

I was afraid, and I shouldn't have been—not if I wanted to survive—but I was afraid of *actual* death.

Maybe my inner screams called out to Bo, because then he held his hand out. My thoughts kept screaming, warning me that his helpful gesture was a trap. I tried looking everywhere else, thinking the earth would drop another hand from the sky, but there was nothing wrong with this hand.

It was a perfectly good hand.

So I let him help me, and I swore I lost part of my humanity when he held my hand.

His eyes turned into pools of honey. His fingers gripped mine, and we melted together, one rock at a time, the maze coming to a standstill.

When we got behind the waterfall, my twists were heavy and dripping with water. We were welcomed with applause from Rico and Jesus, Jesus bowing almost, Rico whistling with his fingers in his mouth.

And it felt good, how that was. How all this was. We were just happening.

Strange. Charlie hugged us both, kissing us on the cheek. That same energy from earlier, pouring from her, rinsing away my doubt, and I tried not to flinch again. Tried.

Bo chuckled at my surprise. He'd been watching me, and his laughter cut in and out like an old radio.

Then.

All of us stood together, on the edge of the rock, and I stretched my arm out to hold the water in my hands. The coldness smashed into my palms, shooting to my clothes, to my nose, and I'd never felt so much power. It was like that day, years ago with Mama. I waited for someone to push me farther into the ground. I waited to fall, but I stood with my chin high, my Senegalese twists loose, thinking about how pretentious metaphors were.

"See?" Bo leaned down to whisper in my ear. His warm breath tickled the side of my face and sent butterflies to my navel. "We were waiting for this moment, and it's already begun."

Bo kissed my cheek, his lips mellow and wet, bouncy, just as I had imagined them.

I wanted to follow the trail of that kiss, to turn and meet him face-to-face, but I scowled at him, feeling so many different things at once. Mostly thinking that if Bo were to kiss me, I'd meet him there. Grab his neck. Force him closer to me.

He scowled back, and then his scowl turned into a smile, but the smile was so different from any of the smiles I'd seen in the past—even different from the one earlier today.

My lips turned up slowly, and my cheeks burned. So much fire there. How could one look make me feel so aware of the entire universe?

A laugh from someone broke our stare. My stomach turned to mush, and when the wind swept past us, I heard the slightest whisper of his soul.

Bo was more alive today than he'd ever been before. It was a cosmic cataclysm, electric energy, a collision creating a whole new realm.

Maybe he wasn't undead after all.

CHAPTER THIRTY-ONE

I JUST ABOUT DIED on the way back up the hill. Tripped but caught myself, a cut forming in the center of my palm from that rock. Could have been worse, though.

Held my hand close to me, falling behind the group again, but Charlie slowed, grasping the straps of the bag on her back, lips twisting.

"Heyyy." Her eyes were big; she looked like a brown anime character.

"Hey..."

"Look, I'm not one for small talk, so I'm gonna jump right in, okay?"

My eyes were as big as hers now. Gulped and blinked, and then she started.

"Mika told me what you asked her earlier. About if I was cool with you being here."

I clamped my eyes shut, held my hand tighter. Shit. I knew asking Mika was a bad idea. Why *wouldn't* Mika tell Charlie? They were best friends.

"Charlie, I didn't mean to impose—"

She shushed me, holing up a finger. Her dark hair bounced as she moved, and I could smell the vanilla scent that escaped it. "No, I want to say this. It's important to me. I wouldn't want you to feel weird being here, and if I made you feel that way in the past, I'm sorry." She looked to her group of friends. They were a few feet ahead of us, but I could see that Bo lingered behind, alert.

"It's just that . . . it's been the six of us for so long, so when you showed up, I was taken off guard. But I'm trying to break out this mold and embrace this life, so if you're Bo's friend, you're my friend, too." She paused, abruptly stopping in front of me. I stopped with her, still so surprised by every word leaving her body.

Charlie held her hand out, tilting her head and smiling. "Friends?"

I shook it immediately, not feeling the pain in my right hand. "Friends," I agreed. Was it weird that Charlie wanted to be my friend?

Sure it was, but if it meant this trip would be better knowing there wasn't any awkwardness between us, I was for it. Like Charlie, I badly wanted to embrace what was coming to me, to mix into the upside-down life that had been thrown at my feet.

And life was too short to wonder if Charlie liked me anyway. Now I knew.

Charlie looked impressed after I shook her hand, a smirk crawling on her face. She walked with me the rest of the way, telling me of her plans to attend RockFest in a couple of weeks. I didn't say much, just listened, and I wondered if this was an accurate glimpse of who she was with her friends. Did she always carry that much yellow on her fingertips?

When we returned to the campsite, I assumed that meant we'd get a chance to relax, but nope.

There was all this talk about "the bridge," but I didn't care about that. I wanted to know if I'd have to *walk* to this bridge, and I think Bo said something to someone when he saw how squished my face was, because soon after, we piled into the van.

The bridge was as literal as it sounded. We pulled off the side of a road and parked behind a couple of cars. Ahead was a cement bridge with long, rusting guardrails hugging the sides, covered in colorful graffiti, and it stretched between clusters of trees. Underneath the bridge was a brown-and-green river, and I wondered if the river and that waterfall connected somehow.

There were already a few people in the murky water. Some had floaties, one person had a chocolate Labrador retriever, and a few people sat off to the side with cans of booze.

The sun rode our backs while we walked closer to the bridge, the whispers of the townies growing at the arrival of seven kids who didn't belong here.

Andrew bounced on his feet. "Let's do this," he hyped, taking off his Rolling Stone T-shirt and throwing it to the rocks. With his shirt off, I could see how slender he was compared to the others, how the shape of his ribs pressed against his skin. "Y'all ready to tear this shit up?" He slapped his chest.

And it hit me. We were at this bridge to jump off it.

I thought I packed all the things, but I didn't think to pack a bathing suit. It was just me, my high-waisted shorts, and this black shirt today.

Then Rico took off his shirt, threw it over his shoulder, and everyone followed, shirts leaving bodies. The boys ricocheted off one another, pumping themselves up. They approached the rail, and I stayed back, behind Mika and Charlie.

While we waited, Charlie and Mika stripped away their shirts, revealing colorful bikini tops and brown skin. They looked at me, thinking I'd do the same, but I hadn't known we'd be swimming. I thought we'd be sightseeing.

"Are you gonna jump with us?" Mika asked, probably wondering why I hadn't also taken off my shirt to reveal a colorful swimsuit.

"Is that what we're doing?"

"Yeah, you ever done it before?" She pulled her curls into a ponytail and glanced over to see if the boys had jumped yet.

I shook my head, staring at the waves in the water. The darkness beneath the layer. There could be anything in there—snakes, fish with big gills and sharp teeth, old Band-Aids.

Charlie grabbed my hand. "You'll have so much fun." She said it like a promise, like it was a present she had wrapped up and saved for this aching moment.

One nod, and we entered the bridge. Bo stood on the ledge now, and I was aware of his entirety. The sun poured its light on his warm, brown skin, every inch of his body glowing, illuminating the muscles in his back and the small bumps of his spine.

Bo looked behind him, searching the crowd until he found me. Enormous smile. White teeth sparkling. He winked and then took a deep breath, his shoulders falling to rest. He wore a chain around his neck, and he brought it to his lips and kissed it before focusing on the river before him.

Andrew cupped his mouth and hollered, "Let's go!" Then Rico held his phone up for a picture, and we all watched Bo complete a backflip into the water.

Freaking effortless.

Jesus was up next, wobbling up the steel, and forcing me to cover my mouth. He steadied himself. "Ta-da!" he said, and he held out his arms as he free-fell, landing with a smack on the water.

The watching crowd ooohed and laughed. I recoiled, looking over the ledge to see if he was okay.

There was a round of applause when Jesus came up for air, and he shouted, "No regrets! I'd do it again!"

We all exhaled together, thankful he was okay. *What a doof.*

Rico shook his head. "Dude is crazy as hell," he said, and he prepped his camera and pointed to us girls. We were next.

Charlie squealed and pushed her forehead to Mika's before she rushed to the bridge.

"You've got this," Mika said after, and we climbed the overhang together. I was sandwiched between the two of them.

"I want us to pose midair," Charlie said. Mika and I nodded in unison.

A sound beneath me, and I wobbled. My stomach tied itself into a ball; I held it with one hand, the other keeping me still.

Another sound. The vibration in my soles. It was Charlie. Both of her hands were in the air, and she shouted nonsense to the sky.

When I looked at the water, Jesus and Bo waved to us, cheering us on, and everything past them and before them was bright orange.

Charlie grabbed my hand and squeezed. "Are you nervous?" she asked, her big eyes full of wonder.

I nodded, and Mika took my other hand. "You will love it," she said, gripping my fingers.

We bent our knees, and I tried not to breathe, tried not to hear the whisper inside me. I could do this. I had to do this.

Mika bellowed, "Three, two, one!"

And we jumped at once, our hands still clasped together, pointing toward the sky. The earth beneath us grew farther and farther away, and I realized we were continuing up instead of down. Somehow, we'd been given flight, and the trees turned into green blobs, and the lots beneath us looked flat and empty. Orange and blue.

We broke through the barrier, passing the clouds, touching the stars momentarily, and I wondered if I was closer to Mama now; I wondered if she could see me.

Back down we went, fast like meteors, smashing into the warm water. It filled my ears. Silence. Bubbles rushed around me, forcing me up, up, up, and I gasped. Laughter. People. Sunlight. The air burned my tongue, and I looked for Bo in the water. He shared a smile with me, and I wanted to do it all over again.

We didn't really fly, but in that moment, it felt like we did. I'd always been so consumed with dance that I'd never considered doing anything else. Never considered camping with strangers and jumping off bridges. Never considered boys who were zombies and friends that made me feel bulletproof.

This undeath was the undoing of an old story I used to tell myself. It was immensely different, yet that was okay. The stitching of these new pieces being pulled together shouldn't feel the same. It should tug and stretch, and I felt that now.

The girls shouted and hugged me, and I hugged them back, excited that I'd actually done another cool thing.

We watched Andrew and Rico jump in together, both doing some sort of flip, and then we went back up, doing it again and again till we were red in the face and our chests were heavy.

On the ride back to the campsite, it was quiet for the first time. A folk song buzzed through the busted speakers, the harmonica wheezing. My fingers danced to the rhythm on my thighs, keeping the tempo. Reminded me of a feeling I'd had before.

Bo sat beside me, and I rested my head on his shoulder, my damp twists seeping into his white shirt, staining it.

He didn't seem to mind, and I saw that he held his hand out, waiting.

That signal could mean anything. Maybe he was relaxing and that was just how his hand looked; maybe he had some sort of internal prayer happening, and his hand was out in receiving mode; and more obvious, maybe he simply wanted to hold my hand.

I slipped my hand into his, weaving our fingers together. He held it tightly, his breathing on my forehead coming quicker.

And I knew I'd thought it before, but there was just something about him, and I wanted to pinpoint it. There was something about the way my head felt on his shoulder. Something about the way his chest rose and fell. Something about this song.

Something.

I'd never felt this way, and I wasn't sure how to describe it, but I was certain if someone opened my skull to look at my brain, it would be a pile of zucchini noodles.

All at once, I wanted to soak up every color Bo was made of. I wanted to tie myself around him and sink so deep into this moment that we crashed to the center of the earth, burning into each other.

Bo kissed the side of my head, and I could feel his lips forming a smile. Could we stay like this, never moving, and be okay?

We inhaled at the same time. Bo squeezed my hand again. "I'm so happy you're here," he whispered, and the words repeated themselves until they were backward and forward; incomplete sentences.

Slow breaths. "I'm glad I am, too," I said, and I closed my eyes, now conjuring new ways to pause the universe.

CHAPTER THIRTY-TWO

AFTER EVERYONE CHANGED out of their wet clothes, we gathered firewood. Mika found a flower and rushed it over to me. She broke part of the stem and placed it behind my ear. I felt like a warrior princess.

She said it complemented me.

As we continued to gather sticks, I noticed Bo watched my every movement with a stupid grin on his face, but I watched his, equally matching that grin and feeling incredibly limitless because of it.

Around eight in the evening, the sun dimmed in the sky, but there was still enough light to see the shimmer of dew in the grass, small beads running down the stems, the croaking of toads in the shadows.

There was a gentle breeze that reminded me of Mama. It tangled itself through the loose twists in my hair and wrapped around my shoulders. Warm and sweet. Slow and gentle. Yellow and blue.

Here and now, we could easily insert ourselves into van Gogh's *Landscape at Twilight.* That was this, exactly. We were stretched, black trees with thin limbs under the golden sky. Layered strokes, clumping on top of each other. We were Impressionists. We were cicadas harmonizing together, and when Jesus lit the fire, we burned blue, green, yellow, and orange.

We pulled lawn chairs out the back of Rico's van and placed them around the fire. Andrew opened a cooler filled with food and passed out hot dogs on sticks.

"We heard you're a vegetarian," Andrew shouted, and he threw me a pack of veggie dogs.

"Wow, okay. Thanks," I said, impressed as hell. I was planning on stuffing my face with potato chips for the next twenty-four hours; this was definitely an upgrade.

Then Rico wheeled in another cooler, and he opened it and passed out small aluminum cans.

When it got to me, I turned it around so I could read it. "Beer?"

Bo leaned over, his arm pressing into mine. "You don't have to drink it."

I popped it open. "YOLO," I said. I was here now. Why not? No one but myself to hold me back. The hike, the bridge, now this. Anything I wanted. I could have it all.

Bo grinned, holding his up. "To the solstice!" he hyped.

We all raised our cans to the fire. "To the solstice!"

The first sip was bubbly and gross, and the second sip wasn't much better, but it was warmer as it slid down my throat. "Is it always like this?" I said to Charlie as I reread the can.

She chuckled, her dark hair wavy now, bleeding into the night. "It gets better. Is this your first one?"

"Yup," I said, taking another sip, and ehhhh. Wasn't a fan. Didn't think I'd *ever* be a fan.

"To the solstice!" Charlie shouted, opening another can, and I wondered if she had a high tolerance.

The crew responded, and Rico ripped out a loud "Ahhhhhh" as he stood, throwing his hands up in the air, beating on his chest like a wild animal.

Then Jesus made a birdcall, to which Andrew responded, then Bo and Rico. The calls bounced over the fire like a volleyball.

Charlie leaned into me, and I realized I was used to it now—used to the idea that we could be friends. "This is how they communicate," she whispered.

After I pulled my veggie dog from the fire, I turned to her. "What does it even mean?"

"Hell if I'll ever know," she said, looking at them, and we both laughed.

A few more dogs were made, a few more drinks were had, and after the chips had run their course, Andrew brought out a guitar.

Mika perked up and clapped, staring at Andrew like he was the golden ticket.

Andrew ran his fingers across the strings and smiled at Mika before giving her a kiss that made me feel as though I shouldn't be watching. Then he plucked a tune that sounded familiar, but I couldn't remember where I'd heard it before.

Mika hummed, low and steady, and when she opened her mouth to sing, I was surprised by the beauty of it—and again, who *were* these people? Andrew joined in, adding a harmony that complemented her so well, you'd think they'd been doing this their whole lives.

At the start of the chorus, I remembered where I'd heard the song. It was in a *Shrek* movie, the "Hallelujah" song covered by Rufus Wainwright.

While they sang, Bo snuck up behind my chair, wrapped his arms around my shoulders, and kissed me on the cheek. His warm nose nestled into the side of my face, and I heard shuffling, Charlie moving beside me, but I ignored it, inhaling Bo's air.

Turned my face slowly, slowly. Paused. Couldn't exhale this time. Our lips almost brushed.

A l m o s t.

We pressed our noses together, and I felt electrified, my whole body blazing at the notion of kissing him. I wanted him, needed to close this space between us for only a second.

To modify the colors of us...

But I pulled away, refocusing on the fire, listening to the song, thinking of how close Bo still was. His smile was on me, I knew it was, I felt it—and then he was gone.

Charlie was gone, too, when I looked. No longer in her chair, she hovered over the cooler, digging and pulling out another can. Opened it, threw her head back. Then Jesus joined her, grabbing a can. He poked her side, and she spat some of her drink on him.

"You're the worst," she said, but he laughed it off, shoulders sagging, and they clanked their cans together.

When the song ended, Charlie returned, and we stood, cheering on Mika and Andrew. They bowed for us, and then Mika skipped over, pressing Charlie into a side hug with a look that begged to know what had happened. She whispered something into her ear, and I heard the sound of her lips parting, catching separated words: *saw . . . do you . . . we can . . . go . . .*

Wondered what it was about, and if Mika would tell me, but Charlie nodded her head, her bottom lip poking out a bit.

"It's okay," she breathed, and Mika let her go.

She turned her attention toward me. "Are you having fun, Z?" Mika tucked her curls behind her ear. Guessed she wasn't going to tell me.

"The time of my life." And when I said it, I felt the alcohol spilling into my body, making me warm.

"Well, let's keep the party going." Mika rushed to grab two more cans. She handed me one, and we opened them at the same time.

"We're throwing them back," she said, and we did, my head feeling lighter than my body.

Jesus connected his phone to a Bluetooth speaker and started a playlist. The first song was one of Kendrick Lamar's, and the girls turned to each other, their eyes wide.

They started jumping and chanting the lyrics, and then they took my hands, making me jump, too. We hopped around the fire, mocking the flames. Each bounce, I felt higher and higher, drifting. They danced, and I mimicked them, letting my gooey limbs flow side to side in the air like an anemone.

When the next song came on, they screamed out the lyrics, scaring the bats, and I swore I saw their souls leave their bodies. I tried singing along, making the words up as I went. Charlie squeezed me tightly, pressing her face against mine, and I truly felt like I'd found my people.

It was like they'd been waiting here, stuck in this painting, and I just needed to get here, years ago. I needed to find them and swim in this never-ending universe until it all made sense again.

The colors smashed together; the world spun. I was no longer in my morphed realities. I was closer to the center of the earth. And we laughed and laughed. Dancing and crashing into the ground.

"Z," Charlie breathed, forehead sweating, the yellow making her face glow. "Damn it. I'm happy you are here. I mean it." Her words broken. "Told myself. Again. To tell you, and I'm doing it. And we're okay. Happy you are here."

"Me? You're happy I'm here? I'm really happy to be here. Thanks for making me feel welcomed," I said, the words drifting to her, the world slightly wobbly.

She smiled, but I rushed to speak again.

"How—how are you so cool? It's like. You know. Everyone loves you."

She put her hand to the sky, inspecting it, and I did the same with mine. The warm colors twisting in my palm like the flames.

"I don't know, Z. I'm just being myself."

Mika jumped beside us. "What are you ladybugs doing? Up!" she demanded, stretching her hands out to us. "No time for talking. We dance!"

And I wanted to dance, but it was nice connecting with Charlie again. She seemed so human. We got up anyway, dancing, doing it all over again. And it was . . . it was everything.

After a breath, I felt a pair of arms around me, lifting me up and taking me away from the crowd. I spun around to find Bo. He towered over me with a smile so big it made my cheeks hurt, and it reminded me of the dream I'd had.

He lured me into *The Starry Night*, his hands around my waist, his lips pressed to the side of my throat. The blood in my veins pumped twice as fast, and my body tingled.

Didn't want to breathe or alter this moment. Just waited. Waited for what would come next.

"Last night, I told the stars about you." He said it in my ear, his lips brushing my lobe.

I swallowed first. "What did they say?"

"They told me to wait for you." His words bled into the air, and in the darkness, his eyes were on me, staring at my mouth.

"And how did you respond?"

"I told them you were worth the wait."

My lips parted, but nothing came out. Had he always wanted to say this? Was this a real, *real* thing? Were these real, *real* words?

It was Bo, he was alive, and I could totally speak to him, try to explain these newfound feelings, but I didn't know how.

All I knew was that I wanted him to stay this close to me. I felt so red and pink, and I was unsure of where to place these colors.

Our chests pressed together, and we swayed to the music in the background, our breathing heavy. It felt like I was dancing backward with him, except we were always on time, never missed a beat, and each outward spin led me to his smile again.

And what was this feeling? My ribs solidified, my feet grew sunflowers, my saliva multiplied. I wanted him so much closer to me, but we were as close as we could get. Maybe these symptoms were signs of being *in like*?

Because love...it was too soon for that...right?

Bo and I slowed our moving, and we were alone in space, our eyes meeting, and I anticipated the moment when he'd warp into the unmentionable thing. He always had, and I knew he would. He *had* to.

But instead, he opened a starship, and in an instance, we were in our own galaxy. The stars twinkling magnificently for us.

Bo pressed his thumb into my cheek, and I held my breath.

And whatever would come next, I wanted him to know that it was okay. That I wanted this, too, so I reached my hand to his face, my fingertips tracing his jaw, following the way it curved. His dark eyes watched me, beaming, until he closed the distance between the two of us.

He kissed me, our lips smashing together like a colorful collision, and we perished almost, falling limp into this novelty. I'd never felt so much energy in my life.

My heart sank into my shoes and poured out my toes in spurts. And I wanted to be so wrapped up in him, but I *couldn't* say it. I wouldn't.

Chemically, he moved me more than anyone had, more than this dance had, and this was the most human I'd been, ever.

For once, the fire stopped flickering and the moon was so bright, it ignited me. I kissed Bo back like a storm, hands on the nape of his neck, crawling up to his curls, tugging at them. Closer. Bo pulled me into him, holding my face, his nose pressed to the side of mine. Breathing. Barely breathing. He was the gravity I wanted to fall into.

And I kept falling,

down,

down,

down,

until we landed in the wet grass, drinking all the air from each other's lungs. And I could keep going, never stopping, but for some reason, I laughed. . . .

Bo laughed with me, looking at me like he was seeing for the first time. "What's so funny?"

I covered my hands with my face and rolled away from him, my back against the ground. "I didn't expect that," I said, catching my breath, and I still couldn't wrap my head around what was happening. Bo kissing me sparked so many questions, but when I sorted it out, it came down to one: *Why?*

I said it out loud then. "Why?" I asked, pressing the grass between my fingers. "Why'd you kiss me?"

"I've wanted to do that since the first moment we met."

The grass snapped from my pulling. "Why didn't you?" I asked, realizing that this *like* thing was a real thing, realizing that maybe it'd been there, under the surface, and I didn't notice it grasping at me until now.

"We just weren't there yet," he said, truth spilling from his eyelids. His palms were sweaty when I took his hand, weaved our fingers together.

"I'm glad you didn't. It probably would have scared me away."

Bo grinned. "It's funny you say that. You always have this wide look in your eyes . . . afraid that I'll eat you or some jazz."

I tried not to gasp. "There have been times when you've looked like a monster."

"Hey." He nudged. "Monsters are humans, too."

I turned to my side, sharing the biggest grin with him.

He turned to his side, too. "Z, there's this energy about you that I can't place. But it feels right, and I know I haven't said this, but you're one of the best people I've ever met. And I want more of it." He looked down. "I want more moments like this with you."

I grabbed him, kissing him, creating more moments. His palm slid to the low of my back, pulling me into his ribs. We moved and breathed in the same way, stitching our worlds together.

This was never the plan. Never part of my ambitions, but Bo was so great and goofy, and he was here. There was no want to undo this.

And if Mama could see me . . .

Pushed the thought away. Didn't want to think about it.

Not now.

But *if* she could see me, she'd be proud.

When we got off the ground, I jumped on Bo's back. "Time for another adventure," I said.

"Where to?" He hiked me up, and we did a quick spin, my arms out.

I pointed to the emptiness ahead of us. "To the moon and never back!"

Bo kicked up dirt and howled. "To the moon!" he said, and he ran fast, the stars blurring. He kept going until he tripped on something, sending us both to the ground.

We laughed, and my phone vibrated in my pocket.

I never wanted any of this to end.

CHAPTER THIRTY-THREE

MY HEAD HURT SO BAD when I stood. It was maybe an hour later, and we were at the campfire, listening to Jesus tell some crazy story about El Chupacabra, and I was presumably two more drinks in. Didn't catch the whole story, but it gave me chills, and I'd forgotten why I stood, so I sat back down.

Think.

The flames flickered with haste, creating shadows on Jesus's face that made him look haunting, and when he spoke, I heard movement behind him. It was quick, rustling in the grass. I stretched my neck and stared down the darkness, trying to make out shapes, but the world kept spinning around me. It was hard to focus.

Croak.

Charlie rubbed my back and asked if I was okay. Her breathing was low, but I didn't look up to see what expression she had on her face. I kept my eyes on the blob in the dark abyss. Focused on what looked more like a figure now, gradually closing in on us. A shadow of a man shaped like a tree.

A man or a tree?

Swallowed. Swallowed the slime in my throat. Blinked to see if anyone saw what I saw. My eyes watered. They were laughing at Jesus. He rolled his hips in a big circle. Slow, then fast.

"Dude, is anyone recording this?" Rico asked.

Someone moved, and the dark figure . . . it twisted, twirling, mixing nothing into nothingness.

It hissed, and the hair pricked on my arms.

Tried to speak, but my lips felt numb. Sat up, and my stomach turned. I coughed, feeling something in the back of my throat. *God, what was that?*

I heard Bo move on the other side of me. "Z, are you okay?"

Coughed again, holding my hand to my throat. Then I felt the sludge making its way up, blurring my vision, and I got out of the way just in time to vomit.

Gah, the smell. Tears spilled from my eyes. "*Ughhh.*" My words shook my body, and I was so thirsty.

Bo was beside me, closer. He grabbed at my shirt. "Oh shit, Z. Let me help you."

I didn't move. I felt it coming again, and then Charlie was beside me, trying to force a plastic water bottle into my hands.

"Drink this," she said, her voice somewhat amused. *Why?*

"Can't." I shook my head, and I could hear hushed voices—one of which was Rico's.

"Your girl can't hang," I heard him say. His deep voice rumbled with laughter after that.

"Shut the hell up!" Bo yelled.

The vomit came again, harder this time, and my throat burned of booze and bile and chips. I couldn't remember how much I drank, but it didn't seem like enough for *this*.

I wanted to cry, but it was bad enough they had to see me hunched over and spilling out my insides. Didn't want to be remembered this way.

Charlie whispered something, and I wanted the world to stop spinning so fast. Wanted the hushed voices to stop growing.

Bo waited, his hand on my arm, his fingers rubbing my skin. "It's okay," he said. "Just take your time. Don't force it."

"We have to get her to her tent," Charlie said. "She needs to lie down."

"Give her a second," Bo whispered. "She's got this."

He was right. I had this . . . well, I *kinda* had this, but I didn't want to lie down. I didn't want to be the girl who left the party first—I'd already been her. Bad idea, Charlie.

I drank some of the water, but even the water tasted awful. "Ew," I mumbled, and Bo laughed. It tasted like La Croix, and I spat it out, only to take another sip from the bottle. Would rather have that on my tongue than the taste of vomit in my mouth.

"I can take care of her," Bo said to Charlie.

Charlie rubbed my back. "You need my help," she said.

"No, I *got* it," he said.

Charlie hissed, "But she's *my* friend, too." There was a pause, and then a huff, her voice lighter now. "C'mon, Abey. Don't fight me on this. *Please…*"

Felt it then, the sudden sleepiness, the heaviness in my eyes, and my limbs giving way to gravity. Charlie was right. Maybe I should lie down, take a break. It would be fine. We were friends now, we could move past this, but we were at a standstill—me hurled over the side of this chair, and an awkward tension floating in the air among the three of us.

Someone shifted.

"Really?" Charlie said, and her voice cracked. Maybe it was a look she saw, or a whisper that was shared.

Bo smacked his lips. "Charlie, *don't* do that….Just don't."

Another shift, and when I finished the water, Bo helped me to my feet, slinging one of my arms across his shoulders. "I'll take care of you," he mumbled, my face close to his chest, safety.

Charlie placed my other arm around her shoulder, and in less seconds than I cared to count, I was sandwiched between two people I never thought I'd be sandwiched by.

Fun.

"I'm helping," she insisted, and Bo sighed.

My stomach flipped with each step, and I looked behind me, past the fire, trying to see if the thing was still there. Nothing.

Where'd it go?

In the night, past the van, Charlie looked my way, but her eyes were on Bo.

His gaze was fixed on what was ahead. Small steps, the silence growing.

I leaned against Bo as Charlie unzipped the tent, and he mumbled something to me I didn't quite catch. Just a rhythm in his chest, a rasp. Then she undid my shoes, and both of them helped me inside.

The ground was uneven, and I shuffled around, trying to get comfortable on the tent floor.

Bo leaned in, pulling a blanket over me. He swayed a little, the alcohol making him blurry. "If you need anything, anything at all, just shout my name. I'll be here. Okay?"

I waited for the glow of his word bubble, but it didn't come. A darkness slid behind his irises instead.

"Okay."

He smiled, but it was broken. His lips peeling and twisted. "Pinky promise." His voice breathy as he held his finger up.

My pinky found his, and they locked.

"Bo, come on," Charlie pressed, and the top of the tent moved.

"Leave her be already." She stuck her head in, and Bo moved out of the way. "Sleep well, Z. Don't let the bedbugs bite," she said, and it made me nervous.

"O-okay." I half waved, and in a blink, the tent was zipped, and they were both gone.

The big orange thing seemed to swallow me, and I felt hot and cold at the same time. Checked my phone, the light so bright my eyes watered. A text from Auntie E:

> We need to speak when u get back

Shit. Those words never meant anything good. Ever. But what did she want to talk about now? Was she just gonna flake again? Pull the job card? Did something come up? Did she need money?

Rested my head with a sigh. A blink, and a flicker. It only took seconds. But then I was in the field outside the tent, standing under the light of the crescent moon. The tree line was closer to me than it should have been, creating a fence of different-sized trees before me.

And I didn't know how I got here, but . . .

My right hand was extended in front of me, and resting in my palm was a warm, beating heart. The ruby blood seeped through the ventricles, down my arm, and into the grass. The blood splattered rhythmically as it landed on the ground, and the sound reminded me of the vibrating pulse in the breakdown of "Thriller."

My attention was drawn upward when I heard something else. It was slow at first, but then the lower tree branches in front of me rustled away from one another, and Bo appeared, entering the clearing.

I rose to the tips of my toes, ecstatic to see him. I missed him. There were so many more questions I had.

Bo stared at me, frozen. His face morphed from joy to fear when he saw what I held.

He yelled, "No, Z! *No!* Get away from here!"

My brows clustered in the middle of my forehead. "What?" I said, but the word was inaudible, and the music grew louder in my head.

Bo tried to move toward me, but thick green vines burst from the ground, and they tied themselves around his legs, up his torso, to his neck. He reached for me, and when I tried to go to him, he begged me to stop, his palms facing me.

Bo gagged and choked, and when he coughed, a sunflower crawled out of his mouth, petal by petal, then dropped to the ground, crumpled.

Bo, I tried again. But nothing.

Then his skin ripped away from his bone, and he morphed into the undead, his red-and-black shirt tattered, his eyes sunken, and his skin emerald green and gray.

His mouth pooled with dark black gunk, and I cried for it to stop, but it would not relent.

It was harder to breathe. I heaved, my chest jolting, and the trees rustled again, their branches shaking, leaves rushing to the ground.

Zombies poured from the shadows, moving to the sound of the pulse.

Throbbing. Throbbing.

They trudged forward, one foot in front of the other, bones snapping, shoulders bouncing. Gusts of thick fog followed them, hiding some of their stares, revealing some of their shredded smiles.

They groaned into the night, the sound echoing off their wet bones.

"*Why?*" Bo cried out, and it was the clearest thing I'd ever heard him say in his zombie form.

I couldn't understand what Bo wanted from me, or what I had done. But Bo seemed farther and farther away from me as the zombies passed him, closing in on me.

Tried to make a run for it, but the same vines that had gotten Bo slithered up my ankles, anchoring me in place.

As I stared in horror at the vines inching up my legs, I noticed a big, gaping hole in my chest where my heart should be. It spilled with blood, making me warm, then hot. The cut was jagged, as if someone had ripped the organ straight from my chest, and I looked at the heart again, then back at my chest.

It was *my* heart that I held in my hand.

My thumping, wheezing heart.

Grunting, I tried to draw my right arm back toward me, but it was locked in place, extending outward.

Why would I do such a thing? Why would I rip my own heart out of my chest? And when, *when* did this happen?

The heart thudded faster when I looked up, practically flopping in my hand like a fish without water. And I tried to move again, to lift my knees, but the unmentionables circled around me with their scorched arms reaching, reaching, reaching and grabbing at my heart.

One got it. Punctured it with its claws. Everywhere now, and it disassembled it with one bite, blood shooting into my eye, covering my face.

Another ripped at my arm, but it wouldn't come off. That pain struck in my jaw, and I screamed, tears mixing with blood. A pop. Disconnecting joints, skin tearing away from my shoulder. Fell to my knees, and I cried out again and again as another got to me. Thoughts drew blackness. And I was done, I was sure I was done, until I woke.

It was only a nightmare.

The sweat was piled on me when I bolted awake, and I felt like I needed to change out of my clothes.

I checked—my heart was still in my chest, and I held my hand there in relief while I waited for my breathing to slow down. What a screwy dream.

After I changed, I realized that the water I drank earlier had finally caught up to me, felt my bladder pressing against my pelvis.

I unzipped the tent, slipped into my Adidas, and stood in the cool night air. The chairs were empty around the campfire, and white smoke rose from the ash, the broken oak still popping and cracking from the heat.

The darkness was overwhelming. It suffocated so much of this clearing, and if I looked for longer than I should, I'd see the thing again. I knew I would. The stillness was hungry.

Checked the moon, and it was tilted in the corner of the sky.

Small, throaty laughs rose from Mika's tent, probably Andrew, and the fabric swished from all the movement. A light flickering. I winced. Didn't care to know what was happening over there. But my thoughts jumped to conclusions anyway.

Pressed my arms close to me, and I headed on a path behind the tents and hammocks to a lone tree a couple yards away—somewhere no one could see me.

I swatted at a couple critters while I peed, peering into the dark, wondering if anything was in the woods watching me. Could be a mountain lion, or a coyote.

A shuffle. Something scurried. Could be the dead.

Pulled up my cotton shorts and moved quickly, my pace doubled until I broke into a jog. I zipped myself back in my tent, my hands shaking, and when I tried to rest, my throat felt dry, parched.

Shoot.

The coolers were by Rico's van, and it would take all of three minutes to grab a bottle of water and make it back. The risk was well worth it if it meant I could sleep okay. And the zombies, they weren't real. They weren't.

Unzipped the tent with a huff, hopped outside, scurried to the coolers. Grabbed a bottle of water, but it fell. *Shit.* A movement again. Sharp whispers coming from nearby. The other side of the van, maybe? I wanted to ignore it, but the voice sounded too familiar to walk away from.

I peeked around the corner, hovering close to Rico's van, pressing my face against the taillight, and it smelled of rusting metal and gas.

What I immediately saw was Bo. He held Charlie's face with both blistered hands, and in the dark, I could clearly see that he was almost a zombie. Bones breaking and popping out of his side.

Charlie's arms were tensed, her fists balled tightly. The moonlight highlighted her protruding lips and dark eyes, her hair purple now.

A groan. Bo's voice sounded like it came from the deepest part of his throat. I'd never heard it so low. "*Please*, Charles. I'm begging you. Just *let it go*."

"But I can't. I thought I could, and I can't. Not today, not tonight. This is too much."

Bo removed his hands from her face, and he limped away from her, creating distance. "You are hurting me. Why can't you see it? I feel like I'm dead on the inside."

When he said it, his words turned me cobalt blue. He was dead on the outside, too.

Charlie grunted, and she kicked at the grass, pulled at her hair. "Listen to me," she said, and I saw the tears. They rushed down her face in streams. Her shoulders drooping, her hands open. "Please, Abe. Please . . . just this one last time," Charlie said, her voice muffled. She studied the ground, paused. Then she ran to Bo, throwing her arms around his neck, and she kissed him, pressing her very alive face into his half-dead one. The squishing. The breaking. The everything reverberating in my ear.

My vertebrae shattered at the sight of it, my jaw falling open. After tonight, I'd thought Charlie was my friend. I'd thought Bo liked me. They had made me feel safe and loved, and now it felt like I didn't know anything anymore.

I stood, and I threw my water bottle to the ground. It picked up dust and skirted toward them. They snapped their heads to see me, Bo's skeletal mouth cracking, Charlie jumping away from him.

We were silent, but the night screamed at us, the smoke curled itself around us, making us small. I tried to find the words, but they were all tied behind my lips, and the yells I held inside made me feel like I was burning.

He was first. "Shit, Z." Bo stumbled forward, his decomposing arm reaching for me. "I swear to you, I swear to God, it's not what you think." The undertone in his voice was laced with moans, his dead side coming through.

And like a werewolf, he fully transformed into the undead under the threatening light that poured from the stars.

We were amber gold then, and I didn't know them.

Everything else Bo said meant nothing to me, literally. He tripped forward, his skin rolling away, and I backed up, my eyes watering, sinking under the weight of the words he tried to say.

He yelled out in groans for me to understand, and I understood nothing. All the while, Charlie paced back and forth, biting her lip, not speaking, not looking up.

I wiped the tears away with the back of my hand. "Enough already," I said, my own voice breaking.

"Z," Charlie started, but I ran away. It didn't matter what she had to say, what *he* had to say, nothing could undo what was already done, and I hated her. I hated him. I hated this.

I fell to the floor of my tent after, my body thudding. The tears kept coming, flooding my eyes. The last time I cried this hard was when Mama died.

And my heart shriveled and split open at the thought of it. It probably wasn't even red anymore. It was black, I was sure it was black.

It was empty but still pumping blood somehow, and if I could, I'd rip it from my chest to stop the heartache, end the madness that felt like an infinity.

I never should have never gotten this close to Bo. Never should have let my guard down. My intentions with him were supposed to be all business.

And *his* friends, who felt like my friends—it would all be gone. What was I supposed to do? Couldn't have them anymore; they'd keep their loyalties to Bo. . . .

Wished they wouldn't, though. Just hours before, we were all so great, but when they found out, it would change. I knew it would.

Then I cried harder, my lungs crushing. They were all monsters. All of them. And they only wanted to hurt me.

And we were terrible, selfish people. Didn't deserve heartbeats. Didn't deserve to feed our needs like we did.

I'd probably never know why Mama died, or why she turned into a zombie. I'd just have to rest on the fact that something had gotten to her somehow.

And no matter what I did, I'd never be able to stop it, because now I knew the spoiler to every story: We all died in the end.

CHAPTER THIRTY-FOUR

BY THE MORNING, my face felt sore and my eyes were puffy.
Bo met me at my tent for breakfast, zombified and reaching for me,
but I ignored him.

Charlie tried to talk to me by the campfire, but I wouldn't look at
her. Mika sensed something was off. I noticed her head tilted to the
side, trying to figure out what had happened, but I disappeared to
pack before she could speak to me.

Jesus helped me take down the tent, making jokes the entire time.
Even when I didn't laugh as hard, he kept going. I think he assumed
it would change how I felt. I wanted to laugh with him, but it wouldn't

come. He offered to finish up the rest, and then he pulled me into a hug, the campfire still lingering in his shirt.

"Hey, Z. Um, um...are you okay? You seem like you have some stuff going on in your head."

My gaze fell to the ground, and when I tried to speak, I felt my eyes swell, so I stopped myself. Placed my hand on Jesus's shoulder, gave him another hug, and walked away.

Charlie came again as I stuffed the rest of my things into the duffel bag. Her brown face gray now. "Zharie," her voice low. "Just give me a minute. That's all I'm asking for."

Got up. "Don't waste your breath."

She stopped me from going forward, blocking my path to the van. And I saw Bo over there, lingering, probably thinking he'd get a chance to come over next. "No, listen. Just listen, okay?" And she smelled like beer. Like last night's betrayals.

"You probably won't believe this, but last night wasn't me. It wasn't who I'm trying to be. I'm not the things that you saw, and it was a moment of desperation. Everything was spinning, and I lost control." Charlie waited; she looked at me with that water in her eyes. Briefly, I wanted to empathize with her, to believe the next thing she'd say, but the last time I did that, she ruined it.

"I really am trying to be a good person. And you probably think I'm a bitch. And I *am*, sometimes. But I wasn't lying when I said I wanted to be your friend. And I wasn't lying when I said I was happy you were here. And if you take anything away from this, just forgive Bo."

She sucked her lip in, tears now. "He's always been the better part of me, and he shouldn't have to lose you because of what I did. And I'm sorry for crossing the line. You didn't deserve that."

I looked to the sky. The clouds blocked the sun, and I tried to digest what Charlie had said. How she wanted to be good but felt bad. How it wasn't as it seemed, and it was a desperate moment for her. How I should forgive Bo. But Bo *wasn't* forced into anything. Charlie didn't tie him down when she kissed him. Didn't threaten him. Maybe my eyes fooled me, but he kissed her, too. It was there, in the moonlight, and had I not walked in, who was to say it wouldn't have continued?

And there had been a point when Bo forced himself into my life. He'd darted in like he was determined to be around forever. Like I was the piece he needed to complete the family he wanted to build, the new group of friends. But now he couldn't even force himself here in place of Charlie. He couldn't revert back. Couldn't do anything but rot like he did. And that was enough for me to want to walk away from him forever.

So as Charlie stared at me with her fawn eyes, I couldn't muster up the desire to believe her. I didn't want to be lured by her presence, and the person she wanted to be. Maybe I'd change my mind about her down the road, maybe I'd think over what she said again and forgive her, but that wouldn't be today.

"Goodbye, Charlie," I said, and I didn't turn to look back at her when I walked away, even though the wind tugged my twists backward, even though a sound rose from behind. Wouldn't do it.

Before we left the campground, I asked Rico if it was cool if I sat shotgun.

Scratched his head and gathered his lips to the side, eyes low. *You good?*

He didn't say it, but I heard it anyway, and my face stung when I shook my head.

Rico cleared the front seat for me, handed me his phone to control the music, and I sighed in relief. Didn't care where Bo or Charlie sat, as long as it wasn't beside me.

At drop-off, I hoped Auntie E was home. I wanted to leave this place, talk about something else, and really, I could go for a burrito. Wouldn't even care if she asked me to look for a job. Didn't matter anymore. But her car wasn't parked in its usual space, and I shriveled a little because Bo followed me to the front door of the apartment. There was a thud when I shut the door on him. Did that infuriate him? Did it turn him inside out, expose him to the world?

I hoped it did. He deserved it.

An hour later, Bo tapped on my window from the fire escape, and it startled the hell out of me. It was weird that he still looked like a zombie—he crossed a world record in *The Book of Zharie*. Too bad I didn't care.

When I closed the blinds, I heard his moans on the other side. He tapped again, and again, and then I turned my music up, threw back my rug, and practiced my steps.

In the evening, he sent me three texts, and I deleted them as they came in:

> Z, i'm really sorry about—

Delete.

> And if u knew that—

Delete.

> I swear that's true. I'd never—

Delete.

I stayed up till midnight, taking out my twists and talking to Mini via FaceTime. She refrained from saying "I told you so," but I told her she was right anyway. It was crazy for me to run off with people I barely knew and think nothing bad would happen. The past me would have slipped away quietly, and they would have forgotten me eventually.

Mini told me that, because of me, she attended her first West Coast Swing class. She said it was weird AF, and that I was "on that white people shit." She wasn't completely wrong. People would say the same thing to Mama.

Mini also said there were a lot of old people. She'd met three elders named Bob. Maybe it was coincidental, but I also knew three elders named Bob at my old studio.

It made me laugh hard, and I cried a little.

"No offense, Z, I don't think it's for me." She shrugged, braiding her sew-in, and then putting on her bonnet.

I told her it was fine. West Coast wasn't for everyone, but I was glad she tried. Wished she would have recorded it, though.

When I was all done with my hair, my fingers felt bruised, my shoulders felt tight. My hair was bigger than it had ever been, longer, and when I looked at my reflection in the mirror, it shocked me.

Leaned in, eyes red, and I studied my tight brown curls. Studied how they zagged in some areas, and how they kept tangling at the ends. My hair looked so much like Mama's, and the thought of it made me cry again.

Life was so effing stupid.

After my shower, I had a missed call and a voicemail from Bo. Listening to it would have been a waste of time. I released a deep sigh, gripping the phone in my hand, wanting to yell, *Just stop, Bo. Leave me alone. Let it be.*

It was too late now.

I blocked his number, turned off my phone, and climbed into bed.

That night, it didn't feel like I slept at all. I tossed and turned until the sun came up, wishing I could go back in time to a different day.

CHAPTER THIRTY-FIVE

THE LAST TIME I SAW Mama happy, like truly, *truly* happy, was a few weeks before she died.

We were at the ballroom, and I was finishing up my geometry homework for the academy. I'd never say it out loud, but I was *legitimately* having fun. Math had always been a hard subject for me, but since I'd had Mr. K (who also doubled as the girls' soccer coach), it clicked. He'd broken down the equations in a way that I could comprehend without second-guessing myself.

When the assignment was complete, I looked up to see Mama practicing with her colleague Jay. Jay had been dancing since he was thirteen, and I remembered learning that he had won like eleven West

Coast Swing Classic Division Championships before he was thirty. Last year, he won Best Swing Choreographer.

Mama and Jay had been dancing together since I was five. When they danced, they glided across the shiny wood like they were an extension of each other, an extension of the music. Their moves were controlled, fluid, and the stuff dreams were made of.

Mama had always been rhythmic, but today, her isolations were on point. Looking at her now reminded me how much she was made for this. If she wanted to, she could be a star, travel the world, teach in new places. But Mama loved her job in KC, she loved her friends, loved her students, and she always said that she wouldn't trade it for the world.

She studied herself in the mirror while she danced with Jay, and I knew she was trying something new because she squinted her eyes and folded her lips.

Even if it messed her up—though no one would EVER be able to know if she messed up because she was *that* good—she tried it anyway. It was her desire to take risks that made her so great, and I only hoped to be as great as her someday.

The tempo sped up, and she laughed, swinging back and forth on the slot. Jay spun her down the length of the dance floor, and she should have been out of breath, but she smiled the whole time, styling her way through the next set of moves.

When the song was over, she reached out for me, sweat dripping down her cheekbones.

"Mama," I said under my breath when I got to her. I was anxious because I didn't want Jay to watch me dance; didn't want him to think that because I was Twiggy's daughter, I'd be as flawless as she was.

And Mama knew I was freaking out. She knew I was reverting back to the last time I competed, and I couldn't get my head out of that space.

"You ready?"

I gulped, tried not to look at her. The music played, and we were in the starter position. I closed my eyes and whispered to myself: *It's only dancing.*

When Mama spun me into the first count, my arms tensed up.

I paused mid-dance, my face squishing. "Sorry."

Mama didn't care that I stopped. She improvised, making my mess-up look like it was part of our routine. "See, you've got it," she said, wiping some sweat away from her brow and smiling at me.

She wanted me to keep going, to *breathe*, because if I were to ever compete again, I needed to get through this roadblock in my head.

And I breathed because it wasn't about messing up, it was about not *giving* up.

When I realized that, I kept going, and Mama's brown eyes burned golden when she saw me fighting for it. I mirrored everything she did, down to the breaths she took, and I could hear Jay applauding and hooting in the background.

Mama and I were one with the song, one with each other, and I wondered if this was what it felt like when she was pregnant with me; we shared the same heartbeat.

When the song ended, Mama gave me the biggest, longest hug. She squeezed me as we both huffed and puffed, and she planted a kiss on my forehead.

She didn't need to tell me how proud of me she was—I knew it. I felt it.

We turned to look at ourselves in the mirror, and we bowed, our reflections following suit. Then she wrapped her arm around my shoulder and pulled me into another hug, her cheek pressing down on my head.

"My Z . . . I love you so, *so* much," she said. She released me, and we walked off the dance floor together. "Z is for *zenith*."

"Zenith?"

"Yes," she said before she grabbed her water bottle. "The highest point in the sky. That's you."

I tried to play it off. "Me? No way."

"Yes, way. Since you were born, you've been my zenith." She took a sip, looking up. "I probably should've named you that, huh?" She smiled, and then she laughed at herself.

I'd never seen Mama happier.

CHAPTER THIRTY-SIX

JULY 3, 9:13 A.M.

The exception: Sometimes, there's the exception. Sometimes there's the guy that looks like a zombie but isn't a zombie at all. Sometimes he's more alive than you are. Sometimes he's the one who can bring you back to humanity once you're dying. Sometimes he's the cure. But the cure is rare. The cure is not to be trusted. Sometimes people don't survive the world of the undead. At some point, we're all going to die. Our wet bones will rot and dry. We'll be meat on sticks, looking for a brain to take over, looking for a heart to own. That's just how it is. Don't look for the cure.

So, what have I learned about zombies, you may ask?

Do *not* trust them.

CHAPTER THIRTY-SEVEN

Hey, Z

It's Mika

Hope it's cool I have ur number

Charlie told me what happened

She feels awful about it, but I understand
if you're not ready to talk to her

I just wanted to reach out to you. You can always
text me. If you need anything, I'm here

& we all enjoyed having you on the trip.
Hope we'll get to see u again soon

Oh, if you hear anything from Bo, let him know that we miss him

Haven't heard from him since everything went down

Read 11:36 AM

CHAPTER THIRTY-EIGHT

AUNTIE E PICKED UP all of the overtime shifts this week. When I wanted to talk to her, try to ask her about her day, she was asleep. And when she was awake, I was asleep. We were like the sun and the moon, always missing each other.

But yesterday, she'd left an envelope on the counter for me. Inside was a receipt of a check from some law firm that had been deposited into my account; it must have been the money Auntie E told me I'd be getting from Mama's house being sold.

Mini was away with her family for a Fourth of July getaway, and I was home alone, trying to remember what normal people did when they weren't analyzing zombies. I lay on the twin-sized bed, my feet against the wall.

Before this "new" normal, I spent most of my free time at the dance studio with Mama—either facilitating check-in, helping with class, or sitting in a corner doing homework.

Tonight, I knew, the dance studio was going to be lit. They always had a huge Fourth of July dance party that ended with a firework display at midnight.

And I couldn't stop thinking about what Luca said: I couldn't avoid the studio forever.

But to dance, I'd have to have a car, and Ubering into the city would be at least twenty bucks, if not more.

Hmm. I turned over, fiddling my phone between my hands. There was always Luca, and since he wouldn't stop texting me about dance, I bet he'd be going tonight. Plus, he'd been aching to give me a ride in his dad's car.

I hopped off the bed and paced. What would people say if I went back? And how would Luca be?

Paced again. Tapped my toes and pressed my fingers to my head. But it couldn't be that bad. If I danced tonight, at least I wouldn't be alone. Wouldn't have to hear Bo creaking around his room upstairs.

I flopped back on the bed and texted Luca.

Hey, are you dancing tonight?

After I sent it, I locked my phone and face-planted into the sheets. Ten seconds later, my phone buzzed.

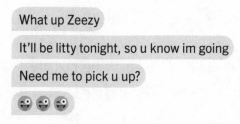

What up Zeezy

It'll be litty tonight, so u know im going

Need me to pick u up?

I rolled my eyes. Dweeb.

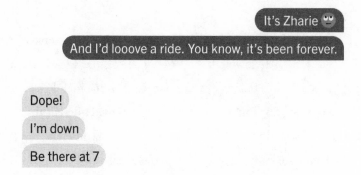

It's Zharie 🙄

And I'd looove a ride. You know, it's been forever.

Dope!

I'm down

Be there at 7

I pumped my fist in the air and squealed. So damn excited. I needed this more than Luca knew...I hoped he wouldn't make it weird tonight. Really, I just needed a friend.

At exactly seven o'clock, Luca texted me, letting me know he was here. I grabbed my cross-body bag, my dance shoes, and met him outside.

The warm air was almost smothering, and fumes filled the sky from the firecrackers the kids popped around us. Then a sound, a whirring, wheels spinning. Looked over my shoulder to see if Bo was nearby on his board. But he wasn't. It was another kid pushing by on a scooter.

Ahead, Luca sat on the hood of his dad's Honda Civic. It was red, and it looked like it'd been freshly washed. He had on a long white shirt and dark blue jeans. His arms, folded across his chest, and his eyes, hidden by black sunglasses. Was he wearing contacts today?

As I jumped over the chalk art on the sidewalk, I could smell Luca. He was heavily doused in cologne.

Eh.

Luca saw my nose wrinkle as he walked me to the passenger side. "It's Burberry." He grinned. And I knew—because I knew Luca— that his energy was ticking upward. He lived on the high I gave him, whatever that was. But he was different already. Different than the last time I'd seen him, and I wasn't sure how he was different, just that behind those sunglasses a newness was there. Like how a house looked beautiful in the evening and strange in the morning.

"Fancy," I said, and I stopped Luca from opening the passenger door. Too much, too soon, but again, it was him pressing. He liked the chase. "I've got it."

He shrugged it off, got in the car, and I did the same.

The car was spotless, smelled of Black Ice, and the leather seat was cool on my legs when I sat down. I rested my dance shoes in my lap and released my breath.

It was an odd feeling in my joints knowing I'd be returning to a place that held so many good memories. And the weirdest part was knowing that I'd be going there without Mama.

"So, what's good?" Luca asked after coming to a four-way stop. He leaned back in his seat, one hand on the wheel, the other resting on the center console. His shades off now, and I could see his dark brown eyes.

I squinted at him. "Wait, didn't you say you don't have your license yet?"

He gave me a single nod. "Yup. But I have my permit."

"But isn't that like for work and school only?"

"It's not like we'll get pulled over. Trust. The cops are looking for other stuff tonight, not underage drivers, Z. Plus, what's a little white lie, anyway? Who's to say we're not coworkers on our way to work?"

Me. I was to say it. Sure, I was down to live a little, but if we got pulled over, I wasn't going to lie to the cops.

But that wasn't true. I'd lie to them, protect us at all costs.

And Luca was right. On the Fourth of July, it was hard to decipher a gunshot from a firework, so theoretically speaking, we should be fine....

I looked out the window. We passed a house that had two boys outside in the driveway. They wore matching red-white-and-blue-striped shirts, and one of them held a smoke bomb in his hand. A violent green spilled out of it, and he lifted it to the sky while the other boy chased him, laughing.

"What have you been up to since the last time I saw you? I like your new hair." Luca wasn't looking at me when he said it, but I could see his lips slowly pulling up at the sides.

"Thanks." I had forgotten it looked different; I was so used to it being twisted up. "I've been all right," I lied, tugging the drawstring on my shoe bag. No part of me wanted to share that I'd been in my room most days, watching YouTube, crying, and blocking out the sound from upstairs. It was a boring story I told myself.

"Have you had the chance to talk to Becca?" Deflection was the key, and part of me desperately hoped he'd found someone since the last time we'd talked.

Luca chuckled, shaking his head, and he sped up a bit to merge onto the highway. "Hell naw. Her and James are still together, no surprise there. Are you seeing anyone?"

"Nope." Double-nope. I could have laughed, but it would have turned into tears. The sucky thing was if I closed my eyes long enough, I could still see Bo and Charlie. I could see Bo's dead fingers pressed into Charlie's stupid, pretty face. I could see Charlie kissing Bo. Bo, who I hoped—for a split second—could be my Bo. For a brief moment in time, it had felt as though our storylines were merging together.

Now we were two sentences without the bridge of a semicolon or comma. Just a period between us. Never connecting.

My heart *literally* hurt when I thought about it, a reminder that even after everything, it was still pressing on. Thudding away. And now it hurt a little more, knowing that Luca and Becca weren't going to work out.

"Have you *ever* seen anyone, Z? You know, I've been with girls, but you, you're always to yourself."

"Does it matter?"

He tilted his head. "I mean, depending on who you speak to … maybe?"

"So *you* care?"

"Me? No."

"You wouldn't ask if you didn't care," I said, trying to call him out on his bullshit. Luca was always on one.

"Yeah, okay," Luca said, the sounds more a scoff than actual words. He turned the dial up. It was a Cardi B song, and Luca grinned at me while he bounced his shoulders.

I reclined the seat and rolled my eyes. Like I said, he was always on one.

After we got off the highway, we kept straight down Johnson Drive, and then Luca turned left and parked at the building with the sparkling lights strung above the entryway.

I took a deep breath, my foot twitching beneath me. Through the dance studio's glass windows, I could see the many bodies congregated on the dance floor, and if I peered harder, I could see my own reflection there, too.

I squeezed my thighs into the leather seat, and I was there. Not here. *There*. In front of the broken stone to my childhood home, a sunflower stretching its neck toward the sun in the flower bed. My fingers pressing my thumb into the wire fence. The one Mama wanted to get repaired but never did. And I was there. My curls twisting into the burning air, a fire lit nearby. I could feel her so close. An inch behind the door, her scent of lavender sweeping under the threshold. But I turned instead, and I was back here. In Luca's dad's car, staring at the window to the studio, watching them.

They looked like they were finishing up a class, smiles stitched into their pale faces. An applause then, some of the dancers flocking off the floor in groups of two and three.

"You all right, Z?"

No. I haven't been all right in a while.

"Um, yeah," I said, undoing the seat belt and grabbing my things. Took another breath, opened the car door.

It would be okay. Another lie I told myself. But I needed it. Sometimes our hearts ate lies when they were hungry. Sometimes it was all that was left in the cupboard.

We walked down the sidewalk, and Luca held the door open for me.

Inside, the sound hit me first. The commercial air system cooling the place down. The low chatter of the people congregating by tables and chairs—some on the dance floor still, practicing what they learned in class. The music, turned at a level too low. Then it was the smell. Food nearby, for the dance party after. Those polished wooden floors. The people, and Lauren.

She stood at the front desk, doing a double take when she saw me. She gasped and held her hands to her mouth. The last time I'd seen her, she had just begun teaching salsa classes. It was odd seeing her on a West Coast night, but maybe she was helping out since I couldn't anymore.

My stomach rumbled, and Lauren left the front counter to welcome me with a hug.

"Zharie, my goodness. It's been too long." She released me to look at me, to see if anything had changed. I wondered if she could see my pure exhaustion, the darkness setting under my eyes. Could she see how much I needed this—how much I needed to dance more than I needed anything else in the world? Anything.

I stared into her emerald eyes, realizing I'd never been this close to her before. It was crazy how grief pulled lives together physically.

Her makeup looked like it'd been professionally done, and though it was the Fourth, she wore all black, the same as me. At least her hair was red; I looked like I was going to a funeral.

Lauren hugged me once more, and then she went back behind the counter. Smiled with a sigh. "Sorry, I got carried away there. It's just really good to see you again. Are you taking the intermediate class tonight?"

"Whoa, wait. I don't ever get a hug like that," Luca interjected. "Don't you miss me when I'm away?"

"Luca, honey, you're always here. You can't be missed if you never leave."

"But that's—"

I cut Luca off and handed Lauren my card. "Yes, please."

Luca bumped me with his elbow. "I would've covered you."

"It's cool. I got it," I said, walking away. I spotted an empty chair by the window. After I sat, I kicked off my shoes and put on my dance boots. Zipped my feet in and felt the suede at the bottom. It had been too long since I'd worn them—didn't have a reason to dance in them at the apartment—but they still felt the same. Still buckled the same. The leather still peeled on the inside, and they still had specks of debris stuck to the bottom of them from the last time I was here.

And I really had missed these stupid, old things. They removed the friction that normal shoes usually caused, which made gliding on the ballroom floor much easier.

There were eyes on me while I got ready. I didn't have to look to know, I just felt it, and I wished I could camouflage myself into these gray walls. Why couldn't that be my superpower? I'd take that over seeing zombies any day.

The murmurs in the ballroom grew, and after I slid my things beneath the chair, I looked up to see Jay. He had on a shirt that said BITTEN BY SWING. It was from some dance event in October that I'd missed out on. But Mama went. She had the same shirt.

A few new things I noticed about Jay: He had peppered hair now. It was mostly on the sides, but still, it was a change. He also had deep lines in his forehead, and very small lines at the corners of his eyes.

That was another thing. His eyes were glossy when he looked at me, quickly turning a light pink.

"Z," he said, holding his knuckle to his top lip. "Wow, look at you." He pulled me into a hug, and I embraced him, pressing my cheek to his chest. Jay was one of Mama's closest dance friends, and hugging him made me feel closer to her. *God.* This was so, so much.

"And your hair." He sniffled; he already had a few tears escaping his eyes. "It's so big, like Twiggy's."

Tried to smile. Tried to suck back my own tears. Because I'd told myself I wasn't going to cry tonight. I'd already cried enough this week. But seeing him got to me; my bottom lip quivered. If Mama was here today, I'd tell her all about Bo. I'd cry into her chest and tell her how boys were so stupid. She'd probably tell me that they weren't, but I'd disagree. I'd tell her they all had degrees in heartbreakology.

She'd probably laugh, tell me to calm down. But I'd tell her that it wasn't funny. That *I* was serious, and she'd just hug me tighter until everything was all right and the world made sense again. Would it ever?

Then I would tell her that I missed her, and that I loved her.

I missed her and loved her so much.

Jay hugged me again, and I was reminded that he wasn't Mama. My gaze zipped around the room when we hugged, seeing the people frozen around us. Hoping Mama would be there in the crowd some-how, but it was wishful thinking.

The room was white. Mama had been the only Black dance instructor here—the only one in the area, actually. It had always stuck with me how few Black dancers or instructors there were in the West Coast Swing world, but I'd always had Mama, so being the only one here today made her absence even more present.

"Phew," Jay said when it was over, and I straightened myself up. "Okay, okay. I've got to get myself together. I'm teaching the advanced class tonight. Are you taking that one?"

"No, I paid for intermediate."

"What? No. Twiggy would want you to be in the advanced class. You're an advanced dancer, Z."

Gulped and looked down, my cheeks still flaming hot. He was right. Mama would encourage me to take the advanced class, but it had been so long since I'd attended a class, I didn't know if I'd meet their standards.

I nodded anyway. "Okay," I said, and before I knew it, they pulled back the big black curtain that divided the dance floor into two different rooms.

Luca was stuck on the other side, and for that, I was ever grateful.

The class wasn't as hard as I imagined it would be. Jay had us warm up by dancing with each other, and I was surprised to find that my body still remembered. Maybe it was this place. It would always be a part of me, and I was certain I'd left fragments of myself in the floor.

In the lesson, we dived into different whip variations, and by the end of it, I was sad it was over. My blood pumped viciously, and I bounced from foot to foot, ready to get back on the floor. More hugs throughout the class. More people asking me where I was and how I'd been. More lies told. More of me trying to push back tears, even though my eyes were probably stained red. Even though my chest was bruised above my heart. Could they see that? Did they know the level of pain I held?

When it was time for social dancing, they opened the curtains, turned the lights down low, and turned the music up so high, it erased some of my thoughts. I grabbed the first person I could find, learning their name in the starter step and forgetting it at the end of it.

I met person after person, never leaving the floor, dancing and smiling and huffing and puffing. I could barely catch my breath, but I didn't want a break. I had to keep going, keep moving. My toes were numb, and I had pit stains that extended down the length of my torso.

When my hair frizzed up, I threw it in a bun. I was unstoppable, climbing to the highest peak in the sky. And no one could reach me. Each song and each person was a different hue. When we danced, our colors bled together, inventing new shades. The floor was our canvas; the syncopation was our medium.

Hours passed, and the seconds were limitless. A quarter before midnight, it finally started to slow down. New faces had come in, but many of those who attended the classes earlier had gone home. The dance floor had more empty space, and I could finally feel the AC on my face. And there was that feeling again. I belonged here.

Gathered myself and drank some water. Up until now, I had managed to dance with everyone except Luca.

He sat on a bench by the window, his shoulders slouched forward, his head low. The twinkle lights shimmered in the whites of his eyes, and he fiddled his thumbs.

When he caught my stare, he stood immediately, his smile growing.

As soon as I noticed he was about to approach me, I looked around to see if there were any open dancers I could introduce him to, but most of them were occupied.

Welp, here goes nothing.

Luca extended a hand when he was closer, and I took it, following him to the center of the dance floor. We stood under the chandelier, and Luca's eyebrows were up high. The way he looked reminded me of when he held my hand last time. How he tried to play it off, even when I knew he wanted to hold it longer. No use ignoring it, I knew Luca liked me. It was as obvious as the day was light. But I'd never felt that for him. And it wasn't how he looked—he looked okay—it was just *who* he was. Maybe that made me a terrible person. And maybe I didn't deserve his friendship at all.

"Hey . . . so, I know I can be too much at times, but I'm glad you reached out to me tonight. It's been weird not having you here."

Yeah, shit. Of course it had. My heart pinched. Pressed my chin against my chest almost, and I waited for the DJ to choose the next song.

"But anyway," Luca continued. "I hope you don't keep running away from dance. I think your mom wants you to be here. Because you're great, and I know you're *meant* for this. You always have been, Zharie."

I looked into Luca's big brown eyes, not feigning a smile this time. He'd done it again, the whole mom thing. *Damn you, Luca.* This time it was so kind and so sincere. He was something else right now, but those words, that was what I needed.

"Luca," I breathed, still stunned by everything. "I really appreciate you saying that." He was right, and I wished I hadn't avoided this place for so long.

All this change had been terrifying, but maybe Mama's spirit lived in this place. Maybe being here was honoring her.

Luca continued to smile, and he was huffing so hard I could feel some of his breath on my face.

I looked away from him, waiting for the song to begin already. The intro was terribly long, and in it, the sound of a door creaking and then—*wait, was that a howl?*

"Yes." Luca answered my question without meaning to, and he effortlessly led me through the starter step. I could tell he'd been practicing, and then we passed each other as soon as the beat dropped. "This is one of my songs."

My throat tightened. It was "Thriller," the literal song that haunted my dreams a couple of weeks ago. And as we danced, I remembered everything. The memories smashing into me, shaking me like a storm. I was in that clearing again. The flat land turning into blackness. The cold night. The mahogany blood pouring out of me. Emptying me. The death in the air. The cracking. Wet bones, wet bones, wet bones.

And when Luca spun me, the people around us morphed into the undead, the unmentionables.

I spun around chairs and then trees.

People and then zombies.

Darkness and then blood.

They glitched in and out, and each time Luca passed me, I hurried to the other side of the slot with haste.

Luca probably thought I was feeling myself, that my movements were a lyrical expression of the song, but really, fear poisoned me, and I felt like I couldn't breathe. It was the zombification of the universe around me.

The room closed, the walls narrowing. Short, raspy breaths. A dragging and sliding. A thud. Another. And the people in the room. All dead and done. No more souls in their eyes. Meat sagging on skin. Bones fresh and pale. And worse, they danced.

They reenacted the routine from the music video. All in sync and together. In a different light, this whole thing could have been comical—what could be better than literal zombies dancing to "Thriller"?

But in this light, in *this* moment, I wanted to scream.

Luca led me through a free spin toward the end of the song, and when I made it back to him, he had transformed into a zombie, too.

The song ended, and I held my breath, my fingers crumpling away from him.

Luca's face, raw skin bloated and ripping away. So dead and thick, pieces of his cheeks sagged, pulling away from his eyes, blood squirting from underneath. He was one of them, except I was in his arms, his claws deep in my shoulder.

He leaned in, the smell rancid, and the blood dripped on my chin in a splat, splat, splattering way. Snarled. Eyes opened, and I froze.

Lips pressed against mine. His scabs scratched me, squishing me, a bruise forming.

And when he pushed his tongue past my teeth, I forced him away from me—a blow to the center of his chest.

Wiped the imaginary blood from my mouth. "What the *hell*, Luca! Why did you do that?" The tears were back, and I didn't try fighting them this time. I needed him as a friend, and he ruined that. All I wanted was to dance with Luca, the babbling Luca. But this? This changed everything.

He barely moved; his breathing labored and pulsed, a puncture deepening in his throat. The blood crawled to the rest of his veins like an ink splotch on paper.

Silence. And I waited for the song to change, waited for the people to glitch back to their normal selves, but no one did.

Death was everywhere.

They all stared at me, bumping into one another and slowly coming forward. Blinked, blinked, blinked, but it didn't help. Stumbled back. Waited for them to change, for my mind to unbreak itself. This wasn't how it usually worked, but I wanted it to. I wanted, so badly, for them to zip out of it. What if my brain had finally broken?

One scurried to the side. Balancing on the tips of its toes. A snarl and a body so decayed, I could see through it. One fell to the ground, skin smacking the floor hard, its jaw popping out of place. Blood thickening in the slots of wood. And Luca came back to me. Purple-and-brown fingers stretched for my heart. The ringing in my ears growing until I screamed.

Ran. Grabbed my stuff and ran as fast as I could out the door, my chest pounding. Kicked off my shoes, and my socks scraped the hot cement as the fireworks roared and exploded in the starless sky, making me run faster.

A zombie behind me. I forced my body to work harder, to go farther, the streetlights flickering as I passed them, and the air stinging my eyes.

I kept going until I couldn't see the ballroom anymore, until the lights were sparse and there was no sign of anyone behind or before me. And then I leaned against a closed building, slid to my butt, and pressed my face into my palms to cry.

My life kept crumbling. It would not stop. It would not give, and what if I had nothing left?

But I needed to get out of here. Wiped the snot away and dug for my phone, my fingers shaking. I sniffled, and tears fell on the screen as I downloaded Uber. My ride found me in less than five minutes.

It was an older Black woman with a navy Toyota.

In the back seat, the world whipping around me, Luca called and texted me. No reason to respond, so I turned my phone off as it vibrated in my hand.

Tonight was supposed to be my night.

For those few hours, I felt alive again, I smelled the sunflowers.

Now I was just numb.

CHAPTER THIRTY-NINE

WHEN I GOT INSIDE the apartment, Auntie E was in the living room, standing by the only piece of furniture in there—the lamp.

Fuckkk.

"Where have you been?" Her arms were crossed against her, and she had on her blue robe, her hair still wrapped in a silk scarf.

I sighed, dropping my keys into the bowl. When I put my bag down, the light flickered, and I realized I never asked for permission to leave tonight. But I didn't think she'd be here. Didn't think it mattered if I was here or there.

"I—"

"And why haven't you been answering your phone? I've called and texted you. I thought someone snatched you up. Are you out of your goddamn mind?"

My shoulders fell forward, and I shrank. When I was at the studio, it didn't occur to me to check my phone. It had become habitual because whenever I was there, the only person who needed me had always been there with me. Now here we were.

"Auntie, I'm sorry, I—"

"*Where* have you been, Zharie? Where could you even be on a day like this—and for *that* long? And if you're pregnant—" She paused, pointing her finger at me. "Damn it. You better not be pregnant. We can't afford another life, Zharie! Shit!"

I pressed my lips so hard, I tasted red, my eyes swelling. When I tried to speak, she cut me off again.

"Tell me where you were!" She stomped her foot and slammed her hand on the wall. The light flickered again.

I flinched, and the words struggled to come out. I didn't get why she was so upset. Did I miss something? Was the house dirty? It had to be more than me forgetting to ask permission. My absence didn't matter before, but the one time I turned off my phone....

"Do you think this is a game?"

"No." I shook my head, feeling my eyes rounding, and I couldn't look at her. Didn't want to see her face, so I stared at her house shoes.

"Well..." She waited.

"I'm not pregnant. I'm not even sexually active." And I was annoyed that she would assume that's what I'd been up to. Was she afraid I'd be like Mama, start my own family young? And maybe I should have. It worked out for Mama. We had each other. We never needed anyone else. But if Auntie were around, if she'd talk to me, give me the chance to take up her space, she'd know most of my free time was spent locked in this stupid, empty apartment.

I pressed my nails into my palms as I spoke. "I was out dancing."

Her arms fell to her side. "With *what* money?"

"My money."

"From *where?* You don't have a job, Z."

"From the sale. *My* money from the sale."

She closed her eyes, her nostrils flaring. "Zharie . . . *that* money . . . how much of it did you spend? You can't just be using it on dance or whatever you want!"

Stood up straight, fingers still pressing into skin, breaking now. "Why not? It's mine!"

"Are you serious? How the hell are we supposed to survive, Z? This world ain't all about you! I wish I could do what I wanted, too! Do you really wanna continue taking cold showers and having little to nothing to eat? We have bills to pay! I'm already struggling as it is. Do you think I'm picking up extra shifts for fun? Do you think my schooling is free?"

"No, but—"

"*But* nothing. I've heard enough. You're selfish, Z. Twiggy spoiled you, and it shows."

"Don't talk about my mom."

Auntie E scoffed, almost laughed. "Girl, calm down. You ain't 'bout to do nothin'."

I stomped my foot. She didn't know what I could do. "Ugh!" I yelled, and I grabbed the closest thing to me—the key bowl—and threw it on the ground as hard as I could. It cracked against the floor, bounced, and just barely missed her.

"Don't you *dare* touch another thing," she said, the words barely escaping her teeth.

I yelled again, loud, the sound ripping from my throat as I stomped down the hallway. "I hate you!" My voice broke. "I hate living here!"

I kicked the bedroom door open, and it slammed against the wall, bouncing back slightly.

Auntie E yelled back. "I hate having you here, too! And don't you even think about—"

I slammed the door. Kicked it again.

"Zharie! If you break anything in there, you're paying for it!"

I could barely hear her words over my own rage. Another kick, and then another. Coming again and again. I kicked everything in sight—my shoes, clothes that weren't put away, the brown box still in the corner.

It was Mama's box. Unopened. Unmoved.

Slammed into it, crushing the items inside, and dust rose as I banged it into the wall. The sides broke open; the contents fell everywhere.

"Why did you have to leave?!" I yelled, every horrible memory from the last year seeping out of my eyes and onto my shirt. Mama on the

couch, blue lips. Mama on the floor, rotten. Packing my things. No chance to say goodbye. Zombies everywhere. Auntie E. This apartment. Bo, dead Bo. Rico, Andrew, Mika. And Charlie. Charlie and Luca, all my hopes. All of it, taken away, all because she died.

"None of this would have happened if you were still here!" I screamed it louder, hoping that Mama would hear me from wherever she was. Hoping that it would somehow make her come back. It wouldn't matter if she was a zombie, if she didn't have a soul in her eyes. Just please. *Please, come back.*

The door busted open, and Auntie E flipped on the light. "What the hell is wrong with you?!" She huffed, rushing to me, trying to grab at my arms.

I kept kicking, yelling, screaming.

"Z! *Stop!*"

I couldn't stop until the box was destroyed.

"Z!" She yanked me away from the box, and I pulled myself from her grasp, fixed my shirt. And I was on fire. I knew I was. But the flames didn't kill me. "You stop it, now!"

I closed my eyes. Dropped to my knees. The world was so black and blue. And I couldn't breathe. My chest shook, my head to the floor now, and *I couldn't* breathe. The universe hated me. I knew it was true. And if it was so disgusted with me, why didn't it take me like it took everything else?

This wasn't fair. If I could go back . . . I'd give anything. *Please. Anything, my soul.*

"Clean it up, Z! Clean all of it up!" Auntie's voice rang, and she didn't stay. Even though she paused. Even though her voice cracked just then, she left, closing the door on her way out.

I crumpled over, sobbing like there was no tomorrow. Everything I loved, ruined, gone.

I had no one. Nothing.

And I hated this life. What was the point of it anyway?

CHAPTER FORTY

IT HAD BEEN AN HOUR. Maybe. I didn't know.

Tried not to move. Wanted to stay still, to not move forward, to be frozen. But my body twitched, a sharp pain growing in my lower back. When I opened my eyes, they felt swollen, probably colored scarlet, and it wasn't till I looked around that I really saw the damage I'd done.

There were three dents in the door, the wood splitting by the knob. The wall by the window was scuffed with dark marks, and the drywall had cracks that looked like spiderwebs. And Mama's box was bent and sunken in.

Haze devoured my insides, torment sinking deep.

The items that used to be in the box were scattered around the room, most of them broken or cracked. I felt my eyes well up, my bottom lip heavy, and I got to my knees to look at my destruction.

Mama's jewelry box and her seashells. The hand-carved wooden box was busted, the metal clasps torn off, and the shells scattered across the floor. I scooped them into my hands, felt them in my palms. Different sizes and colors, some cracked now, chipped away. Mama got them from the beach in California before I was born. She always said she wanted to take me to the same beach so we could squish our toes in the sand, treasure hunt the day away, but we never went.

My old Bear. Light brown and scraggly, a button eye hanging by a thread. I didn't know he was in there. Grabbed him quickly, placed him to my nose, against my cheek. Used his hand to wipe away a few tears. He smelled faintly of our old home—sandalwood and citrus. I tucked him under my arm after—didn't want to ever let him go again.

A picture frame, the glass broken, the edges falling apart. The photo inside was of Mama and me on the day I was born. Her hair was in shambles, and she had on a hospital gown. I was bundled like a burrito, wrapped in a white blanket. She held me close to her chest, and despite the fact that she was looking down, I could tell she was smiling. She told me her life changed forever after that.

Mama's favorite book. It was *A Walk to Remember* by Nicholas Sparks. I used to make fun of her for liking it, told her she could do better, but she said I didn't get it. Maybe I would when I was older, so she hid the book away from me, somewhere tucked high in her room. The pages were bent now, the cover torn, and there was a yellow envelope poking out of it.

I opened the book to grab it, and the envelope—along with a small folded piece of paper—fell onto the floor.

In the book, Mama had highlighted a paragraph on this particular page:

"I don't think that we're meant to understand it all the time. I think that some-times we just have to have faith."

I went for the folded paper first. It looked old, real old. It crumpled when I opened it, and I could see that the edges of it were rough, like they'd been ripped away from something. The back of an old flyer maybe? The paper didn't say who it was from, just a note scribbled inside. The words almost faded:

I'll always dance with you. Always. I'm forever yours, Twig.

Hmm. Furrowed my brows and turned it over again to try and make out what the flyer had been for previously. All I could pinpoint was a tiny dance icon.

Set it down and went for the envelope. When I turned it over, I saw the return address was from California. San Diego, California.

What? The sperm donor lived in California.

I opened the envelope and pulled out a white piece of lined journal paper. There were watermarks on parts of it, the ink bleeding.

When I unfolded the letter, I found this:

Twiggy,

Know that this is one of the hardest things I've ever had to write. It's also one of the toughest things I've ever had to do.

We've known each other for seventeen years, and I never thought I'd have to see this day, but I'm writing to you as a formal goodbye.

I can no longer be a participant in our love affair. Like you, I used to think that our little family would work out some day, but we need to stop lying to ourselves.

You are a wonderful dancer, the best I know in the industry, but I haven't felt that deep love for you in a very long time, and I refuse to force it anymore.

I have my own family, a wife, kids, and I love them.

You have Zharie. That was part of the deal.

Don't try to contact me after this. I prefer we go on as if we never happened.

Please, Twiggy, let me go.

The best to you and yours.

Sincerely,

Devin Sinclair

What? I reread it again, quickly. Mama was having an affair with the sperm donor? For how long? When? I flipped the envelope over, finding the date it was stamped: October 25. Nine days before her death.

Mama never lied to me. Never, ever. But was this why she never dated? Because she was secretly dating my birth father?

I swallowed hard, sinking into the floor, my chin pointing toward the ceiling. It felt like my life was imploding, my organs twisted, turning teal.

Closed my eyes, skimming through all my memories of her in my head. She never dated anyone. She always said it was hard to date in the industry. She also said it was hard to date *outside* the industry. She stayed busy, worked late. She lived in her phone. It stayed locked. I tried, but I could never crack the code. She was up late, traveled often. Sometimes to California. Sometimes for multiple days at a time.

Damn. It made sense.

But more than that, I remembered now. Remembered seeing this creased envelope, and I didn't think this piece of paper could hold so much intensity in it, but now I wished I would have asked Mama about it the day I saw it.

It was *before* I watched her zombification. She was in the kitchen, eyes low as she stood in front of the sink. She gripped the counter with one hand. With the other, she held this envelope.

I didn't think she saw me because then she paced the laminate floor saying, "What . . . *what* did I do? Where did it go wrong?"

But I couldn't see her eyes when she turned. Only saw how her lips twisted, how this new light in my imagination painted her oxford blue.

When I moved, the floorboard creaked, and she jumped. "Jesus, Z. You scared me," she said, tucking the paper under her armpit. The bags beneath her eyes were dark gray, puffier than usual, and her cheeks looked hollow.

I entered the kitchen and stood under the dim, canary light. A foot away from her, close enough to know her breathing was labored. "Sorry, Mama. Got up for water. Are you . . . okay? You seem worried."

Her shoulders relaxed, and then I watched her move the envelope from her armpit to her robe pocket. "I'm . . ." She huffed. "I'll be fine."

"You sure?" I asked, approaching the cupboard to grab a glass and fill it with water. I leaned against the counter, took a sip.

She nodded, her curly hair pulled back into a tight bun, her bottom lip trembled. I didn't get what was bringing her down.

"Is it your competition?" I knew she was traveling to San Jose for the South Bay Dance Fling competition. She had a new partner for this one, someone whose name I didn't catch.

Mama's brows rose. "Actually, I'm looking forward to it being over with."

"Really?" I set my glass down to give her a hug. "Mama, you're so great, though," I said, squeezing her.

She squeezed me back, then smoothed down my hair. "Thanks, Z. It's just that I haven't competed like this since . . . since before I had you."

I wanted her to see it through my eyes; I wanted to be able to replay the way she moved on the ballroom floor so she could know how magical it was. "You've got this. That's what you always say. And even if you mess up, who cares. At least you can say you did it."

She half smiled, and she kissed me on the forehead. "I hear you, Z. Now, go on back to bed, crazy girl."

Lips thin, I waited a beat more, tried to find the words she didn't say. We resolved the issue, I thought. At least partly, but there was something hiding there. *Something.*

Before I left, I winked at her. "All right. Sleep tight!" I said it, but I didn't know if she ever went to sleep that night. It was the first time I'd heard a cracking; something being stripped apart. Her light was still on when I passed by to go to the bathroom, and I heard hushed words coming from her room. It was unclear what was being said, just that it seemed awful.

The day after, she forgot to pick me up from school. It wasn't like her. But even when she arrived, the light in her eyes was dim, gloom settling in her irises. She brushed it off, said she got sidetracked. That evening, she cooked jambalaya with her shoulders slumped over the stovetop. Hands brittle, almost pale. She kept folding her lips together like she was trying to hold life in. Like if she opened her mouth, some-thing would crawl out of there. After, she spent dinner in bed. But Mama was never still, always doing, always on the go. A smile fixed in her soul like it was sewn there. I'd never seen this side of her. Didn't know this version of Mama. But she *promised* she wasn't sick, swore it.

When she returned from the competition, she was just so frozen. I thought she'd messed up her routine, but no, it turned out she placed in her division, taking home a great title. I told her we should celebrate with chips and salsa. Maybe tres leches. But she slipped deep into the middle of the couch, eyes glazed. All she wanted to do was rest.

"Later," she had said, but later never came.

And then day one began.

CHAPTER FORTY-ONE

JULY 5, 3:01 A.M.

This has nothing to do with zombies, but everything to do with my life.

As an echo of seeing zombies (okay, I lied. This does involve zombies—this has everything to do with zombies), I realized that Vincent van Gogh has been stuck in my head, too.

When *The Starry Night* was found, this letter was attached:

"Looking at the stars always makes me dream . . . Just as we take a train to get to Tarascon or Rouen, we take death to reach a star. We cannot get to a star while we are alive any more than we can take the train when we are dead. So to me it seems possible that cholera, tuberculosis and cancer are the celestial means of locomotion. Just as steamboats, buses and railways are the terrestrial means.

"To die quietly of old age would be to go there on foot."

When van Gogh was at the weakest point in his life, when everything and *everyone* betrayed him, he still had his brother.

His brother never stopped believing in him or his talents.

But for van Gogh, that love was simply never enough. It didn't fill his cup the way he wanted it to, and I wonder if it was the same for Mama.

We could only love her so much; we could only give her so much. Her heart exploding was inevitable, and maybe it was too much of the wrong kind of love that attacked her body like a virus and turned her into a zombie.

Maybe too much of the wrong love has the potential to kill you.

And if this logic is true, why haven't I turned into a zombie yet?

Am I immune?

CHAPTER FORTY-TWO

COULDN'T SLEEP. Couldn't lie in bed with this. I paced back and forth, back and forth. My knees were weak, something moving in my thighs. I kept picking at my nails and chewing on them, going over the details I'd discovered.

Another hour passed, and the pressure in my back made my feet swell. It felt like something twisted up my spine in small increments. My eyes felt heavy when I sat on the floor. But I kept Bear close to me, next to my ribs. I went through more photos of Mama, pinched them between my fingers, chewed my lips. Sifted through them again. Needed to see her face. Needed her near me.

With all I had, I wished she could speak to me, tell me all about this whole thing with her and my birth dad. It was still hard knowing that she'd lived this whole other life in secret. How could anyone do that and be happy? What did she think would come from it?

I punched the floor, my knuckles bleeding, anger ripping through my throat. *Why?* Why didn't she tell me? And that rage mocked me. Maybe she hoped it would make me happy? Did she think her love alone wasn't enough for me? That I ever needed him?

Sometimes it did suck. No father-daughter dances, just him across the ballroom, dancing with literally anyone else. Not looking at me. No playing catch with him or knowing how he liked his coffee. No Father's Day celebrations. No one else to embarrass me at family cookouts.

But those moments had always been in the smallest increments. Mama was always everything.

Or maybe it was just that she really did love him, and she wanted to make it work—not for me—but for her own sanity.

Maybe there was something about him that she couldn't let go of.

Another thirty minutes passed, a ticking from somewhere. My chin kept nodding to my chest, couldn't keep my eyes open. Footsteps squeaking on the floorboards above me. Pressed my head against the wall underneath the window, next to all the stuff I'd broken. Only wanted to close my eyes for a moment.

Drifted. Silence. Long exhales, and the dreams rushed in.

But I woke, told myself to get up. I'd cleaned my mess before getting into bed, slowly gathering up all Mama's items and placing them on top of the box I'd broken. It was hard to look away from them, hard to leave them like that.

It was almost five in the morning when I fell asleep. In my sleep, I dreamed of Mama.

She was in the clearing this time—the same one from the camping trip—her feet bare and covered in mud. She had on her favorite baggy pants and a tribal-print shirt. I remembered the shirt—it was in my closet now. She'd found it at a flea market.

Mama stood still in the darkness, her eyes low. She settled into third position, her arms held out in front of her. Mama completed a series of chaîné turns, moving closer to me with each spin, her hair tossing, her lips pulling into a smile.

She paused a few feet away from me and waved.

Mama? I thought, but I couldn't speak. My words were trapped. When I waved back, the sun came up, highlighting the dark greens and browns from the earth. Blue birds flew in the sky, chirping once they made it to the sycamore trees, and sunflowers sprouted rapidly, bringing the buzzing bees with them. She glowed under the immense sunlight, and I wanted to go to her, hug her, but my feet wouldn't move.

Her smile faded when she saw a small envelope descend from the heavens. We watched it drift down slowly, and she held her hand out; it landed in her palm.

She opened the envelope, finding a letter inside.

Mama! I tried again. It was the letter from my birth father, and I didn't want her to read it. I needed to save her this time.

But nothing I did worked, and her face transformed into utter sadness as she read the words on the page. She fell to her knees helplessly, and I mirrored her.

"I'm so sorry, Z," she uttered, tears sliding down her cheeks like thick raindrops. "I thought it would be different this time. I thought he'd choose us. I thought he'd love us...I thought he loved me."

The paper and envelope disintegrated, and she held her hand to her chest. She gasped, her eyes widening, her mouth agape. To the ground she fell, disappearing into the overgrown grass, dying as she had before. Her heart broke all over again, and this time I heard it snap in two.

I screamed when her body disappeared, my voice finally tearing through the barrier. My limbs could barely function as I cried out for her to come back, to *please* stay with me.

There was a flicker, and then it was night. The sunflowers had gone; the air was still and quiet. It smelled of fresh rain.

I scanned the darkness, trying to grasp what was happening.

Another flicker, and Bo appeared.

The stars twinkled when he arrived, and he approached me. He sat in the grass, his legs crisscrossed. Bo had on a pair of white joggers and a plain white tee. He shared a cautious smile with me, and then four words appeared on the center of his shirt: DO YOU TRUST ME?

My head hurt, and I wiped the water from my eyes. "You lied," I said, the words loud, echoing into the night.

Bo shifted, chewing his lips, and the words on his shirt changed: YOU DON'T KNOW THE WHOLE STORY.

I shrugged, and Bo sighed at my reaction.

He sat up, the words changing again: DO YOU TRUST ME?

I tugged at the grass, aggravated. Why was he asking again? What did it matter?

Bo leaned forward, his gaze locking to mine. The words on his chest flashed, waiting.

"I used to trust you, but things have changed."

Three more words appeared: BUT YOU DID?

I nodded.

Bo nodded, too. He looked down, his fists balling, and then his brown freckles disappeared, and he transformed into the undead.

Held my breath as he fell apart, and I stared in shock as I watched his shirt type out five more words: DO YOU TRUST ME NOW?

"What?" I leaned away from him, and when I did, a green vine ripped from the earth again, wrapping itself around Bo.

He yelled for my help, his eyes full of fear and color. Tighter, the vines twisted him, clutching his already torn skin. They kept making it worse, and I couldn't let them take him. Didn't want to lose another person if I could help it.

I tried reaching for him, but another set of vines slithered around my legs and pulled me away from Bo.

We tried reaching for each other, fingertips amiss, but we couldn't. The vine squeezed and squeezed, wrapping around me until I could no longer breathe. I felt my body crushed beneath the weight of it all, felt that ticking thing inside me shrivel and stop. Why was this happening?

Another flicker. The vines vanished, releasing me. My chest expanded; I could breathe again. The sun was back, painted in the sky with swirls that seemed to never end.

The earth sparkled with primary colors. Dandelions rose from the ground in subtle sprigs, small seeds bouncing away from them. Sunflowers sprouted around them, and I could smell their sweet intensity filling my lungs.

A breeze came, tangling itself around me, helping me to my feet, and in a flash, Vincent van Gogh appeared.

I blinked. Once, then twice, and again. I knew I was dreaming, but this was surreal.

There was a brightness that made his body glow. He stood so angelically, his palms at rest, his body almost floating. His red beard was decorated with small daisies, and his eyes flashed from brown, to green, to blue, and then brown again.

He reached for me, and I took his hand. When I did, a sunflower grew beneath us, and it pushed us toward the swirly yellow sky.

We sat on a velvety smooth petal, and I spoke first. "What happened to you?" I asked. I wanted to know so bad. From what I'd read about him, no one really knew where his mind was the day he shot himself. Yet he didn't die in that moment; he lived for two more days.

Van Gogh smiled, his eyes blue. He pulled a small bag out of his pocket and handed it to me.

I gasped. In the plastic bag was his ear and more daisies.

When I gave it back to him, he shrugged, tucking the bag safely back into his pocket.

"The heart of man is very much like the sea, it has its storms, it has its tides, and in its depths it has its pearls, too."

Nodded, half-heartedly agreeing. "Do you know when I'll see her again?" He probably didn't know Mama, and I'm sure he had no idea what I spoke about, but it was worth it to try.

"I'm afraid I do not have an answer. It could be a lifetime, forever perhaps."

"But how long is forever?"

"Sometimes it's only a second."

I looked away, folding my lips.

"Z is for *zenith*," he said, his voice the color orange.

"How did you know?" I sat up and tilted my head to the side.

"Everyone knows." He smiled. "But it's you who has to make a choice. Time is fleeting. Someday death will take us to another star." He stood, and around us, several buckets of paint appeared on the sunflower. "We shall paint," he said, and I stood, too.

I walked around each bucket, but all the paint was the same. It was either yellow or blue. Since I didn't have a brush, I dipped one hand into yellow, the other into blue, and when I brought them out of the buckets, they were both green.

I knew it was weird, but I joined van Gogh anyway.

He pulled the sky closer to us, and we painted the clouds with our hands, making a mess, the paint dripping everywhere.

I reached to paint the sun, the light blinding me, burning my fingers, and it was that pain that forced me awake.

My eyes snapped open, and I woke to the sound of Mac Miller and an acoustic guitar in my ears. My earbuds had stayed in all night; I'd hardly moved; Bear was still stuck under my arm, safe.

Said where are you going? Can I come, too?

When I took a deep breath, my lungs rattled like the sound of air leaking out of a balloon, and it felt like someone was sitting on my chest, pressing me deeper into the bed.

I didn't move, not because my chest felt heavy, but because I couldn't stop thinking about this new revelation I'd had last night.

The truth was clear as day, and it squeezed me: Mama died of a broken heart.

She loved him, but he didn't love her.

It was like he held all this power in his hands, and her body couldn't push the blood through her veins anymore.

For some reason, witnessing this, and not knowing it, sent my brain into panic mode. It was why my imagination turned her into this horrible, horrible thing. It was why it turned anyone who'd been affected by the wrong love into zombies, even if I knew nothing about their personal lives. Like every time I saw Bo around Charlie, or if Bo ever thought about Charlie, he morphed.

I cringed at the realization.

Why did humans hurt each other? What was the point of producing that kind of pain?

All we did was create scars, create zombies.

There weren't enough consequences.

He, my birth father, had no consequences. He got to live in sunny California with his new life, his new family, and I'd be damned if he thought, for another second, he could continue living his fairy-tale life without owning up to all the destruction he'd caused.

I would die before I let him get away with it, set myself on fucking fire.

It was time to get up, to do something. But when I did, it was hard to breathe, my throat felt raw. Reached for my phone to stop the music, but...

But...

My hands. They looked like mush. The flesh sagged, exposing oozing tendons and bones. My knuckles were scarred, and the skin was discolored—yellow and green—the sign of an infection.

No, no, no. Please, God, no.

Ripped the blankets away from me, every move inflamed, my legs and feet looked like my arms and hands. They bled and gaped and were bruised.

I made a choking sound when I moved, like a centipede crawled up my throat, little by little. Coughed, only it wouldn't come out. And my heart raced, and raced, and raced, on the verge of exploding.

THE UNDEAD TRUTH OF US

Staggered out of bed, my body feeling like it weighed a thousand pounds, and when I got to the mirror, I gaped in horror at my new reflection.

My brown eyes had green rings around the irises, and the veins above my cheeks were stained purple. The skin looked like it had been burned down to the white bone beneath in certain places, tissue seeping out in clumps, and my jaw was dislocated, my tongue torn, staining my teeth a cherry red.

I was the unmentionable thing I feared. I was a zombie, like Mama, like Bo, like all the others.

It had finally happened, and maybe I felt part of the deadness inside me after seeing Bo and Charlie. Maybe I knew that feeling but ignored it. Couldn't place my finger on it. But the discovery of Mama's secret affair must have driven my body over the edge. I wasn't immune to my made-up disease. I breathed it in, no way to escape it.

The rattling, the rattling, the rattling.

Good Lord. What was I supposed to do? I pinched myself. Even if this was all in my head, it *felt* real. Would I be like this forever now? I didn't know. I needed to know.

Paced again, slowly, broken breaths. My legs kept dragging behind me, making it harder to line my joints up the way I wanted to. I needed a plan, but I swore, my mind was blank. Any idea landed with a clunk. Kept running in circles up there, surprised and shocked that this could happen to me.

Minutes had passed, then an hour. The clock wouldn't stop ticking.

I dug through all Mama's things again, looking, searching for anything that had more answers. I checked her old purse; it was tucked away in my closet. I pulled out old receipts, gum, and ChapStick. Nothing gave me the answers I needed, and I wasn't quite sure what that answer would even look like; I just knew I needed to fix this.

With a perturbing thud in my sides, I went back to the letter—reading it once, twice, a third time. How the hell was I supposed to fix this? I sunk to the floor; my skin folded beneath me. How did anyone fix this? I needed to get out of my own head. My thoughts spun out of control.

Think.

Think.

Think.

But it was so hard to think. I could barely function.

Think.

Think.

Think.

I gasped, my thoughts coming to a thumping halt. I limped to my phone, scrolling through the texts I had with Bo. My eyes skimmed the words quickly, searching for the right one. Scrolling, scrolling. When I landed on what I was looking for, I clicked it. There.

Bo had texted me about the book we'd read together. It was that very pulling paragraph about being stuck in the labyrinth that highlighted the word *forgiveness.*

In order to survive, we had to forgive.

In order to *live*, we needed to forgive.

And it was this ultimate truth that haunted me because I knew it would be the cure. Yet, for the smallest millisecond, I didn't know if I *could* forgive.

But I was going to. I'd figure it out somehow, because no one person could simply defeat a zombie apocalypse—you had to survive it. And if I was going to *survive* this death and forgive, I needed to confront the sperm donor and get answers.

I needed to know why he did what he did, or I'd never move on.

But first, I needed to see Bo.

CHAPTER FORTY-THREE

I LAY ON THE FLOOR, my head pressing into the rug, gravity forcing the ripped parts of my skin away from me. I stared at the speckled ceiling. Bo was up there, living or dying.

I thought about how I'd forgive him, how I'd open my blue veins and let him back in. Not that it mattered. Everything I knew in my world was a lie, and I craved the truth. Maybe this truth shit might get me my life back.

That and forgiveness. Right. Because I couldn't forget that piece.

Deep inside, a moan. I was still decaying. Every breath that left my body made me feel frozen. My chest kept caving in when I moved, and putting on shorts was almost equivalent to running up three flights of steps.

When I was dressed, I grabbed my phone and opened my bank app to check how much money I had left. It was enough to get me to California and back.

Then, a quick text to Mini:

Shit is crazy.

You're gonna think I'm freaking out and that I've lost my mind, but please don't try to stop me

I'm going to California to see the sperm donor

Apparently him and my mom were having an affair

I know it's crazy, but I promise I'll catch you up

Also, I'm a zombie now

That's also crazy, I know

But I'm fine

Kind of

It will be ok. Need to talk to Bo.

I'll call you later

After the texts were sent, I silenced my phone, and as I approached the window to climb out, I felt the memories rush in.

Bo beside me on the grass, catching a piece of cotton that fell from the sky. Bo holding my hand, leading me in a left-side pass. His eyes never leaving my face. Bo towering over me, his freckles the stars in the night sky. His lips on my lips. His hands on my waist.

Back again, and I slumped up the steel steps of the fire escape, my legs dragging behind me. His window open, and I could see parts of him: phone in hands, legs stretched across his twin-sized bed.

Knocked, the sound loud in my ears. He didn't move at first, and that scared me, waiting any longer killed me. I tapped my foot, but the tapping hurt, so I huffed, a croak releasing.

Bo pulled back the curtain. We exhaled together. His dark brown eyes held a taste of hope and an ounce of despair. He was the human Bo, *my* Bo, and the place where my stomach would be—if it weren't hanging to the side of my abdomen—fluttered.

But then my throat burned, angry again.

He rubbed his eyes, opened the window, a sweetness rushing out. "Hey," he said, his voice soft. Bo's curls were fluffy today, longer, and they bounced when he moved.

I waved, lips flat, and I focused my gaze on his butt chin. It was the only part of his face I could look at without feeling numb. "Can I talk to you?"

"Why would you want to do that? We haven't spoken since—" He paused and looked past me, his Adam's apple bobbing while he swallowed the venom in his throat. He was remembering it, too. How I shut him out after. How I refused to respond to his texts, his calls. How I tried to pretend we never existed together.

"Whatever. Why do you want to talk now? What's the point?"

"Look, do you want to talk or not?"

His head fell back, and he grunted. "Fine. You can come in."

Bo stepped away from the window, and I crawled through, stumbling to the fuzzy white carpet.

He tried to help me up, and I waved him away. He smacked his lips, plopped on his bed. The blankets were pulled back, but I could see he had Spider-Man printed sheets.

Wiped my decaying hands on my shorts. "Cool sheets," I joked, sitting in his gamer chair. My skin made a squishing sound beneath me. It wasn't a time for jokes. Why did I even make a joke? Nothing here was funny.

When I looked around, I noticed Bo had a lot of posters in his room; he even had some original sketches. Green lights hung from the ceiling. Photos. Skater boy shit. An emo band. Chance the Rapper. Him and his brother. How had I missed the opportunity to see Bo's room this entire time? What else had I missed during my excursion to zombietopia?

Bo didn't react to my comment. Cleared my throat, pressed the toe of my Chucks into the carpet. "I'm not here to yell at you, but I want to so bad," I said, and I remembered the book again, remembered that I needed to get myself out of this maze.

I crossed my legs and then uncrossed them, realizing that the gunk on them made it hard for me to sit comfortably in this ridiculous chair. Took another deep breath. "I'm pissed at you, Bo. What happened with Charlie ... seeing you *with* Charlie. That killed me. I liked you. I trusted you. We connected, and I've never connected with anyone like that except my mom," I said, my heart pounding.

Bo had his arms resting on his knees, his fingers laced together. He was still, and I wasn't used to seeing him like that. He was always so fidgety, always moving. But no words now. His lips never parted.

I spoke again. "We were friends. How could you play me like that? I felt so stupid. I thought you liked me."

He cocked his jaw and clenched his teeth. "I *do* like you, Zharie!" He said it fast, but his words were more of a whisper-shout. It had only just occurred to me that maybe his parents were home, and he didn't want them to know I was here. If not his parents, then maybe his brother, and I could not meet a new person today. Not right now. Not like this.

Bo leaned forward and continued, "I never wanted any of that to happen. Any of it. Charlie, she ..." Bo slid his hands down his face and exhaled, his nostrils flaring. "Fuckk. No, I'm not gonna do that. I'm not gonna blame this on anyone. I'm just going to tell you the truth. I'm going to tell you what happened from the beginning."

I bit my lip, unsure if I wanted to know. This could change us forever.

"Charlie and I have known each other since we were three. Our moms grew up together. We essentially know everything there is to know about another person. And when we were thirteen, she told me she liked me as more than a friend. I was surprised, but it was cool, you know? Isn't that the dream at some point, for someone? Date your best friend?"

I waited, wondering if that was how Mama felt about the sperm donor. She'd said they'd been best friends, but I never wanted to hear how she fell in love with him.

Bo kept going. "And it was great for a while, but right after we turned fifteen, she told me she wanted to be with other people. So, I thought it was over, because what the hell does a person do with that kind of information? I wanted to move on, but...I don't know. She kept coming back to me, like she didn't want to let me go. And I let her." He gazed at the carpet. "It was our secret, and it didn't matter if she was with some other guy, because behind closed doors, she was still with me."

"You were *a secret*? While she dated other guys?"

He nodded, his eyes graying. And there it was. The first sign. "I mean, our friends knew. And it's not like she kept me hostage. I knew the choice I was making, and she deserved to know what it's like to be with other people. Everyone ain't high school sweethearts. But... she's always loved me in a way that made me feel seen, and I didn't know if I'd ever get that with anyone else." He couldn't look me in the eye when he said it, his fingertips peeling away from the skin, flakes falling to the floor.

"And I tried, for a year, to be the backup guy. I swore to her I'd try, and I did. For her, I did. And maybe also for me. But it got too hard for me. And I failed her, Z." His lashes fluttered, then he sat up again, the sunlight catching on him now. "Call that shit selfish, but watching the one person you love love everyone else was like standing in the middle of a battlefield. It broke me more than I could ever be broken."

"What happened after that?" I said, and I watched the room paint itself blue; the walls expanding, vines tearing their way out the ceiling.

"I told her I couldn't do it anymore. I didn't want to be the side guy. And I said we could still be friends, but that was all I could give her. She told me she understood, and we left it at that."

"And that was it?" I asked, breathing it in now. It made sense. Charlie loved Bo, but Bo loved Charlie more. Classic unrequited love. It was why Bo kept turning into a zombie, why he kept glitching. Charlie was Bo's bokor, and maybe Bo felt like he was forever bound to her.

"Yeah."

"But what happened on the camping trip? What was that? I thought it was over between the two of you?" The green, fuzzy vines were on the floor now, slithering around his feet.

"It *is* over, Z. It is. But I slipped up. I let my guard down. After I walked you to your tent that night, Charlie opened up to me. She said she had too much to drink, and she was feeling low. She kept apologizing for how she strung me along. How it wasn't right. She said she liked you for me, that we'd be great together. And then she just started crying, and I couldn't leave her by the campfire by herself," he said, his eyes breaking like glass. "But she thought my kindness was because things weren't over. I tried to leave after that, I put out the fire, but she didn't want me to go. What you saw was me trying to explain to her that we could never be together and that I wanted to be with you, and I needed her to be okay with that. Then she kissed me, and that's when you appeared."

My chest felt less condensed, less like it was tied in knots. A sunflower there, by his ankles, blooming from the end of the vine, stretching its way up to Bo.

And now Charlie's words sat with me, rested on my lap while I sorted through them. She said it wasn't what it seemed. She was trying to be better, to be a good person. That I should forgive Bo. "But why didn't you ever tell me about you and Charlie?" I understood love wasn't a straight line. I wouldn't have judged them.

Bo stared at me, life coming back, brown filling his irises. And his room was golden now. "I didn't want you to look at Charlie differently because she's a good person. *She is.* And she needs friends. We all need friends."

Fiddled with my nails, and my hands looked normal again. Except I wasn't entirely sure what to do with this new information. Where did that leave Bo and me?

When Bo sat up, the vines slithered to me, blooming on the way over. "I get that this changes stuff for us, and I'm really sorry I hurt you, Z." He said it, and his word bubble appeared, right in the middle of us, floating in the air.

"I'm sorry," he said it again, another one.

Sucked my lips in, but I couldn't say anything.

His shoulders dropped. "I get it, and you don't have to forgive me. I understand if you don't want to be around me. I have a lot of baggage, shitty baggage."

Same. "We all have baggage."

He looked at me, curious—his eyes squinting, pressing to know more—and I told myself I'd tell him the entirety of it all, even if it would hurt me later.

"I forgive you..." I said, and I meant it, my bubble merging into his. With everything I had, I truly meant it. Life was too damn short, and I saw Mama in my head again, on the floor. That was the issue with us. We always thought we had more time. We always thought there was tomorrow. But that wasn't always the case.

A smile now, breaking on his face, and our bubbles vanished. "You never really told me why you were here. I thought I'd never see you again...."

"Right..." Shit. Okay, how would I do this? How could I explain this? And it felt like there were flowers in my lungs when I took another breath. It tickled. "Remember how you said you thought I was stuck in the labyrinth? How I was stopping myself from really living my life?"

He gave me a single nod.

"You were right. I've been kind of stuck, but it's not why you think."

Bo smirked, and the vines worked their way up my leg, sewing it back together, the deadness crawling away.

"It's actually way more than that," I continued. "It's because, since my mom died, I've been seeing zombies. . . ."

"Zombies?"

I gulped, and when he said the word back to me, I cringed. "I know it sounds crazy, and it *is* crazy, and I'm not quite sure what's going on in my head. It's like a surrealist explosion up there, and every day, ordinary things aren't as they appear." And I waited for something else to happen. Another bubble, more flowers, the undead.

But Bo adjusted himself, the bed squeaking a little.

"And before my mom died, she experienced a heartbreak that turned her into this undead thing—not literally." I shrugged. Or maybe literally. "But in my head. I just . . . I didn't know it was in my head until I realized no one else could see it. And there were more zombies, all around me, but it wasn't everyone . . . just a few people. It's why I was drawn to you."

Bo pointed to himself with his entire hand, his fingers directed to the center of his chest. "Wait, wait, wait. You saw *me* as a zombie? *Me?*"

"Yes, you."

"Do I look like a zombie right now?"

"No. Um, I'm actually the one who looks like a zombie right now." And when I said it, the vines slid through my scalp, around my curls. A blooming there, the smell of flowers.

His mouth fell open, and I knew I was making it worse. That same look, like everyone before him—Auntie, Grandma, Mini. He was clearly confused. I mean, his eyes were comically big, *cartoonishly* big.

Didn't know if I should continue anymore. I could take these flowers with me and slide out the window, disappear into the light.

Bo closed his mouth. The vines were around him, too, the flowers also there. And if I left, I'd be taking him with me either way, so I shut my eyes so I could envision the words. "I think the reason I've been seeing zombies . . . or why some people appear as zombies . . . is because they've been hurt by someone they loved, or someone they *thought* loved them."

Opened my eyes and he was closer, the sunflowers blooming in his curls, too.

"Like, for example. I think the reason why you looked like a zombie was because of your relationship with Charlie. And you didn't always appear as a full zombie—sometimes it was just part of you that looked that way."

"Hmph," he mumbled, thinking. But the wait burned a new question inside: *Why did we* love *love, when love seemed to hate us?*

"It's like your brain antenna is tuned into an alternate universe."

"Yeah . . ." I hadn't thought of it like that before. But that was it.

"Okay." He took a breath, the room forcing us even closer together, and I felt like I should stand. I could now, my legs were pieced back together, and my chest wasn't so heavy, but I couldn't move.

"So you're seeing zombies, but they're not like the I'm-gonna-kill-you-and-take-your-brains zombies, they're *metaphorical* zombies?"

"Exactly. Metaphorical. And I think the only way to get past it is to confront the issue."

He rubbed his chin, only a little hair there. "And if *you're* a zombie right now, then what do you need to confront?"

But I was already feeling so much better. "You. Clearly, you. Because I like you, Bo. You're the only person I want to be around these days, and I think the Charlie thing threw me over the edge. It was just so damn confusing."

"You still like me . . . after everything?"

My cheeks warmed, and a flower tickled my ear. "*Like* is a broad word, right? Technically, you can like anything, *anyone*. And don't flatter yourself too much; you're not the only person I need to confront. There's unfinished business with my birth father."

Bo held his hand up, a vine twirling around his finger. "Pause . . . but *you* like me?"

I pinched my lips together, trying to fight the smile. "Yes, I like you," I said, and I rolled my eyes, feeling like I should really stand now. When I stood, some of the petals fell to our feet.

And Bo's lips pulled at the corner. "Cool, *cool*." He broke eye contact with me. "I mean, it's dope. It *really* is dope." He cleared his throat, still cheesing. "But enough about that. You mentioned unfinished business with your 'birth father'? His title has updated, I see."

"No. Not really. He's always going to be the sperm donor to me, but I'm trying the forgiveness thing. Though, I doubt it's gonna be any of that when I meet him. I could care less about an apology. I just need answers."

"*Meet?* You're going to see the sperm donor? For real? When? *Why?*"

"Tomorrow. It'll be a short trip, but it was the cheapest one I could find. And because these are the facts, Bo. My mom died of a broken heart, I know she did, and my birth father broke her heart. There's proof of it. I need to know why he did this."

"Dang, for real? Um . . . okay, how are you getting there? Because if you need help, if you need a ride, I can help. I'll even go with you . . . if you need someone. I can—I can be there for you."

"You'd do that?"

"Zharie." He touched me then, his hands on the outside of my arms, his vines merging into mine. "I wouldn't want anything else. And if this means you get closure from some scumbag who hurt you—who *hurt* your mom—I want to make sure you do it. I'm here for you, and I mean it."

Closer. The vines forced me closer to him. "Okay," I said, my chest tightening again.

Then Bo held his arms out, creating a Z-shaped hole for me to fit into. "I feel like we need to hug. Can we?"

I fiddled with the idea of it, keeping my feet planted, and then I pulled a Bo, flashing the hang loose sign.

"You're the worst," he said, laughing under his words. "The worst and the best."

And I smiled, pressed into him, placed my head against his chest, and the vines tied me there. We mashed together, and he kissed my forehead. Bo was adventure, spring rain.

And I knew it would be okay. Because if he was the rain, I was the mud, new life springing out of me.

His warm breath against my eyelids now, his thumbs pressed into my neck. His eyes rounded and he said, "I really, *really* like you, Z. And I don't ever want to lose you again."

Looked into his eyes, thinking they'd decay like mine, but they didn't. "I don't want to lose you, either." When I said it, I caught the tiniest reflection of myself in Bo's window. I was mostly human, but there were still dead parts. Still parts of me hurting for Mama.

And in a single moment...

Our foreheads pressed together. Lashes interlaced. Darkness now. Skin to skin. Nose to nose. Lips to lips. His fingers crawled to my hair, flowers falling out, and I pressed into him, drinking his sweet air until our hips smashed together, our bellies touched.

And we were brown, we were brown, we were brown.

We drifted to another universe, and in our world, there were two new truths: I was a paradox, and he was a motif.

CHAPTER FORTY-FOUR

JULY 5, 11:00 P.M.

My life is still in shambles, but maybe there's hope.

Somehow. Somewhere.

Hope is good, right?

The cure:

- Forgiveness?
- Letting go?

Next steps:

- Off to San Diego

CHAPTER FORTY-FIVE

THERE IS PEACE EVEN IN THE STORM. That's what Vincent van Gogh said, and that's what I was trying to hold on to before I left the next morning.

I texted Luca when I woke. The thought of what happened at the studio still stuck to me, not quite gone yet.

> Listen, I'm not mad at you, but what you did the other day wasn't cool

> If I ever made you feel like we were more than friends, then i'm sorry that was never my intention

You're a great guy, Luca. You're just not my guy.

And I think you deserve someone who wants to be as crazy for you as you are for them.

They should be chasing after you.

Don't settle for the Becca's in the world. Hell, don't even settle for the Z's in the world.

If you're too caught up in someone who doesn't want to be with you, it could keep you from meeting the person you're supposed to be with

And the person you're supposed to be with will be worth it.

At least that's what they say

Anyway, I'd like to still be friends, but I need time to process all this craziness.

I hope you understand.

Also, don't respond to this text

Rolled out of bed then. Slipped off my satin bonnet, opened my window. The flowers were there, stuck to the glass. Undid the latch, grabbed one till it snapped, and stuck it behind my ear on the dead side. The weirdness, the sunflowers, the sounds—all of it was comforting. In a way, it pulled me closer to Mama. Even in death, she kept me close to her, reminded me she was here.

Bag packed, hair moisturized, and the smell of coffee stirred through the apartment. A beeping then, like an alarm, and I tilted my head in confusion. Auntie E never made coffee before work. I honestly wasn't sure if she liked it.

Shifted my weight and settled into my heels. I should go out there, apologize, be the first to say it. Not because Mama would want me to, or because it would change things, but because it was a habit I wanted to break. Since I moved in with Auntie, I waited for life to happen to me, for someone to tell me how to move forward, and I didn't want to be in that rotation anymore.

The door creaked when I opened it, the dent by the knob staring at me. Eyes forward, shoulders back, and I trailed down the hallway, following the coffee and the light that poured in from the kitchen.

When I turned the corner, Auntie E was at the peninsula, pouring milk into a Disney-themed coffee mug. She didn't look at me when I appeared, but she spoke.

"Good morning," she said, her voice soft. Auntie had on a set of blue scrubs, and her hair was in long braids, small beads at the ends of them. I wondered when she'd done that; it was a nice look on her. By her chest, a glimmer. She had her name tag on today. She never wore it. Her first name, Eyanna, was printed across in thick black letters.

"Good morning," I said, matching her tone.

She sat the milk down, twisted the top on it. "You know, Twiggy had a thing for coffee. I never did, couldn't stand the taste, but she bought me this bag of grounds for my birthday." A smiled appeared, her eyes sparkling, remembering. "Could you believe that? It was like her to do that, too. She always wanted me to step out of my comfort zone. You know she was a barista before she had you. Before she started dancing full-time."

I nodded, remembering some of the stories Mama would tell me about when she was a barista. Some of her dance friends worked with her, too. They'd even carpool together, she'd said. She'd also told me her favorite drink to make was a café au lait, one part steamed milk, one part coffee. She made it for me once, but it was gross. *Sorry, Mama.*

"Here." Auntie pushed the milk toward me. "Grab a cup."

I did as she said, picking an old Saint Vincent de Paul mug from the cupboard. From the corner of my eye, I spotted the bag of coffee grounds resting on the off-white laminate countertop while I filled my cup. It was Starbucks signature blonde roast—the only stuff Mama would drink from there.

Before I joined Auntie at the peninsula, I pressed the rim of the cup to my nose. It smelled like Mama; it smelled how our house smelled twice a day. My throat swelled, and I felt that warmth pushing behind my eyes.

A year ago almost, but I could see it: her hands holding a spoon, stirring the cream in her coffee. The clink, her smile, all of it faded now.

I returned to the peninsula, poured milk into my cup, already knowing that milk alone would not satisfy me, but I couldn't remember if we had sugar.

The silence felt like forever. I stirred the coffee, listening to the spoon scrape the inside of the porcelain mug, waiting for Auntie E to say more.

Her lips were at rest, and her young eyes still seemed exhausted from the shift before. She was focused on her coffee, a pretty mocha like the color of her skin.

I remembered now. I needed to break the cycle. "I'm sorry about the other night," I said, my words splitting through the stillness. "I shouldn't have worried you, and I did. I should have told you where I was going. . . . I should've checked my phone." Took a sip, it wasn't as bitter as it could have been, but it still needed sugar. "Honestly, I didn't think you really cared."

She looked at me, her brow raised. "Why would you think that?" she asked, and my body heated, perspiration dripping from my armpits. Did she not know? It was carved in these walls still, the words from the other night. She *hated* that I lived here. But that was obvious. She barely looked at me sometimes, her gaze drifting. She was in and out, always. School, work, the world outside of this place—the reminder that out there, she was free. In here, she had me.

I looked at the coffee, swirling, swirling. "You've made it evident, and we don't really talk anymore. Not like we used to, *before* . . . Mama. And you're always upset, always huffing. It's just this feeling that I've done something wrong, but I don't know what it is."

She folded her lips, her eyes still down.

"So, yeah . . . it doesn't seem like you care. It's like you're just waiting for me to graduate and move out."

"I care. I do care. Um . . ." She paused, and I recognized what was happening. The puffiness growing above her cheeks, the wetness in her rims. She took another sip, cleared her throat, and just then, I imagined us sitting in a greenhouse. It was one that I'd been to years ago with Mama. It was a greenhouse and a coffee shop combined. I think it was called Café Equinox.

Around us now: ferns, caladiums, and succulents. Lots of succulents, big and small. Birds bouncing on the cement, low chatter from the bodies moving with carts in the distance, and the air thick in my lungs.

Inhaled the sweetness and the smell of dirt, the blocked sun warm on my eyelids.

"I do care about you, Zharie. And, um, I—I apologize if I've made it seem like I'd rather be doing something else." Her shoulders sank, and the tears poured from her eyes, falling off her chin. It was like the funeral again, all dressed in black, Grandma tucked to her side, her world spinning off a cliff.

"It's just that I'm mourning Twiggy, too. She was my only sister, my only anything . . . I didn't even get that much time with her, Z. And every time I see you walk by, I'm reminded of her. You both sound the same, you know that? Whenever I close my eyes, it's like I'm hearing her. And it's frustrating. It's not fair. We were supposed to be best friends when we grew up, but I did my own thing. She did her own thing, and we just kept forgetting to get back to that." She wiped her tears away, and I felt my own forming. I didn't know she felt that way—that I reminded her of Mama, or that they had promises that weren't kept.

"All that to say, I do care about you, Zharie. I love you so much, but sometimes it's hard to be around you. Do you get that? It's hard to be reminded that my sister's never coming back, and—" She couldn't speak anymore. A lump sliding in her throat, her fingers pressing into the mug, blue birds picking remnants from the ground.

I nodded in response to her, not knowing what to say, focusing on one of the plants. I forgot that Auntie E was grieving, too. I'd been so focused on my own path of sadness that I'd never considered Auntie's anger was due to the loss of her sister. I let the idea manifest that she hated me, but she didn't, she hated the reason why she had me— Mama gone forever, her sister, and then me, her crooked reflection. A reminder that she'd never see Twiggy again.

Auntie's fingers relaxed, and she turned her mug. "I'm sorry I was hard on you the other night—that I'm hard on you in general. It's that *this* shit is hard. Life is hard. No one prepares people for this kind of tragedy, Z. And I was already struggling when you were dropped off with me. I haven't got it together yet. I'm working on that. But give me time. Please be patient with me. It won't be like this forever, I promise."

I believed Auntie because I knew who she was before this. I knew she was bright-eyed with a dream in her hands. And I didn't know if Mama ever told Auntie E this, but she looked up to her younger sister.

Thought she was talented, and smart, and going as far as she could. "Thank you, Auntie. I appreciate you saying that," I said. "I didn't know, but it means a lot. I miss her, too."

She nodded her head, lashes low.

"And also," I started, gripping the white handle of the mug. "I'm going to California to see my birth father today."

Her eyes were wide, probably thinking I'd lost my mind again. Then she shook her head. "Okay," she said.

But I couldn't believe it. With a flash, we were back in the apartment again, leaning over the peninsula. The fluorescent light seeming less bright now that the sun was pouring in. "Really?"

"Yes, ma'am. I'm not gonna stop you from seeing your dad if that's what you wanna do. It ain't like he ever answers his phone anyway. No offense, but your dad is kind of a dick, Z."

I took a gulp of coffee. "None taken," I said, hoping she wouldn't change her mind.

She raised her brow and straightened out the cardigan over her scrubs. "Well, anyway, I'm off to work." She put her mug in the sink and grabbed her lunch bag.

"Okay, have fun doing whatever it is you do at the nursing home."

"I'll be sure to give my best smile while I wipe old white people's asses all day." She smirked, grabbing her purse and her keys. "Let me know when you're out, and please text me when you land."

I waved goodbye. "I will," I said, sinking into my feet. That went so much better than planned. We needed that.

A half hour later, Bo texted me, letting me know the Uber would be picking us up in ten. I grabbed my bag and the letter before I headed out.

When I descended the staircase, Bo was there—hands in his front pockets, bag on his back, a smile deep in his face. A look he shared with a feeling I couldn't name.

"What?" I said.

Eyes low when he said it, but he couldn't hide. "Everything."

When I got to him, I remembered how the vines wrapped themselves around us, and I felt it a little, where his hands touched me last. My shoulders, my hips, my legs. It should have been comforting, but it amplified my nerves, and I could barely breathe in these high-waisted shorts.

Because it wasn't just that there was Bo. It was also that in a few hours, I'd probably be seeing the sperm donor for the first time outside of a dance setting. For the first time without Mama, and I still wasn't sure how I felt about that.

Bo took my hand, and with the other, he twisted a curl, close to the flower tucked above my ear, close to the part of my face where the flesh ripped away from the bone. So dead there, and I could feel a moving in my skin, trudging toward my nose. Flinched and the feeling went away.

And I wished Bo could see it. Wished, when he looked at me, he saw how undead I was, how I fell apart. Wished he saw the sunflower in my ear, stretching toward him. Then I wouldn't be alone with this truth.

A horn honking, and when we turned, a light blue Ford Fusion pulled into an empty spot in front of us. The person inside waved us down. "That's him," Bo said, and we loaded our stuff in the car.

Before we drove off, my phone buzzed with a text from Mini:

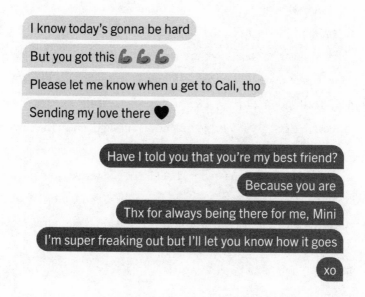

I know today's gonna be hard

But you got this 👏 👏 👏

Please let me know when u get to Cali, tho

Sending my love there 🖤

Have I told you that you're my best friend?

Because you are

Thx for always being there for me, Mini

I'm super freaking out but I'll let you know how it goes

xo

We made it to the KCI airport around eight a.m., and since it was early, or maybe it was the day, we were checked in and seated in thirty minutes.

And while the flight attendant went through the motions, telling us what we should do in case of an emergency, I stared out the window, the land golden and blue.

I couldn't keep up. I hadn't thought this through, but I was already buckled in. Too late. *What if I get to California and he's not there? What if he's competing? What if it's an old address and he's moved since then? What if no one's home?*

If any of that turned out to be true, I'd be wasting this money that could have gone to Auntie. And if I failed to confront him, my life might not push forward in the way I wanted it to.

Bo tightened his grip on my hand.

"Hey, you good?" he asked, his eyes piercing me.

"Yes," I said quickly, but then I changed my mind. "No. Frick. No, I'm not really good. I'm bad. I feel awful. I don't really know how this is supposed to go?" We were soaring now, pulling through the clouds.

"What part is scary?"

"All of it. I just . . . I don't know what he's gonna be like, or what he's gonna say. What if he doesn't want to see me?" And after I said it, the other seats disappeared. Now it was just Bo and me, surrounded by windows in the sky.

It was a thought I always had: What if he didn't want to see me? What if he refused, slammed the door in my face?

Clearly, there was a reason why I belonged to Mama and *not* him. Our stories were just a bunch of blank paragraphs. Was he there when I was born? When I got my first tooth? Did he ever reach out for any of my birthdays?

What I knew about him was terribly thin. He danced. Apparently, he had a family. He broke my mom's heart. A true freaking dingle-berry.

"We will make him see you," Bo said, my thoughts fleeting. "He doesn't have a choice."

Bo was right. I had to do this regardless. "Wait, you never told me how you got money for a ticket and an Uber?"

He stuck his tongue out and did that stupid sign again. "It's better I don't tell you."

"C'mon, really?"

"Let's just say, when I get back, I'll probably be grounded for the rest of the summer."

"Oh, God. *Bo.*"

"It's fine, it's fine. This is worth being grounded for."

I put my head back on the seat. "I surely hope so."

CHAPTER FORTY-SIX

SAN DIEGO, CALIFORNIA, was sunny and green, and the air made my open wounds pulse with blood.

After we landed, we had a car drop us off in Point Loma, a neighborhood in San Diego, close to the ocean. I couldn't see the water while we were on the ground, but the air smelled like salted candy and wet concrete. I knew we were close.

Tall palm trees, small colorful buildings, and narrowing streets. People flocking the sidewalks; they reminded me of Mika, the way she dressed, the way she moved, and I wondered how she was. I should text her back, maybe even see if I could meet up with all of them. They still felt like they were my people, like they cared for me. Even

Charlie. I wondered how she was, how life had been, how this whole thing had changed her.

Bo and I walked to a nearby Chipotle for lunch. We both ordered burrito bowls, but I could barely take five bites. My stomach kept twisting, and it felt like small bugs tried to pierce their way out.

Bo looked at me, his head tilted, his curls springing. He saw it in me, and he tried. Tried to stop my leg from bouncing. Tried to trade me his favorite shiny Pokémon. Tried to hold my hand.

But I couldn't think about that. My thoughts popped out of my brain, floated away from me, and there was no end to the anxiety. All of us, we spun out of control with no sign of the end.

My belly still empty, and we were on the sidewalk now, the sun shining on our necks as we headed toward the Whole Foods next door.

"It's gonna be okay," he said as he followed me down the aisle. My lips twisting, the dead and the human side meshing together. *Bo doesn't know that. He can't swear it.*

"What are you looking for?" he asked as he trailed behind me. Next aisle, next aisle, next aisle.

"Bergamot orange essential oil." Mama used to say that the smell alone could calm any nerves or anxiety. And I needed her here any way I knew how.

I was out five dollars after, and outside, I opened the bottle and dabbed a few drops on my wrists. Bo looked at me funny, but he said he wanted some, too.

"It's like I'm being blessed by the Holy Trinity."

I laughed, inhaling it now. "What's holy about this?"

"You, the oil, and everything before us."

Turned away from him, tucked the oil in my bag, hid a smile. What a dweeb.

Bo and I found two electric scooters. He offered to pay for both of them, and I put the sperm donor's address in my phone. Only two miles away from here; it would take us less than ten minutes to get there.

I hadn't realized how close we were. Did the sperm donor shop at that Whole Foods? Did he take his family to eat at that Chipotle? Did he get gas and Slurpees at the 7-Eleven? Did he pass the same tower apartments, hair salon, and thrift shop?

Maybe the people knew him here. Maybe his studio was nearby. Maybe he had his own daughter who loved dance, and maybe he took her to the ballroom, and she sat in on all his classes. Maybe she was really good and didn't know she was. Maybe she looked like me and walked like me.

And maybe not.

It wasn't long before we entered a neighborhood with little houses and little yards, the vines chasing us as we sped by. It seemed like each yard had its own palm tree, and all the homes here were so colorful— pinks and yellows, greens and whites.

The lots we passed were noticeably small, the roofs nearly touched one another, and many of the people who lived in them parked on the single street they shared, their cars crammed bumper to bumper.

We turned left onto Spruce Street, and the house was less than a foot away.

Slowed when the GPS declared we'd arrived, and I tried to catch the air in my lungs, but they wouldn't fill fast enough.

His house was unlike any house in the neighborhood. It was two stories, complete with olive-green siding. A modern, wooden door with horizontal windows, and a small twine wreath in the center of it.

"Whoa." Bo gasped. "Your donor is pretty damn loaded."

I eyed the place down, looking at the freshly paved driveway, the very green grass, and the pretty landscaping. "Eh," I said. "I mean, it's not that big, Bo."

"Z . . . a place like this, out here by the ocean. *Shiddddd.* Dude's rich."

Parked the scooter and held on to the straps of my backpack as I stared down the house. A sound again, a gasping somewhere. And the thing moved in my cheek, slithering through the gooey stuff.

If I stood here long enough, I'd never have to knock on the door. They'd see us at some point, they'd notice two lost kids in their front yard. They'd probably tell us to go away.

"So now what?" Bo stood beside me, and I sank a little, the concrete rippling.

"Want me to knock on the door?" he asked.

"No." The word rushed out. This was my issue to confront. "I'll do it," I said, and I walked up the steps, counting each one. Six total. If I needed to run away, I could hop over three of them, cut through the yard, and be gone. But then Bo would still be here, looking dumb as hell, wondering where I ran off to.

Something clumped in my throat when I made it to the last step, and I stood on a brown doormat that said WELCOME HOME.

I rolled my eyes, annoyed by the irony. *Breathe*, I told myself, and I exhaled deeply through my nostrils. Behind me, Bo stood on the sidewalk, shifting to the side. He smiled, his head nodded forward.

With my next crooked breath, I rang the doorbell.

Shuffling inside, distant laughter. More hushed voices, and then I could see a shadow on the other side of the door.

A clicking sound. Then a twist.

With a gush of air, the door was open, and I could see directly into the living room—a misplaced sock, toys on the ground, the back of a couch. A flat-screen TV mounted on the wall, the smell of fried fish. A small boy peeked around the corner, a silly smile on his face, a toy truck in his hand.

Before me stood a man in sweatpants and a gray shirt. MÉLANGE DANCE STUDIO was printed in white ink across his chest, and my lips cracked, salt on them now. That was Mama's studio. That was where we danced in KC. He didn't deserve to wear that shirt.

Studied the rest of him. Warm brown skin, hazel eyes, and short dark hair. It was thick, loose curls. Oddly shaped nose, rounded. Reminded me of my own.

He held a little girl in his arms, her hair wild and curly, flat on one side. She sucked on a yellow pacifier, and she looked like she was maybe one or two. Big, tired green eyes. Little hands gripping his shirt, tiny dangling toes.

"Can I help you?" he said, sounding out of breath, and I had hoped that his voice would sound familiar, but it didn't. It wouldn't.

That last competition I'd seen him at, I distinctly remembered he had spotted me in the crowd. We saw each other, and it looked like he almost smiled, his lips thinning out at one corner. I watched him walk off the dance floor that evening, his head down. I waited for him to look up, to just see me again, but he never did.

Now he was seeing me. No choice but to. Devin's eyes squinted. Then dilated. And he looked on the edge of curious when he stretched his neck to see who was on the sidewalk behind me.

His jaw loosened, suddenly closing the door a bit. "Excuse me, do I know you?"

I took another breath. "Um, hi, Devin. I'm Zharie."

When I said it, I imagined the words came out in slow motion because Devin's skin looked white, like he could see me decaying, parts of me falling on the ground before us. The vine wrapping itself around the door. The world turning, turning, turning.

He repositioned the baby in his arms, and she rubbed her eyes.

"Honey, who is it?!" someone yelled from inside. It sounded like a woman.

He stepped onto the porch, closing the door behind him. "How... how'd you get here?"

"I flew in today."

"For wha—I..." He noticed the bag on my back. "Oh, Zharie, I—"

"I'm not trying to stay with you." I said it fast. "I just have some questions to ask you."

He released a breath, his skin filling with color again. "Oh, okay," he said, and it looked like he feigned a smile. "I'm sorry. Excuse my manners, I forgot to introduce you to Lily. Lily, this is Zharie."

Lily smiled at the sound of my name. She didn't really move, though. Kind of just stayed still, her head resting on his shoulder.

"Well, um. I'd love to talk. I can bring you and your friend some water." He tipped his chin in Bo's direction when he said it. "We can talk on the patio." He pointed to the fence on the side of the house. "If you push that gate open, I'll meet you back there."

"Okay," I said, and I didn't move. Just watched.

Devin disappeared into the house with Lily. When the door latched, there was shuffling on the other side. Lowered voices. Stillness.

"What happened?" Bo rushed over to me.

My face felt blank while I stared at where the sperm donor just was. Tried to see through the glass, to see more. Couldn't believe that was him. "He wants me to meet him on the patio."

Bo tried to get me to turn, to see his face. "Who was that girl?"

Shrugged. "He said her name was Lily."

He stood behind me, wrapped an arm across my chest, rested his chin on my head. "You think that was your sister?"

Shrugged again and Bo let go. "Probably," I said, and the words didn't seem real. Never thought I could have a sister, but there were some parts of her that felt familiar. And then that boy in there, was that their son? Was that Lily's brother? It didn't register till now: I was an older sister. I had half siblings. And if we knew each other, what would that be like?

Bo was in front of me now. "Want me to go back there with you?"

"No," I said because I knew I needed to do this part alone, too.

I knew he understood because of how his eyes set in mine, and when we hugged, I held on to his smell, locked it in my memory for when I'd need it later.

I took the folded envelope out of my pocket, and I handed my backpack to Bo. He watched me follow the path to the side of the house, and he said he'd be a call away if anything went down.

My fingers pressed into the wooden gate, pushing it open. The backyard wasn't big like my old one, but it looked like they made the most of the space they had.

A small garden in the left corner, and in it, I spotted cilantro, parsley, and green and red tomatoes. There was a plastic kid slide, a soccer ball, and a small toy treasure chest.

To the left, the patio took up most of the space. It was HGTV beautiful, surrounded by paneled wooden walls, lights, and an assortment of leafy plants. A couch with gray, cushioned seats, and one of those neat firepit tables in front of it. On the other side of the patio, closer to the door, there was a wooden table with four chairs.

I sat down in a chair at the table and waited. From where I was, I could see through the sliding glass door into the dining room of their home. A small light flickering, and then the little boy I'd seen earlier was there, pressing his nose into the glass and waving his truck around so I could see it.

Lips pressed thin, I nodded my head, acknowledging the red-and-blue truck.

A woman appeared beside him, making him move away from the door. She never looked back to see me, but I saw she had long brown hair and fair skin. Was that Devin's wife?

Then he appeared, stepping onto the patio with his black flip-flops and two glasses of water in hand. "Where'd your friend go?" he asked, smiling a bit as he set the glasses on the table.

I didn't respond, and Devin scratched the side of his head and closed the door to the house. He sat across from me, relaxing into the chair.

So this was it. This was the person Mama was in love with. This was the person who didn't want me.

And I hated it, but in this sunlight, I could see myself in him. More than before. Not only did we share the same nose, but we also shared the same lips, the same eye shape, the same, confused scowl.

"Zharie, it's . . . it's truly good to see you. You've grown so much." His facial features softened, potentially recalling a few memories.

Was it *really* good to see me, Devin? That was hard to believe. "It's been a long time," I said, shifting in the seat.

He mumbled something I didn't catch. "So, what questions do you have?" he asked, and I watched him lace his hands together.

I set the envelope on the table, my fingers trembling from the weight of the situation, the pulling inside me, the vines stitching through the dead parts. A blink, and I could almost see Mama.

Devin stared at the paper on the table, his eyes big, his chest folding like origami. "What are you doing with that?" He leaned in.

"I found it, and I want to know what happened between you and my mother."

He straightened himself, and he reached for the letter but stopped midway, recoiling. Fingers to his face now. "Zharie, your mom and me—it was all in the past."

"It wasn't that long ago," I said, recalling the date on the letter.

Devin massaged his eyebrows and sat up. "What do you want to know?"

"All of it," I said, the pulsing thick inside me.

He looked at the house for a moment, his pupils ticcing, and then he whispered, "Look, what happened with Twiggy and me, that was almost two decades ago. I loved her when we were together, but it wasn't a thing we were ever really serious about. We were just kids, young and ignorant. I called it off before you were born."

"Why?"

He jerked. *"Why?"* he said, repeating it like I misspoke. "Because."

Waited. Saw her again. Mama twirling in place, hair tossing. In and out of the wind like particles in the air.

"Because. We were too young to have a family, to have kids."

"But I was born anyway."

"*I know,*" he said, clenching a fist. Leaned back, looked over his shoulder again. "I let her have full custody of you."

"Why?"

His chest stopped moving, his jaw locking. "I—" He broke our gaze. "That's neither here nor there."

I didn't move; I waited, waited to know what happened next. There was more, I knew there was more. Mama's heart didn't break over anything that simple.

Devin sighed again. "Look, Zharie, I don't know what more you want. Here." He pulled a checkbook and a pen out of his pocket. "What do you want? Do you need money? Is that why you're here?"

"No, that's not why I'm here," I said, and I watched him fill out the check, watched the pen draw zeros.

I banged my fist on the table. A thud, but he didn't move. He kept writing, signing his name at the very end.

"I want to know what happened with you and my mom. I want the full story. It's in the letter—the two of you were having an affair," I said, and Devin looked to the door again, eyes low.

Back at me, he whispered, "*What?*" Ripped off the check and slid it across the table. It was several thousand dollars. "I need you to go, leave." A growl almost. Was that a threat?

Banged my fist again, and he flinched. "I'm not leaving until you tell me what else happened. I *will* yell," I demanded. "And then everyone in your entire neighborhood will hear about it."

His nostrils flared, and he squeezed the pen in his hand before tossing it on the wood between us. "I just—I didn't love your mom anymore." He shook his leg under the table, and he sat up straight.

My eyes narrowed in on him.

"I never really loved her like that, okay? Is that what you want to hear? Everything I told her was a lie." He said it with venom, his hands turning into fists. "The only reason I came around was because I wanted her to take me under her wing, teach me everything she knew. I wanted to know what her coaches taught her, and shit. I couldn't afford that. Not some scrawny kid from KC. I wasn't about to waste time working, paying for lessons when I knew I had talent. But Twiggy saw that fire in me, and she didn't charge me. She made sure we were competition ready, and once we got on the big stage, we started winning. Then the money started coming in, and so did the opportunities."

"And that's it? You used her to get what you wanted and then you left?" When I said it, it made me more upset. What an asswipe.

"That's it. That's the story. Now it's time for you to leave."

Dug myself deeper in the chair and crossed my arms, mocking him. I wasn't going anywhere. "There's more. I know there's more. Why would you even string her along the whole time? It doesn't make sense."

He stood. "This is ridiculous, Zharie. You need to leave. I told you what happened, I wrote you a check. Just get out of here." He paced, his brown skin turning red.

And it upset me that he paced, that he walked the same way I did. That was mine. I swore that was mine.

He stopped, realizing that I wasn't leaving. Sat back down, crossed his arms like me, and his chest rumbled when he spoke. "Look, the truth is . . ." And he clenched his teeth, spit still shoving its way out. "I was never attracted to your mother, not like that. But she was always around when I needed her, and I took advantage of that because I could. Simple as that. Twiggy was just another opportunity. And it went on longer than it should have. That's why I put a stop to it. I couldn't play games anymore. I needed to be a good man for *my* family."

I died again, my bottom lip dropping, the blood on the tip of my tongue. *His family?* He thought he was doing a service by abandoning his past life for his current one? He was more awful than I could ever imagine. And he played Mama because she was his opportunity out of the city. She was his opportunity to live out his dream.

And she knew. Good God, *she knew.* That's why she said people made bad decisions when they were desperate. Why love could make you do weird things. And she held on anyway. Because she still had hope. Because he kept giving her that hope. Because she'd do anything for him, even if she shouldn't have.

But it was *that* love.

And maybe Mama thought no one could love her the same way he pretended to love her. She didn't think she was strong enough to see past the fog.

Hearing this now, knowing this: It killed me. Because she never needed him, but it was too hard for her to understand how incredible she was without him. She always had the power, and she never used it.

Devin's face softened when I didn't respond, his hands relaxing, and he shifted in his seat. "I'm sorry it happened how it did. I'm sad she's gone. I am. What happened to her was tragic, and I'm terribly sorry for your loss."

But.

He wasn't. Mama's death was a way out for him. She loved him so much, and I couldn't unsee that anymore. Couldn't unsee her body, shriveled on the floor. Her hand, crumpled beneath her chest. Her heart, broken.

How could he be this person? If he had seen her, like she was, how could he turn away from that?

And I felt the vines pull me together as my voice broke. "No. You're not sorry. She loved you, and you used her! She would have done anything for you, and how dare you *lie*. How dare you decide. She didn't have a choice, and you did!"

He recoiled, his eyes flinching at how loud my voice had grown. "That's just life, and—"

I threw my glass of water on him, and I stood, his face filling with rage. "You think I care about what you're going to say? You don't get to do that to me. You don't get to lie!" I grabbed the check from the table and shoved it in my pocket, hoping he wouldn't move.

And he didn't move; he sat with his arms up, spitting out the water that got in his mouth.

Then I dumped the other glass of water on him, and the water forced his hair straight, dripped down his nose, and soaked his shirt. "And that's for my mom, and all the pain you caused us, you fucking piss-poor excuse for a person. I hope your wife finds out about this! I hope all your clients leave you, and your career turns to shit!" I shouted so loud I heard movement in his house. "You don't deserve any of this. You cheated your way to the top, and you lied," I said, and I threw the cup against him.

Devin tried to catch it but couldn't. His mouth agape as the cup rolled on the ground. I picked the other one up then, threw it at the house. And when it shattered, the pieces filled with light. "I hope all your dance shoes get water on them. That they all fall apart. That you can never wear suede again." And it was the last thing I said to him. Didn't look back when I left, but he didn't chase after me.

Slammed the gate, kicked the trash can beside the house, watched the items tumble onto the grass.

Wanted to yell again, but my vision blurred, and I used my knuckles to wipe away the wetness in my eyes.

Bo didn't move when he saw me dashing his way, and I grabbed my bag from him, hopped on the scooter, and kicked it into go.

Bo followed in a hurry behind me, confused. He said something, but his words slipped away.

The world felt small as the scooter sped up, the California breeze racing through my tight curls. Mama somewhere, close beside me. And I needed to see the water.

CHAPTER FORTY-SEVEN

JULY 6, 5:07 P.M.

"And in the end, we were all just humans . . . drunk on the idea that love, only love, could heal our brokenness."

—Christopher Poindexter

CHAPTER FORTY-EIGHT

I'D HEARD SOME PEOPLE say that when you change, you *feel* it.

They said it was like a tugging and stretching on your bones, as if someone pulled and twisted your tendons specifically for the world to measure them out. It was supposed to mark a milestone. A feeling of immense pain. A varied period of highs and lows.

Today, I felt that.

My joints didn't hurt, my muscles weren't sore, but there was this tingle buried deep inside me that I couldn't shake. A change happening. A truth spilling out.

The ocean was next, and even from a foot away, I could hear the seashells singing for me, could feel the gritty salt in my nostrils. And seeing it for the first time, it was everything I hoped it would be.

Knees weak when I dropped the scooter in the sand. My Converse off now, and I rushed to the shoreline, falling, legs pressing into the warm earth.

Bo was beside me on the ground as I put my hands in, the water rushing to my skin, stinging my dead parts. And I didn't care that I was wet now. Didn't care that my shorts were soaked, and that my tears wouldn't stop. Scooped the ocean in my hands, and I wasn't here anymore.

There again. At the porch of my childhood home. The fiery breeze bruising my face. The wooden door closed before me, her smell still sweeping past it. And I was there. My hand on the knob, twisting it until it pushed open.

And she was there.

Her eyes big and rushing toward me until we collided. Until my face was pressed into her, breathing in her curls as I cried. And we sank to the floor. Her hands around me, her heart beating into my ear. And she loved me so much. She wouldn't stop saying it. Wouldn't let me forget. Squeezed me till I remembered it all.

Then I was here again. The ocean before me, roaring. The water rippling forward, splashes against my face, the sun in my eyes.

And if Mama were water, she'd be the sea and the never-ending tides.

I'd be the shore, and she'd always come back to me, soaking me with her love, leaving behind seashells, and always looking for me, always running to me.

I'd wait, breathless, just for her to splash around me again so we could dance together. So we could sing around the fire, watch it melt into the horizon over and over again.

I couldn't move after I was soaked, and Bo didn't make me. We sat in the sea for a long time, and we didn't speak, and it was okay.

CHAPTER FORTY-NINE

IT WAS TOO HARD TO leave the ocean, so I spent some of Devin's money on a hotel that sat facing the beach. The sun would be down soon, and I hoped to be near the water again, but I was in the hotel bathroom, pacing back and forth.

A knock on the door, a voice coming through. "You almost ready, Z?"

It had been half an hour since I'd stepped foot in here. After the exchange between Devin and me, I just wanted to shower, wash the thought of seeing him out of my hair. He was the past now, and every memory of him belonged down the drain. He didn't deserve a spot in my headspace anymore, and I felt so much better now that it was over, now that I knew Mama's truth.

When I stared at my reflection, I was me again. No more zombie. No more deterioration. Just brown skin and some old acne scars. I was Zharie Young. I was Twiggy's legacy. I was at the start of my new beginning. I was at the *zenith* of my being.

I finger-detangled my hair, doused it with conditioner, and shimmied back into my high-waisted shorts and one of Mama's shirts.

Ready to see the ocean again, but I couldn't leave this bathroom. Held my phone in one hand, picked my lip with the other. I couldn't decide if I should reach out to Mama's dance studio back home or not. I had an email opened, the subject title: *Hello again.* The body of the email empty.

If I asked them for a job at the ballroom, would they give me one? And if they did, could I handle being at the studio again, seeing everyone dance, knowing that Mama would never walk through the door?

Leaned against the bathroom door. Sighed. I didn't know, but I knew dance was my life, that I would certainly compete again, that I would run away from that fear I once had. Dance had always been the reason for everything. And if I turned away from it, I'd only be turning away from a piece of myself—a piece of Mama.

Without another thought, I typed out a few words and sent the email. Hoped I'd hear back from them soon. But even if I didn't, I'd be there next week.

Left the bathroom and opened the door to see Bo sitting on the bed. He put his phone away quickly, shoving it under his leg. His eyes were clear, glistening like the fading sunlight that poured through the window. And his smile came in slow motion, shooting electricity through the palms of my hands.

"Hey."

"Hey," I said, my cheeks and lips warm.

"Ready?"

I nodded, and then the two of us left the hotel room and took the elevator down to the ground level. It only took us a few minutes to get to the beach, and I pressed Bo's hand when we arrived.

To the shoreline I ran, my feet sinking into the wet sand. Bo followed, and we both laughed as the tide pushed the cold water between our toes. Kicked up some of the water, and it landed on Bo, startling him. I laughed at how big his eyes were, how half of him dripped with seawater. He tried to get me back, but I took off, running down the beach and away from him.

But Bo was fast, faster than the tide, and he tackled me into the water, drenching us both.

We came out of the ocean laughing, my hair stuck to my face, and Bo looking like an excited puppy, ready for round two.

"I can't believe I get you," he said, huffing.

I sat up, the sand everywhere, and I pressed a finger to his nose, thinking the same old thing I always thought. "That was cheesy AF."

"You always think I'm cheesy."

I grinned. "It's because you are. It's cute, though," I said, placing some sand into Bo's hand now. He crumbled it through his fingers. "We still have so much to learn about each other."

Bo stuck his chest out. "I know everything I need to know about you, Zharie Young."

"Ha! You absolutely do not."

Bo leaned against me, pressing his lips to my shoulder. "Okay, maybe I don't, but I'm learning." He was silent for a second, and I listened to the water toss, saw the waves creep closer and closer. "Z, can I tell you something?"

"Anything," I said, watching three people in the water. They kicked around, threw their hands in the air, and shimmied under what was left of the sun. In the middle of it all, one of them morphed into a zombie, their skin breaking in the salt water, blood pooling around them.

It was strange that I was still seeing them, but it didn't bother me so much anymore.

Whatever their story was, I hoped they'd make it through to the other side.

"I'm really, *really* proud of you. What you did back there, confronting your birth dad, that was insane. I wished I had the balls to do some of the stuff you did. I know I need to talk to my parents again. Make them listen. Straight up tell them how their dreams for me aren't what I want."

"It's hard. But it's so worth it. You gotta do it for you," I said, and that was the thing about love. It wasn't a printed piece of the same thing. It was crooked and unfocused sometimes. It depleted us, consumed our brains, ripped our hearts from our chests, turned us into the undead.

Sometimes we were sagging skin and moldy bones.

"I'm happy I'm here with you," I said to Bo.

Bo rubbed his fingers across my jawline and smiled. His smile was growing to be one of my favorite things in this realm, and if he didn't kiss me soon, it would be a cruel joke.

"I bet you'd never done anything like this before, huh?" he said, his eyes locked on me; they flashed a burning yellow.

"*Never*," I said, looking down to his knees, blushing. He made me feel so orange on the inside.

Bo pressed his lips against mine, kissing me slowly, and I'd never felt like I belonged anywhere more than beside the ocean with my heart in his lungs, and my face smashing into his.

Together, we were our own metaphysical realities. And we could be anything. We could do anything.

I wrapped my arms around Bo, rested my chin on him, spotted a sunflower growing beside the tide, breathed in this moment.

His shoulders tensed after a while. "Z, do you *see* that?"

"See what?" I released him to look around. A dog rolling in the sand, a kid crying in the distance. A couple strolled by, both of them part of the undead. Nothing particularly out of the ordinary.

Squinted, searching for more, searching for what Bo might have

BRITNEY S. LEWIS

noticed, too. Was it the sunflower? "No," I said, still looking around. "What do you see?"

Looked at him. His eyes big, full of something so terrifying it made me move closer to him. "Bo, what is it?"

He squeezed my arm, and he pointed with his other hand, jaw dropping when he said it. "They're everywhere, Z. The zombies. I see them, too."

Gasped. My eyes following his pointer finger to see what he saw. To see what I'd already seen. And then the twisting, the pulling, the creaking. All of it thumping inside me like a drum. *"What?"* I choked the word out.

And I could not believe it. Could not believe it. Could not.

I thought I was the only one.

355

ACKNOWLEDGMENTS

THIS BOOK CAME TO ME my last semester of college as I wondered why every relationship I tried to be in never worked. Not in middle school. Not in high school. Not in college. The original pitch I had for this book was literally: "Girl falls into a metaphorical trap of believing boys are zombies who want to eat her heart out. Her life then becomes hollower once she falls in love with one."

It's hard to see that sentence and not laugh because that's not the story anymore. It was true, though. At that time in my life, I thought I wasn't worthy of love from another human being who didn't *have* to love me (you know, like my parents, siblings, my dog, or my cat). In my head, I had a list of reasons for why that was, but in the end, none of it was true. This story turned into how love can change you—good love, bad love, and everything in between. Love plays a main character in so many parts of our lives, and I am thankful for how love has transformed me, and how love has transformed this story.

There are so many people I have to thank. I wouldn't be the person I am today without my parents. I think they always knew I was the weird middle child. There was something about me that didn't quite fit, but I was still theirs, and I know that today they are very proud of me. To my siblings, thank you for loving me, for calling, texting, or stopping by. I know, *I know.* I'm the worst communicator.

To my grandfather, the other writer in my family. Thanks for reading my early work, for all your long rants, and for your abundance of short stories.

To Nana, the woman who pushed me to be the author I am today. For letting me use your printer and ink to print endless literary agents' names and for your stamps to send snail-mail queries to New York. Thanks for letting me read for hours while you watched the news, and for watching me write stories from the green couch you used to have. Thanks for all the library trips and for sharing your love of art with me.

Big thanks to all of my family and friends who've supported me. I appreciate you.

A world of thanks to my amazing literary agent Katelyn Detweiler who saw this story and this pitch and read it all within a day's work. Your enthusiasm and love for my story is unmatched, and I appreciate you tremendously. You're the best advocate, the best business partner, and overall, just a sincerely amazing human. You're also a very talented writer. To anyone reading this, please buy her books.

Also, thanks to Jill Grinberg for reading my story, being immersed in Z's world, and believing Katelyn would champion my work. You were right. She's the best.

Thanks to everyone else at Jill Grinberg Literary Management who helped with this story, and many thanks to Sophia Seidner for answering all my tedious contract questions.

All of the thanks and praise to Emily Meehan for buying this book, and to Christine Collins for being the literal best assistant editor ever. Another thanks to Brittany Rubiano for being the most wonderful senior editor. All three of you have spent countless hours on shaping this book and helping this story become what it is. Another thanks to Christine and Britt for rooting for me, for being my voice, for championing this project, and for getting everyone on the Hyperion team as excited as you were about this story. I couldn't have done any of this without you. I appreciate you both.

To the wonderful team at Hyperion, you all have made me feel like a princess. Thank you for helping bring *The Undead Truth of Us* to the world.

Infinite thanks and gratitude to the managing editorial and copyediting team: Sara Liebling, Guy Cunningham, Jody Corbet, Jacqueline Hornberger, Meredith Jones, and David Jaffe. Thanks to the design team for making this book so pretty to look at and easy to read: Marci Senders and Zareen Johnson. Thanks to Adekunle Adeleke for making me cry with a stunning cover that really touched my heart. Thank you Marketing and Publicity for being my engine for this book. All of you deserve eternal gratitude: Holly Nagel, Dina Sherman, Andrew Sansone, Seale Ballenger, and Christine Saunders.

A special thanks to Amanda Pavlov, the most incredible author-friend and critique partner. I don't know where I'd be without you and that Reddit forum. Another special thanks to Morgan G. Thanks for reading all my stories, for sharing your own stories, and for talking to me for hours on end. You're a great friend.

To Laura Averil for sitting through endless hours of me dreaming about being a writer, listening to my stories, and being the best friend I could ever ask for. You make life great and full of adventure—and of course, a big thanks to you and Yale for pushing me to be more competitive and get out of my comfort zone.

Thank you to some of the great English teachers I've had at KCK public schools, more specifically the wonderful Kim Applebury.

Thanks to Liz Watkins for introducing me to West Coast Swing and being such a wonderful teacher and friend. There's a light in you that forever shines. And to my West Coast Swing community in Kansas City and all the teachers and ballrooms I've spent hours and hours practicing in. Thanks to Jesse Lopez, Ariel Peck, Liz Watkins, Kris Haney, Hailee Vargas, Kayla Sloan, Ashley Meeker, Kris

Swearingen, Kyle Patel, and Carrie and Jake Gansert. To Allegro Ballroom, Mélange Dance and Events, Overland Park Ballroom, and Viva Dance and Events.

Tremendous thanks to the outstanding Kianna Asberry for inspiring the lovely Mini character and for being such an anchor for me in high school. I love you, friend.

To the Lit Squad for cheering me on every step of the way and being so gracious and full of humor and hope. To every author who has inspired me, listened to me, encouraged me, given me advice, mentored me. I'm so appreciative of you: Tracy Deonn. Dhonielle Clayton. Zoriada Córdova. Nicola Yoon. Emily X.R. Pan. Nic Stone. Kalynn Bayron. Melissa Albert. J.Elle. Rebecca Podos. Jay Coles. Justin A. Reynolds. Jason Reynolds. John Green. Tiffany D. Jackson. Elise Bryant.

And all my thanks to Michael. My bear. My rock. My anchor. My best friend. My husband. My everything, everything. Thank you for believing in my dream and supporting me through every high and low of it. Thank you for your patience in me as I continue to grow into the person that I want to be, and thank you for loving me, even when I thought something like that could be impossible. I appreciate you, and you deserve every good thing coming your way.